THE HOUSE OF ARDEN

A STORY FOR CHILDREN

BY
EDITH NESBIT

ABOUT EDITH NESBIT

Edith Nesbit (married name **Edith Bland**; 15 August 1858 – 4 May 1924) was an English writer and poet, who published her books for children as E. Nesbit. She wrote or collaborated on more than 60 such books. She was also a political activist and co-founder of the Fabian Society, a socialist organisation later affiliated to the Labour Party.

Nesbit was born in 1858 at 38 Lower Kennington Lane, Kennington, Surrey (now classified as Inner London), the daughter of an agricultural chemist, John Collis Nesbit, who died in March 1862, before her fourth birthday. Her mother was Sarah Green (née Alderton).

The ill health of Edith's sister Mary meant that the family travelled for some years, living variously in Brighton, Buckinghamshire, France (Dieppe, Rouen, Paris, Tours, Poitiers, Angoulême, Bordeaux, Arcachon, Pau, Bagnères-de-Bigorre, and Dinan in Brittany), Spain and Germany. Mary was engaged in 1871 to the poet Philip Bourke Marston, but later that year she died of tuberculosis in Normandy.

After Mary's death, Edith and her mother settled for three years at Halstead Hall, Halstead, north-west Kent, a location that inspired *The*

Railway Children, although the distinction has also been claimed by the Derbyshire town of New Mills).

When Nesbit was 17, the family moved back to Lewisham in south-east London. There is a Lewisham Council plaque to her at 28 Elswick Road.

In 1877, at the age of 18, Nesbit met the bank clerk Hubert Bland, her elder by three years. Seven months pregnant, she married Bland on 22 April 1880, but did not initially live with him, as Bland remained with his mother. Their marriage was tumultuous. Early on, Nesbit found that another woman believed she was Hubert's fiancée and had also borne him a child. A more serious blow came in 1886, when she discovered that her friend, Alice Hoatson, was pregnant by him. She had previously agreed to adopt Hoatson's child and allow Hoatson to live with her as their housekeeper. After she discovered the truth, she and her husband quarrelled violently and she suggested that Hoatson and the baby, Rosamund, should leave; her husband threatened to leave Edith if she disowned the baby and its mother. Hoatson remained with them as a housekeeper and secretary and became pregnant by Bland again 13 years later. Edith again adopted Hoatson's child, John.

Nesbit's children by Bland were Paul Cyril Bland (1880–1940), to whom *The Railway Children* was dedicated, Mary Iris Bland (1881–1965), who married John Austin D Phillips in 1907, and Fabian Bland (1885–1900). Bland's two children by Alice Hoatson, whom Edith adopted, were Rosamund Edith Nesbit Hamilton, later Bland (1886–1950), who married Clifford Dyer Sharp on 16 October 1909, and to whom *The Book of Dragons* was dedicated, and John Oliver Wentworth Bland (1899–1946) to whom *The House of Arden* and *Five Children and It* were dedicated. Nesbit's son Fabian died aged 15 after a tonsil operation; Nesbit dedicated several books to him, including *The Story of the Treasure Seekers* and its sequels. Nesbit's adopted daughter Rosamund collaborated with her on *Cat Tales*.

Nesbit admired the artist and Marxian socialist William Morris. The couple joined the founders of the Fabian Society in 1884, after which their son Fabian was named, and jointly edited its journal *Today*.

Hoatson was its assistant secretary. Nesbit and Bland dallied with the Social Democratic Federation, but found it too radical. Nesbit was a prolific lecturer and writer on socialism in the 1880s. She and her husband co-wrote under the pseudonym "Fabian Bland", However, the joint work dwindled as her success rose as a children's author. She was a guest speaker at the London School of Economics, which had been founded by other Fabian Society members.

Edith lived from 1899 to 1920 at Well Hall, Eltham, in south-east London, which makes fictional appearances in several of her books, such as *The Red House*. From 1911 she kept a second home on the Sussex Downs at Crowlink, Friston, East Sussex. She and her husband entertained many friends, colleagues and admirers at Well Hall.

On 20 February 1917, some three years after Bland died, Nesbit married Thomas "the Skipper" Tucker in Woolwich, where he was captain of the Woolwich Ferry.

Towards the end of her life, Nesbit moved first to Crowlink, then to "The Long Boat" at Jesson, St Mary's Bay, New Romney, Kent, where probably suffering from lung cancer (she "smoked incessantly"), she died in 1924 and was buried in the churchyard of St Mary in the Marsh. Her husband Thomas died at the same address on 17 May 1935. Edith's son Paul Bland was an executor of Thomas Tucker's will.

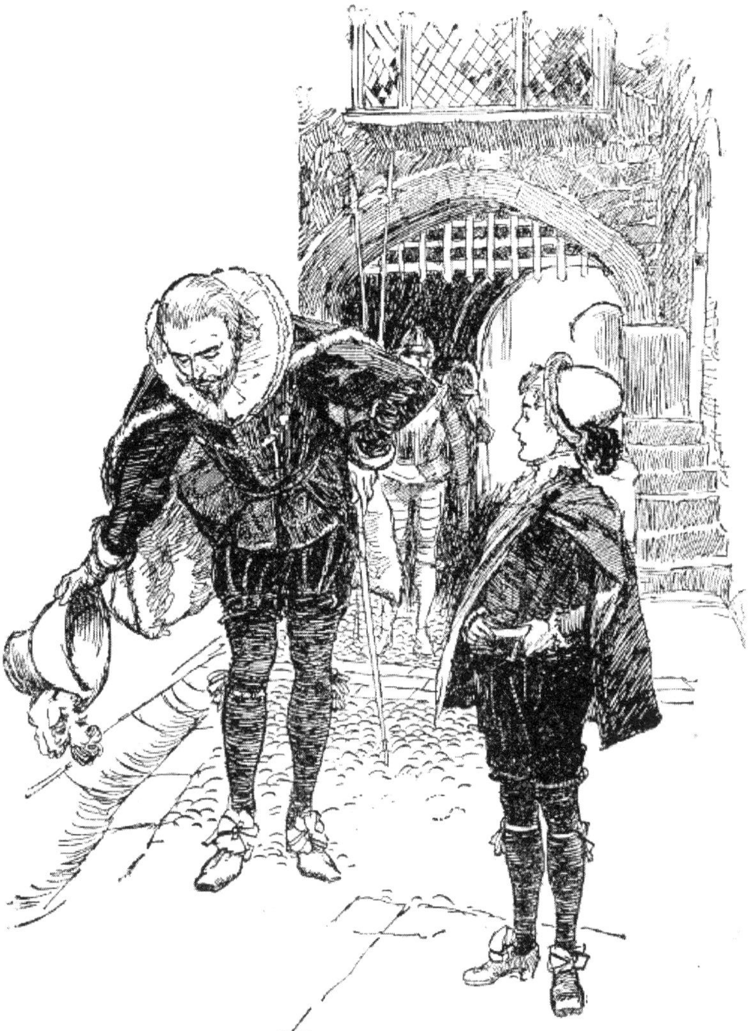

CONTENTS

CHAPTER I   ARDEN'S LORD 1

CHAPTER II   THE MOULDIWARP 29

CHAPTER III   IN BONEY'S TIMES 57

CHAPTER IV   THE LANDING OF THE FRENCH 75

CHAPTER V   THE HIGHWAYMAN AND THE ——............ 87

CHAPTER VI   THE SECRET PANEL..107

CHAPTER VII   THE KEY OF THE PARLOUR......................131

CHAPTER VIII   GUY FAWKES 149

CHAPTER IX   THE PRISONERS IN THE TOWER 173

CHAPTER X   WHITE WINGS AND A BROWNIE................193

CHAPTER XI   DEVELOPMENTS 213

CHAPTER XII   FILMS AND CLOUDS 237

CHAPTER XIII   MAY-BLOSSOM AND PEARLS....................251

CHAPTER XIV   THE FINDING OF THE TREASURE..........267

CHAPTER I
ARDEN'S LORD

It had been a great house once, with farms and fields, money and jewels—with tenants and squires and men-at-arms. The head of the house had ridden out three days' journey to meet King Henry at the boundary of his estate, and the King had ridden back with him to lie in the tall State bed in the castle guest-chamber. The heir of the house had led his following against Cromwell; younger sons of the house had fought in foreign lands, to the honour of England and the gilding and regilding with the perishable gold of glory of the old Arden name. There had been Ardens in Saxon times, and there were Ardens still—but few and impoverished. The lands were gone, and the squires and men-at-arms; the castle itself was roofless, and its unglazed windows stared blankly across the fields of strangers, that stretched right up to the foot of its grey, weather-worn walls. And of the male Ardens there were now known two only—an old man and a child.

The old man was Lord Arden, the head of the house, and he lived lonely in a little house built of the fallen stones that Time and Cromwell's round-shot had cast from the castle walls. The child was Edred Arden, and he lived in a house in a clean, wind-swept town on a cliff.

It was a bright-faced house with bow-windows and a green balcony that looked out over the sparkling sea. It had three neat white steps and a brass knocker, pale and smooth with constant rubbing. It was a pretty house, and it would have been a pleasant house but for one thing—the lodgers. For I cannot conceal from you any longer that Edred Arden lived with his aunt, and that his aunt let lodgings. Letting lodgings is one of the most unpleasant of all possible ways of earning your living, and I advise you to try every other honest way of earning *your* living before you take to that.

Because people who go to the seaside and take lodgings seem, somehow, much harder to please than the people who go to hotels. They want ever so much more waiting on; they want so many meals, and at such odd times. They ring the bell almost all day long. They bring in sand from the shore in every fold of their clothes, and it shakes out of them on to the carpets and the sofa cushions, and everything in the house. They hang long streamers of wet seaweed against the pretty roses of the new wall-papers, and their washhand basins are always full of sea anemones and shells. Also, they are noisy; their boots seem to be always on the stairs, no matter how bad a headache you may have; and when you give them their bill they always think it is too much, no matter how little it may be. So do not let lodgings if you can help it.

Miss Arden could not help it. It happened like this.

Edred and his sister were at school. (Did I tell you that he had a sister? Well, he had, and her name was Elfrida.) Miss Arden lived near the school, so that she could see the children often. She was getting her clothes ready for her wedding, and the gentleman who was going to marry her was coming home from South America, where he had made a fortune. The children's father was coming home from South America, too, with the fortune that he had made, for he and Miss Arden's sweetheart were partners. The children and their aunt talked whenever they met of the glorious time that was coming, and how, when father and Uncle Jim—they called him Uncle Jim already—came home, they were all going to live in the country and be happy ever after.

And then the news came that father and Uncle Jim had been captured by brigands, and all the money was lost, too, and there was nothing left but the house on the cliff. So Miss Arden took the children from the expensive school in London, and they all went to live in the cliff house, and as there was no money to live on, and no other way of making money to live on except letting lodgings, Miss Arden let them, like the brave lady she was, and did it well. And then came the news that father and Uncle Jim were dead, and for a time the light of life went out in Cliff House.

This was two years ago; but the children had never got used to the lodgers. They hated them. At first they had tried to be friendly with the lodgers' children, but they soon found that the lodgers' children considered Edred and Elfrida very much beneath them, and looked down on them accordingly. And very often the lodgers' children were the sort of children on whom anybody might have looked down, if it were right and kind to look down on any one. And when Master Reginald Potts, of Peckham, puts his tongue out at you on the parade and says, right before everybody, "Lodgings! Yah!" it is hard to feel quite the same to him as you did before.

When there were lodgers—and there nearly always were, for the house was comfortable, and people who had been once came again—the children and their aunt had to live in the very top and the very bottom of the house—in the attics and the basement, in fact.

When there were no lodgers they used all the rooms in turn, to keep them aired. But the children liked the big basement parlour room best, because there all the furniture had belonged to dead-and-gone Ardens, and all the pictures on the walls were of Ardens dead and gone. The rooms that the lodgers had were furnished with a new sort of furniture that had no stories belonging to it such as belonged to the old polished oak tables and bureaux that were in the basement parlour.

Edred and Elfrida went to school every day and learned reading, writing, arithmetic, geography, history, spelling, and useful knowledge, all of which they hated quite impartially, which means they hated the whole lot—one thing as much as another.

The only part of lessons they liked was the home-work, when, if Aunt Edith had time to help them, geography became like adventures, history like story-books, and even arithmetic suddenly seemed to mean something.

"I wish you could teach us always," said Edred, very inky, and interested for the first time in the exports of China; "it does seem so silly trying to learn things that are only words in books."

"I wish I could," said Aunt Edith, "but I can't do twenty-nine thousand and seventeen things all at once, and——" A bell jangled. "That's the seventh time since tea." She got up and went into the kitchen. "There's the bell again, my poor Eliza. Never mind; answer the bell, but don't answer *them*, whatever they say. It doesn't do a bit of good, and it sometimes prevents their giving you half-crowns when they leave."

"I do love it when they go," said Elfrida.

"Yes," said her aunt. "A cab top-heavy with luggage, the horse's nose turned stationward, it's a heavenly sight—when the bill is paid and—— But, then, I'm just as glad to see the luggage coming. Chickens! when my ship comes home we'll go and live on a desert island where there aren't any cabs, and we won't have any lodgers in our cave."

"When I grow up," said Edred, "I shall go across the sea and look for your ship and bring it home. I shall take a steam-tug and steer it myself."

"Then I shall be captain," said Elfrida.

"No, I shall be captain."

"You can't if you steer."

"Yes, I can!"

"No, you can't!"

"Yes, I can!"

"Well, do, then!" said Elfrida; "and while you're doing it—I *know* you can't—I shall dig in the garden and find a gold-mine, and Aunt Edith will be rolling in money when you come back, and she won't want your silly old ship."

"Spelling next," said Aunt Edith. "How do you spell 'disagreeable'?"

"Which of us?" asked Edred acutely.

"Both," said Aunt Edith, trying to look very severe.

When you are a child you always dream of your ship coming home—of having a hundred pounds, or a thousand, or a million pounds to spend as you like. My favourite dream, I remember, was a thousand pounds and an express understanding that I was not to spend it on anything useful. And when you have dreamed of your million pounds, or your thousand, or your hundred, you spend happy hour on hour in deciding what presents you will buy for each of the people you are fond of, and in picturing their surprise and delight at your beautiful presents and your wonderful generosity. I think very few of us spend our dream fortunes entirely on ourselves. Of course, we buy ourselves a motor-bicycle straight away, and footballs and bats—and dolls with real hair, and real china tea-sets, and large boxes of mixed chocolates, and "Treasure Island," and all the books that Mrs. Ewing ever wrote, but when we have done that we begin to buy things for other people. It is a beautiful dream, but too often, by the time it comes true—up to a hundred pounds or a thousand—we forget what we used to mean to do with our money, and spend it all in stocks and shares, and eligible building sites, and fat cigars and fur coats. If I were young again I would sit down and write a list of all the kind things I meant to do when my ship came home, and if my ship ever did come home I would read that list, and—
— But the parlour bell is ringing for the eighth time, and the front-door bell is ringing too, and the first-floor is ringing also, and so is the second-floor, and Eliza is trying to answer four bells at once—always a most difficult thing to do.

The front-door bell was rung by the postman; he brought three letters. The first was a bill for mending the lid of the cistern, on which Edred had recently lighted a fire, fortified by an impression that wood could not burn if there were water on the other side—a totally false impression, as the charred cistern lid proved. The second was an inquiry whether Miss Arden would take a clergyman in at half the usual price, because he had a very large family which had all just had measles. And the third was THE letter, which is really the seed, and beginning, and backbone, and rhyme, and reason of this story.

Edred had got the letters from the postman, and he stood and waited while Aunt Edith read them. He collected postmarks, and had not been able to make out by the thick half-light of the hall gas whether any of these were valuable.

The third letter had a very odd effect on Aunt Edith. She read it once, and rubbed her hand across her eyes. Then she got up and stood under the chandelier, which wanted new burners badly, and so burned with a very unlighting light, and read it again. Then she read it a third time, and then she said, "Oh!"

"What is it, auntie?" Elfrida asked anxiously; "is it the taxes?" It had been the taxes once, and Elfrida had never forgotten. (If you don't understand what this means ask your poorest relations, who are also likely to be your nicest, and if they don't know, ask the washerwoman.)

"No; it's not the taxes, darling," said Aunt Edith; "on the contrary."

I don't know what the contrary (or opposite) of taxes is, any more than the children did—but I am sure it is something quite nice—and so were they.

"Oh, auntie, I *am* so glad," they both said, and said it several times before they asked again, "What is it?"

"I think—I'm not quite sure—but I think it's a ship come home—oh, just a quite tiny little bit of a ship—a toy boat—hardly more than that. But I must go up to London to-morrow the first thing, and see if it really is a ship, and, if so, what sort of ship it is. Mrs. Blake shall come in, and you'll be good as gold, children, won't you?"

"Yes—oh, yes," said the two.

"And not make booby traps for the butcher, or go on the roof in your nightgowns, or play Red Indians in the dust-bin, or make apple-pie beds for the lodgers?" Aunt Edith asked, hastily mentioning a few of the little amusements which had lately enlivened the spare time of her nephew and niece.

"No, we really won't," said Edred; "and we'll truly try not to think of anything new and amusing," he added, with real self-sacrifice.

"I must go by the eight-thirty train. I wish I could think of some way of—of amusing you," she ended, for she was too kind to say "of keeping you out of mischief for the day," which was what she really thought. "I'll bring you something jolly for your birthday, Edred. Wouldn't you like to spend the day with nice Mrs. Hammond?"

"Oh, *no*," said Edred; and added, on the inspiration of the moment, "Why mayn't we have a picnic—just Elf and me—on the downs, to keep my birthday? It doesn't matter it being the day before, does it? You said we were too little last summer, and we should this, and now it is this and I have grown two inches and Elf's grown three, so we're five inches taller than when you said we weren't big enough."

"Now you see how useful arithmetic is," said the aunt. "Very well, you shall. Only wear your old clothes, and always keep in sight of the road. Yes; you can have a whole holiday. And now to bed. Oh, there's that bell again! Poor, dear Eliza."

A Clapham cub, belonging to one of the lodgers, happened to be going up to bed just as Edred and Elfrida came through the baize door that shut off the basement from the rest of the house. He put his tongue out through the banisters at the children of the house and said, "Little slaveys." The cub thought he could get up the stairs before the two got round the end of the banisters, but he had not counted on the long arm of Elfrida, whose hand shot through the banisters and caught the cub's leg and held on to it till Edred had time to get round. The two boys struggled up the stairs together and then rolled together from top to bottom, where they were picked up and disentangled by their relations. Except for this little incident, going to bed was uneventful.

Next morning Aunt Edith went off by the eight-thirty train. The children's school satchels were filled, not with books, but with buns; instead of exercise-books there were sandwiches; and in the place of inky pencil-boxes were two magnificent boxes of peppermint creams which had cost a whole shilling each, and had been recklessly bought by Aunt Edith in the agitation of the parting hour when they saw her off at the station.

They went slowly up the red-brick-paved sidewalk that always looks as though it had just been washed, and when they got to the top of the hill they stopped and looked at each other.

"It can't be wrong," said Edred.

"She never told us not to," said Elfrida.

"I've noticed," said Edred, "that when grown-up people say 'they'll see about' anything you want it never happens."

"I've noticed that, too," said Elfrida. "Auntie always said she'd see about taking us there."

"Yes, she did."

"We won't be mean and sneaky about it," Edred insisted, though no one had suggested that he *would* be mean and sneaky. "We'll tell auntie directly she gets back."

"Of course," said Elfrida, rather relieved, for she had not felt at all sure that Edred meant to do this.

"After all," said Edred, "it's *our* castle. We *ought* to go and see the cradle of our race. That's what it calls it in 'Cliffgate and its Envions.' I say, let's call it a pilgrimage. The satchels will do for packs, and we can get half-penny walking-sticks with that penny of yours. We can put peas in our shoes, if you like," he added generously.

"We should have to go back for them, and I don't expect the split kind count, anyhow. And perhaps they'd hurt," said Elfrida doubtfully. "And I want my penny for——" She stopped, warned by her brother's frown. "All right, then," she ended; "you can have it. Only give me half next time you get a penny; that's only fair."

"I'm not usually unfair," said Edred coldly. "Don't let's be pilgrims."

"But I should like to," said Elfrida.

Edred was obstinate. "No," he said, "we'll just walk."

So they just walked, rather dismally.

The town was getting thinner, like the tract of stocking that surrounds a hole; the houses were farther apart and had large gardens. In one of them a maid was singing to herself as she shook out the mats—a thing which, somehow, maids don't do much in towns.

"Good luck!" says I to my sweetheart,

"For I will love you true;

> And all the while we've got to part,
>
> My luck shall go with you."

"That's lucky for us," said Elfrida amiably.

"We're not her silly sweetheart," said Edred.

"No; but we heard her sing it, and he wasn't here, so he couldn't. There's a sign-post. I wonder how far we've gone? I'm getting awfully tired."

"You'd better have been pilgrims," said Edred. "*They* never get tired, however many peas they have in their shoes."

"I will now," said Elfrida.

"You can't," said Edred; "it's too late. We're miles and miles from the stick shop."

"Very well, I shan't go on," said Elfrida. "You got out of bed the wrong side this morning. I've tried to soft-answer you as hard as ever I could all the morning, and I'm not going to try any more, so there."

"Don't, then," said Edred bitterly. "Go along home if you like. You're only a girl."

"I'd rather be only a girl than what *you* are," said she.

"And what's that, I should like to know?"

Elfrida stopped and shut her eyes tight.

"Don't, don't, don't, don't!" she said. "I won't be cross, I won't be cross, I won't be cross! Pax. Drop it. Don't let's!"

"THEY WENT SLOWLY UP THE RED-BRICK-PAVED SIDEWALK."

"Don't let's what?"

"Quarrel about nothing," said Elfrida, opening her eyes and walking on very fast. "We're always doing it. Auntie says it's a habit. If boys are so much splendider than girls, they ought to be able to stop when they like."

"Suppose they don't like?" said he, kicking his boots in the thick, white dust.

"Well," said she, "I'll say I'm sorry first. Will *that* do?"

"I was just going to say it first myself," said Edred, in aggrieved tones. "Come on," he added more generously, "here's the sign-post. Let's see what it says."

It said, quite plainly and without any nonsense about it, that they had come a mile and three-quarters, adding, most unkindly, that it was eight miles to Arden Castle. But, it said, it was a quarter of a mile to Ardenhurst Station.

"Let's go by train," said Edred grandly.

"No money," said Elfrida, very forlornly indeed.

"Aha!" said Edred; "now you'll see. *I'm* not mean about money. I brought my new florin."

"Oh, Edred," said the girl, stricken with remorse, "you *are* noble."

"Pooh!" said the boy, and his ears grew red with mingled triumph and modesty; "that's nothing. Come on."

So it was from the train that the pilgrims got their first sight of Arden Castle. It stands up boldly on the cliff where it was set to keep off foreign foes and guard the country round about it. But of all its old splendour there is now nothing but the great walls that the grasses and wild flowers grow on, and round towers whose floors and ceilings have fallen away, and roofless chambers where owls build, and brambles and green ferns grow strong and thick.

The children walked to the castle along the cliff path where the skylarks were singing like mad up in the pale sky, and the bean-fields, where the bees were busy, gave out the sweetest scent in the world—a scent that got itself mixed with the scent of the brown seaweed that rises and falls in the wash of the tide on the rocks at the cliff-foot.

"Let's have dinner here," said Elfrida, when they reached the top of a little mound from which they could look down on the castle. So they had it.

Two bites of sandwich and one of peppermint cream; that was the rule.

And all the time they were munching they looked down on the castle, and loved it more and more.

"Don't you wish it was real, and we lived in it?" Elfrida asked, when they had eaten as much as they wanted—not of peppermint creams, of course; but they had finished them.

"It is real, what there is of it."

"Yes; but I mean if it was a house with chimneys, and fireplaces, and doors with bolts, and glass in the windows."

"I wonder if we could get in?" said Edred.

"We might climb over," said Elfrida, looking hopefully at the enormous walls, sixty feet high, in which no gate or gap showed.

"There's an old man going across that field—no, not that one; the very green field. Let's ask him."

So they left their satchels lying on the short turf, that was half wild thyme, and went down. But they were not quite quick enough; before they could get to him the old man had come through the field of young corn, clambered over a stile, and vanished between the high hedges of a deep-sunk lane. So over the stile and down into the lane went the children, and caught up with the old man just as he had clicked his garden gate behind him and had turned to go up the bricked path between beds of woodruff, and anemones, and narcissus, and tulips of all colours.

His back was towards them. Now it is very difficult to address a back politely. So you will not be surprised to learn that Edred said, "Hi!" and Elfrida said, "Halloa! I say!"

The old man turned and saw at his gate two small figures dressed in what is known as sailor costume. They saw a very wrinkled old face with snowy hair and mutton-chop whiskers of a silvery whiteness. There were very bright twinkling blue eyes in the sun-browned face, and on the clean-shaven mouth a kind, if tight, smile.

"Well," said he, "and what do *you* want?"

"We want to know——" said Elfrida.

"About the castle," said Edred, "Can we get in and look at it?"

"I've got the keys," said the old man, and put his hand in at his door and reached them from a nail.

"I s'pose no one *lives* there?" said Elfrida.

"Not now," said the old man, coming back along the garden path. "Lord Arden, he died a fortnight ago come Tuesday, and the place is shut up till the new lord's found."

"I wish *I* was the new lord," said Edred, as they followed the old man along the lane.

"An' how old might *you* be?" the old man asked.

"I'm ten nearly. It's my birthday to-morrow," said Edred. "How old are you?"

"Getting on for eighty. I've seen a deal in my time. If you was the young lord you'd have a chance none of the rest of them ever had—you being the age you are."

"What sort of chance?"

"Why," said the old man, "don't you know the saying? I thought every one knowed it hereabouts."

"What saying?"

"I ain't got the wind for saying and walking too," said the old man, and stopped; "leastways, not potery." He drew a deep breath and said—

"When Arden's lord still lacketh ten

And may not see his nine again,

Let Arden stand as Arden may

On Arden Knoll at death of day.

If he have skill to say the spell

He shall find the treasure, and all be well!"

"I *say!*" said both the children. "And where's Arden Knoll?" Edred asked.

"Up yonder." He pointed to the mound where they had had lunch.

Elfrida inquired, "What treasure?"

But that question was not answered—then.

"If I'm to talk I must set me down," said the old man. "Shall we set down here, or set down inside of the castle?"

Two curiosities struggled, and the stronger won. "In the castle," said the children.

So it was in the castle, on a pillar fallen from one of the chapel arches, that the old man sat down and waited. When the children had run up and down the grassy enclosure, peeped into the ruined chambers, picked their way along the ruined colonnade, and climbed the steps of the only tower that they could find with steps *to* climb, then they came and sat beside the old man on the grass that was white with daisies, and said, "Now, then!"

"Well, then," said the old man, "you see the Ardens was always great gentry. I've heard say there's always been Ardens here since before William the Conker, whoever *he* was."

"Ten-sixty-six," said Edred to himself.

"An' they had their ups and downs like other folks, great and small. And once, when there was a war or trouble of some sort abroad, there was a lot of money, and jewelry, and silver plate hidden away. That's what it means by treasure. And the men who hid it got killed—ah, them was unsafe times to be alive in, I tell you—and nobody never knew where the treasure was hid."

"Did they ever find it?"

"Ain't I telling you? An' a wise woman that lived in them old ancient times, they went to her to ask her what to do to find the treasure, and she had a fit directly, what you'd call a historical fit nowadays. She never said nothing worth hearing without she was in a fit, and she made up the saying all in potery whilst she was in her fit, and that was all they could get out of her. And she never would say what the spell was. Only when she was a-dying, Lady Arden, that was then, was very took up with nursing of her, and before she breathed her lastest she told Lady Arden the spell." He stopped for lack of breath.

"And what is the spell?" said the children, much more breathless than he.

"Nobody knows," said he.

"But where is it?"

"Nobody knows. But I've 'eard say it's in a book in the libery in the house yonder. But it ain't no good, because there's never been a Lord Arden come to his title without he's left his ten years far behind him."

Edred had a queerer feeling in his head than you can imagine; his hands got hot and dry, and then cold and damp.

"I suppose," he said, "you've got to be *Lord* Arden? It wouldn't do if you were just plain John or James or Edred Arden? Because my name's Arden, and I would like to have a try?"

The old man stooped, caught Edred by the arm, pulled him up, and stood him between his knees.

"Let's have a look at you, sonny," he said; and had a look. "Aye," he said, "you're an Arden, for sure. To think of me not seeing that. I might have seen your long nose and your chin that sticks out like a spur. I ought to have known it anywhere. But my eyes ain't what they was. If you *was* Lord Arden—— What's your father's name—his chrissened name, I mean?"

"Edred, the same as mine. But father's dead," said Edred gravely.

"And your grandf'er's name? It wasn't George, was it—George William?"

"Yes, it was," said Edred. "How did you know?"

The old man let go Edred's arms and stood up. Then he touched his forehead and said—

"I've worked on the land 'ere man and boy, and I'm proud I've lived to see another Lord Arden take the place of him as is gone. Lauk-alive, boy, don't garp like that," he added sharply. "You're Lord Arden right enough."

"I—I can't be," gasped Edred.

"Auntie said Lord Arden was a relation of ours—a sort of great-uncle—cousin."

"That's it, missy," the old man nodded. "Lord Arden—chrissen name James—'e was first cousin to Mr. George as was your grandf'er. His son was Mr. Edred, as is your father. The late lord not 'avin' any sons—nor daughters neither for the matter of that—the title comes to your branch of the family. I've heard Snigsworthy, the lawyer's apprentice from Lewis, tell it over fifty times this last three weeks. You're Lord Arden, I tell you."

"If I am," said Edred, "I shall say the spell and find the treasure."

"You'll have to be quick about it," said Elfrida. "You'll be over ten the day after to-morrow."

"So I shall," said Edred.

"When you're Lord Arden," said the old man very seriously,—"I mean, when you grow up to enjoy the title—as, please God, you may—you remember the poor and needy, young master—that's what you do."

"If I find the treasure I will," said Edred.

"You do it whether or no," said the old man. "I must be getting along home. You'd like to play about a bit, eh? Well, bring me the keys when you've done. I can trust you not to hurt your own place, that's been in the family all these hundreds of years."

"I should think you could!" said Edred proudly. "Goodbye, and thank you."

"Goodbye, my lord," said the old man, and went.

"I say," said Edred, with the big bunch of keys in his hand,—"if I *am* Lord Arden!"

"You are! you are!" said Elfrida. "I am perfectly certain you are. And I suppose I'm Lady Arden. How perfectly ripping! We can shut up those lodging-children now, anyhow. What's up?"

Edred was frowning and pulling the velvet covering of moss off the big stone on which he had absently sat down.

"Do you think it's burglarish," he said slowly, "to go into your own house without leave?"

"Not if it *is* your own house. Of course not," said Elfrida.

"But suppose it isn't? They might put you in prison for it."

"'AYE,' HE SAID, 'YOU'RE AN ARDEN, FOR SURE.'"

"You could tell the policeman you thought it was yours. I say, Edred, let's!"

"It's not vulgar curiosity, like auntie says; it's the spell I want," said the boy.

"As if I didn't know that," said the girl contemptuously. "But where's the house?"

She might well ask, for there was no house to be seen—only the great grey walls of the castle, with their fine fringe of flowers and grass showing feathery against the pale blue of the June sky. Here and there, though, there were grey wooden doors set in the grey of the stone.

"It must be one of those," Edred said. "We'll try all the keys and all the doors till we find it."

So they tried all the keys and all the doors. One door led to a loft where apples were stored. Another to a cellar, where brooms and spades and picks leaned against the damp wall, and there were baskets and piles of sacks. A third opened into a tower that seemed to be used as a pigeon-cote. It was the very last door they tried that led into the long garden between two high walls, where already the weeds had grown high among the forget-me-nots and pansies. And at the end of this garden was a narrow house with a red roof, wedged tightly in between two high grey walls that belonged to the castle.

All the blinds were down; the garden was chill and quiet, and smelt of damp earth and dead leaves.

"Oh, Edred, do you think we ought?" Elfrida said, shivering.

"Yes, I do," said Edred; "and you're not being good, whatever you may think. You're only being frightened."

Elfrida naturally replied, "I'm not. Come on."

But it was very slowly, and with a feeling of being on tiptoe and holding their breaths, that they went up to those blinded windows that looked like sightless eyes.

The front door was locked, and none of the keys would fit it.

"I don't care," said Edred. "If I am Lord Arden I've got a right to get in, and if I'm not I don't care about anything, so here goes."

Elfrida almost screamed, half with horror and half with admiration of his daring, when he climbed up to a little window by means of an elder-tree that grew close to it, tried to open the window, and when he found it fast deliberately pushed his elbow through the glass.

"Thus," he said rather unsteadily, "the heir of Arden Castle re-enters his estates."

He got the window open and disappeared through it. Elfrida stood clasping and unclasping her hands, and in her mind trying to get rid of the idea of a very large and sudden policeman appearing in the garden door and saying, in that deep voice so much admired in our village constables, "Where's your brother?"

No policeman came, fortunately, and presently a blind went up, a French window opened, and there was Edred beckoning her with the air of a conspirator.

It needed an effort to obey his signal, but she did it. He closed the French window, drew down the blind again, and——

"Oh, don't let's," said Elfrida.

"Nonsense," said Edred; "there's nothing to be frightened of. It's just like our rooms at home."

It was. They went all over the house, and it certainly was. Some of the upper rooms were very bare, but all the furniture was of the same kind as Aunt Edith's, and there were the same kind of pictures. Only the library was different. It was a very large room, and there were no pictures at all. Nothing but books and books and books, bound in yellowy leather. Books from ceiling to floor, shelves of books between the windows and over the mantelpiece—hundreds and thousands of books. Even Edred's spirits sank. "It's no go. It will take us years to look in them all," he said.

"We may as well look at some of them," said Elfrida, always less daring, but more persevering than her brother. She sat down on the worn carpet and began to read the names on the backs of the books nearest to her. "Burton's Atomy of Melon something," she read, and "Locke on Understanding," and many other dull and wearying titles. But none of the books seemed at all likely to contain a spell for finding treasure. "Burgess on the Precious Metals" beguiled her for a moment, but she saw at once that there was no room in its closely-printed, brown-spotted pages for anything so interesting as a spell. Time passed by. The sunlight that came through the blinds had quite changed its place on the carpet, and still Elfrida persevered. Edred grew more and more restless.

"It's no use," he kept saying, and "Let's chuck it," and "I expect that old chap was just kidding us. I don't feel a bit like I did about it," and "Do let's get along home."

But Elfrida plodded on, though her head and her back both ached. I wish I could say that her perseverance was rewarded. But it wasn't; and one must keep to facts. As it happened, it was Edred who, aimlessly running his finger along the edge of the bookshelf just for the pleasure of looking at the soft, mouse-coloured dust that clung to the finger at the end of each shelf, suddenly cried out, "What about this?" and pulled out a great white book that had on its cover a shield printed in gold with squares and little spots on it, and a gold pig standing on the top of the shield, and on the back, "The History of the Ardens of Arden."

In an instant it was open on the floor between them, and they were turning its pages with quick, anxious hands. But, alas! it was as empty of spells as dull old Burgess himself.

It was only when Edred shut it with a bang and the remark that he had had jolly well enough of it that a paper fluttered out and swept away like a pigeon, settling on the fireless hearth. And it was the spell. There was no doubt of that.

Written in faint ink on a square yellowed sheet of letter-paper that had been folded once, and opened and folded again so often that the fold was worn thin and hardly held its two parts together, the writing was fine and pointed and ladylike. At the top was written: "The Spell Aunt Anne Told Me.—December 24, 1793."

And then came the spell:—

> "Hear, Oh badge of Arden's house,
>
> The spell my little age allows;
>
> Arden speaks it without fear,
>
> Badge of Arden's house, draw near,
>
> Make me brave and kind and wise,
>
> And show me where the treasure lies."

"To be said," the paper went on, "at sun-setting by a Lord Arden between the completion of his ninth and tenth years. But it is all folly and not to be believed."

"This is it, right enough," said Edred. "Come on, let's get out of this." They turned to go, and as they did so something moved in the corner of the library—something little, and they could not see its shape.

Neither drew free breath again till they were out of the house, and out of the garden, and out of the castle, and on the wide, thymy downs, with the blue sky above, where the skylarks sang, and there was the sweet, fresh scent of the seaweed and the bean-fields.

"Oh," said Elfrida, then, "I am so glad it's not at midnight you've got to say the spell. You'd be too frightened."

"I shouldn't," said Edred, very pale and walking quickly away from the castle. "I should say it just the same if it was midnight." And he very nearly believed what he said.

Elfrida it was who had picked up the paper that Edred had dropped when that thing moved in the corner. She still held it fast.

"I expect it was only a rat or something," said Edred, his heart beating nineteen to the dozen, as they say in Kent and elsewhere.

"THEY WERE TURNING ITS PAGES WITH QUICK, ANXIOUS HANDS."

"Oh, yes," said Elfrida, whose lips were trembling a little; "I'm sure it was only a rat or something."

When they got to the top of Arden Knoll there was no sign of sunset. There was time, therefore, to pull oneself together, to listen to the skylarks, and to smell the bean-flowers, and to wonder how one could have been such a duffer as to be scared by a "rat or something." Also there were some bits of sandwich and crumbled cake, despised at dinner-time, but now, somehow, tasting quite different. These helped to pass the time till the sun almost seemed to rest on a brown shoulder of the downs, that looked as though it were shrugging itself up to meet the round red ball that the evening mists had made of the sun.

The children had not spoken for several minutes. Their four eyes were fixed on the sun, and as the edge of it seemed to flatten itself against the hill-shoulder Elfrida whispered, "Now!" and gave her brother the paper.

They had read the spell so often, as they sat there in the waning light, that both knew it by heart, so there was no need for Edred to read it. And that was lucky, for in that thick, pink light the faint ink hardly showed at all on the yellowy paper.

Edred stood up.

"Now!" said Elfrida, again. "Say it now." And Edred said, quite out loud and in a pleasant sort of sing-song, such as he was accustomed to use at school when reciting the stirring ballads of the late Lord Macaulay, or the moving tale of the boy on the burning deck:—

"'Hear, Oh badge of Arden's house,

The spell my little age allows;

Arden speaks it without fear,

Badge of Arden's house, draw near,

Make me brave and kind and wise,

And show me where the treasure lies.'"

He said it slowly and carefully, his sister eagerly listening, ready to correct him if he said a word wrong. But he did not.

"Where the treasure lies," he ended, and the great silence of the downs seemed to rush in like a wave to fill the space which his voice had filled.

And nothing else happened at all. A flush of pink from the sun-setting spread over the downs, the grass-stems showed up thin and distinct, the skylarks had ceased to sing, but the scent of the bean-flowers and the seaweed was stronger than ever. And nothing happened till Edred cried out, "What's that?" For close to his foot something moved, not quickly or suddenly so as to startle, but very gently, very quietly, very unmistakably—something that glittered goldenly in the pink, diffused light of the sun-setting.

"Why," said Elfrida stooping, "why, it's——"

CHAPTER II
THE MOULDIWARP

And it was—it was the living image of the little pig-like animal that was stamped in gold above the chequered shield on the cover of the white book in which they had found the spell. And as on the yellowy white of the vellum book-cover, so here on the thymy grass of the knoll it shone golden. The children stood perfectly still. They were afraid to move lest they should scare away this little creature which, though golden, was alive and moved about at their feet, turning a restless nose to right and left.

"It *is*," said Elfrida again, very softly, so as not to frighten it.

"*What?*" Edred asked, though he knew well enough.

"Off the book that we got the spell out of."

"That was our crest on the top of our coat-of-arms, like on the old snuff-box that was great-grandpapa's."

"Well, this is our crest come alive, that's all."

"Don't you be too clever," said Edred. "It said *badge*; I don't believe badge is the same thing as crest. A badge is leeks, or roses, or thistles—something you can wear in your cap. *I* shouldn't like to wear *that* in my cap."

And still the golden thing at their feet moved cautiously and without ceasing.

"Why," said Edred suddenly, "it's just a common old mole."

"It isn't; it's our own crest, that's on the spoons and things. It's our own old family mole that's our crest. How can it be a common mole? It's all golden."

And, even as she spoke, it left off being golden. For the last bit of sun dipped behind the shoulder of the downs, and in the grey twilight that was left the mole was white—any one could see that.

"Oh!" said Elfrida—but she stuck to her point. "So you see," she went on, "it can't be just a really-mole. Really-moles are black."

"Well," said Edred, "it's very tame. I will say that."

"Well——" Edred was beginning; but at that same moment the mole also, suddenly and astonishingly, said, "Well?"

There was a hushed pause. Then——

"Did *you* say that?" Elfrida whispered.

"No," said Edred, "*you* did."

"Don't whisper, now," said the mole; "'tain't purty manners, so I tells 'ee."

With one accord the two children came to their knees, one on each side of the white mole.

"I *say!*" said Edred.

"Now, don't," said the mole, pointing its nose at him quite as disdainfully as any human being could have pointed a finger. "Don't you go for to pretend you don't know as Mouldiwarps 'as got tongues in dere heads same's what you've got."

"But not to talk with?" said Elfrida softly.

"Don't you tell me," said the Mouldiwarp, bristling a little. "Hasn't no one told you e'er a fairy tale? All us beastes has tongues, and when we're dere us uses of en."

"When you're where?" said Edred, rather annoyed at being forced to believe in fairy tales, which he had never really liked.

"Why, in a fairy tale for sure," said the mole. "Wherever to goodness else on earth do you suppose you be?"

"We're here," said Edred, kicking the ground to make it feel more solid and himself more sure of things, "on Arden Knoll."

"An' ain't that in a fairy tale?" demanded the Mouldiwarp triumphantly. "You do talk so free. You called me, and here I be. What d'you want?"

"Are you," said Elfrida, thrilling with surprise and fear, and pleasure and hope, and wonder, and a few other things which, taken in the lump, are usually called "a thousand conflicting emotions,"—"are you the 'badge of Arden's house'?"

"Course I be," said the mole,—"what's left of it; and never did I think to be called one by the Arden boy and gell as didn't know their own silly minds. What do you want, eh?"

"We told you in the spell," said Elfrida.

"Oh, be that all?" said the mole bitterly; "nothing else? I'm to make *him* brave and wise and show him de treasure. Milksop!" it said, so suddenly and fiercely that it almost seemed to spit the words in poor Edred's face.

"I'm not," said Edred, turning turkey-red. "I got into the house and found the spell, anyway."

"Yes; and who did all the looking for it? *She* did. Bless you, I was there; I know all about it. If it was showing *her* the treasure, now, there'd be some sense in it."

"I think you're very unfair," said Elfrida, as earnestly as though she had been speaking to a grown-up human being; "if he was brave and wise we shouldn't want you to make him it."

"You ain't got nothing to do with it," said the mole crossly.

"Yes, she has," said Edred. "I mean to share and share with her—whatever I get. And if you could make me wise I'd teach her everything you taught me. But I don't believe you can. So there!"

"Do you believe I can talk?" the mole asked, and Edred quite definitely and surprisingly said—

"No, I don't. You're a dream, that's all you are," he said, "and I'm dreaming you."

"And what do *you* think?" the mole asked Elfrida, who hesitated.

"*I* think," she said at last, "that it's getting very dark, and Aunt Edith will be anxious about us; and will you meet us another day? There isn't time to make us brave and wise to-night."

"That there ain't, for sure," said the mole meaningly.

"But you might tell us where the treasure is," said Edred.

"That comes last, greedy," said the mole. "I've got to make you kind and wise first, and I see I've got my work cut out. Good-night."

It began to move away.

"Oh, *don't* go!" said Elfrida; "we shall never find you again. Oh, don't! Oh, this is dreadful!"

The mole paused.

"I've *got* to let you find me again. Don't upset yourself," it said bitterly. "When you wants me, come up on to the knoll and say a piece of poetry to call me, and I'll come," and it started again.

"But what poetry?" Edred asked.

"Oh, anything. You can pick and choose."

Edred thought of "The Lays of Ancient Rome."

"Only 'tain't no good without you makes it up yourselves," said the Mouldiwarp.

"Oh!" said the two, much disheartened.

"And course it must be askin' me to kindly come to you. Get along home."

"Where are *you* going?" Elfrida asked.

"Home too, of course," it said, and this time it really *did* go.

The two children turned towards the lights of Ardenhurst Station in perfect silence. Only as they reached the place where the down-turf ends and the road begins Edred said, in tones of awe, "I say!"

And Elfrida answered, "Yes—isn't it?"

Then they walked, still without talking, to the station.

The lights there, and the voices of porters and passengers, the rattle of signal-wires and the "ping, ping" of train signals, had on them the effect of a wet sponge passed over the face of a sleeper by some "already up" person. They seemed to awaken from a dream, and the moment they were in the train, which fortunately came quite soon, they began to talk. They talked without stopping till they got to Cliffville Station, and then they talked all the way home, and by the time they reached the house with the green balconies and the smooth, pale, polished door-knocker they had decided, as children almost always do in cases of magic adventure, that they had better not say anything to any one. As I am always pointing out, it is extremely difficult to tell your magic experiences to people who not only *will* not, but *cannot* believe you. This is one of the drawbacks of really wonderful happenings.

Aunt Edith had not come home, but she came as they were washing their hands and faces for supper. She brought with her presents for Edred's birthday—nicer presents, and more of them, than he had had for three years.

She bought him a box of wonderfully varied chocolate and a box of tools, a very beautiful bat and a cricket-ball and a set of stumps, and a beetle-backed paint-box in which all the colours were *whole* pans, and not half ones, as they usually are in the boxes you get as presents. In this were beautiful paint-brushes—two camel's-hair ones and a sable with a point as fine as fine.

"You are a dear, auntie," he said, with his arms very tight round her waist. He was very happy, and it made him feel more generous than usual. So he said again, "You *are* a dear. And Elfrida can use the paint-box whenever I'm out, and the camel's-hair brushes. Not the sable, of course."

"Oh, Edred, how jolly of you!" said Elfrida, quite touched.

"I've got something for Elfrida too," said Aunt Edith, feeling among the rustling pile of brown paper, and tissue paper, and string, and cardboard, and shavings, that were the husks of Edred's presents. "Ah, here it is!"

It was a book—a red book with gold pictures on back and cover—and it was called "The Amulet." So then it was Elfrida's turn to clasp her aunt round the waist and tell her about her dearness.

"And now to supper," said the dear. "Roast chicken. And gooseberry pie. And cream."

To the children, accustomed to the mild uninterestingness of bread and milk for supper, this seemed the crowning wonder of the day. And what a day it had been!

And while they ate the brown chicken, with bread sauce and gravy and stuffing, and the gooseberry pie and cream, the aunt told them of her day.

"It really *is* a ship," she said, "and the best thing it brings is that we shan't let lodgings any more."

"Hurrah!" was the natural response.

"And we shall have more money to spend and be more comfortable. And you can go to a really nice school. And where do you think we're going to live?"

"Not," said Elfrida, in a whisper,—"not at the castle?"

"Why, how did you guess?"

Elfrida looked at Edred. He hastily swallowed a large mouthful of chicken to say, "Auntie, I do hope you won't mind. We went to Arden to-day. You said we might go this year."

Then the whole story came out—yes, quite all, up to the saying of the spell.

"And did anything happen?" Aunt Edith asked. The children were thankful to see that she was only interested, and did not seem vexed at what they had done.

"Well," said Elfrida slowly, "we saw a mole——"

Aunt Edith laughed, and Edred said quickly—

"That's all the story, auntie. And I *am* Lord Arden, aren't I?"

"Yes," the aunt answered gravely. "You are Lord Arden."

"Oh, ripping!" cried Edred, with so joyous a face that his aunt put away a little sermon she had got ready in the train on the duties of the English aristocracy—that would keep, she thought—and turned to say, "No, dear," to Elfrida's eager question, "Then I'm Lady Arden, aren't I?"

"If he's lord I ought to be lady," Elfrida said. "It's not fair."

"Never mind, old girl," said Edred kindly. "I'll *call* you Lady Arden whenever you like."

"How would you like," asked the aunt, "to go over and live at the castle *now*?"

"To-night?"

"No, no," she laughed; "next week. You see, I must try to let this house, and I shall be very busy. Mrs. Honeysett, the old lady who used to keep house for your great-uncle, wrote to the lawyers and asked if we would employ her. I remember her when I was a little girl; she is a dear, and knows heaps of old songs. How would you like to be there with her while I finish up here and get rid of the lodgers? Oh, there's that bell again! I don't think we'll have any bells at the castle, shall we?"

So that was how it was arranged. The aunt stayed at the bow-windowed house to arrange the new furniture—for the house was to be let furnished—and to pack up the beautiful old things that were real Arden things, and the children went in the carrier's cart, with their clothes and their toys in two black boxes, and in their hearts a world of joyous anticipations.

Mrs. Honeysett received them with a pretty, old-fashioned curtsey, which melted into an embrace.

"You're welcome to your home, my lord," she said, with an arm round each child, "and you too, miss, my dear. Any one can see you're Ardens, both two of you. There was always a boy and a girl—a boy and a girl." She had a sweet, patient face, with large, pale blue eyes that twinkled when she smiled, and she almost always smiled when she looked at the children.

Oh, but it was fine, to unpack one's own box—to lay out one's clothes in long, cedar-wood drawers, fronted with curved polished mahogany; to draw back the neat muslin blinds from lattice-paned windows that had always been Arden windows; to look out, as so many Ardens must have done, over land that, as far as one could see, had belonged to one's family in old days. That it no longer belonged hardly mattered at all to the romance of hearts only ten and twelve years old.

Then to go down one's own shallow, polished stairs (where portraits of old Ardens hung on the wall), and to find the cloth laid for dinner in one's own wainscoted parlour, laid for two. I think it was nice of Edred to say, the moment Mrs. Honeysett had helped them to toad-in-the-hole and left them to eat it—

"May I pass you some potatoes, Lady Arden?"

Elfrida giggled happily.

The parlour was furnished with the kind of furniture they knew and loved. It had a long, low window that showed the long, narrow garden outside. The walls were panelled with wood, browny-grey under its polish.

"Oh," said Elfrida, "there must be secret panels here."

And though Edred said, "Secret fiddlesticks!" he in his heart felt that she was right.

After dinner, "May we explore?" Elfrida asked, and Mrs. Honeysett, most charming of women, answered heartily—

"Why not? It's all his own, bless his dear heart."

So they explored.

The house was much bigger than they had found it on that wonderful first day when they had acted the part of burglars. There was a door covered with faded green baize. Mrs. Honeysett pointed it out to them with, "Don't you think this is all: there's the other house beyond;" and at the other side of that door there was, indeed, the other house.

The house they had already seen was neat, orderly, "bees-whacked," as Mrs. Honeysett said, till every bit of furniture shone like a mirror or a fond hope. But beyond the baize door there were shadows, there was dust, windows draped in cobwebs, before which hung curtains tattered and faded, drooping from their poles like the old banners that, slowly rotting in great cathedrals, sway in the quiet air where no wind is— stirred, perhaps, by the breath of Fame's invisible trumpet to the air of old splendours and glories.

"THE CHILDREN WENT IN THE CARRIER'S CART."

The carpets lay in rags on the floors; on the furniture the dust lay thick, and on the boards of corridor and staircase; on the four-post beds in the bedchambers the hangings hung dusty and rusty—the quilts showed the holes eaten by moths and mice. In one room a cradle of carved oak still had a coverlet of tattered silk dragging from it. From the great kitchen-hearth, where no fire had been this very long time, yet where still the ashes of the last fire lay grey and white, a chill air came. The place smelt damp and felt——

"Do you think it's haunted?" Elfrida asked.

"Rot!" was her brother's brief reply, and they went on.

They found long, narrow corridors hung crookedly with old, black-framed prints, which drooped cobwebs, like grey-draped crape. They found rooms with floors of grey, uneven oak, and fireplaces in whose grates lay old soot and the broken nests of starlings hatched very long ago.

Edred's handkerchief—always a rag-of-all-work—rubbed a space in one of the windows, and they looked out over the swelling downs. This part of the house was not built within the castle, that was plain.

When they had opened every door and looked at every roomful of decayed splendour they went out and round. Then they saw that this was a wing built right out of the castle—a wing with squarish windows, with carved drip-stones. All the windows were yellow as parchment, with the inner veil laid on them by Time and the spider. The ivy grew thick round the windows, almost hiding some of them altogether.

"Oh!" cried Elfrida, throwing herself down on the turf, "it's too good to be true. I can't believe it."

"What *I* can't believe," said Edred, doing likewise, "is that precious mole."

"But we saw it," said Elfrida; "you can't help believing things when you've seen them."

"I can," said Edred, superior. "You remember the scarlet toadstools in 'Hereward.' Suppose those peppermint creams were enchanted—to make us dream things."

"They were good," said Elfrida. "I say!"

"Well?"

"Have you made up any poetry to call the mole with?"

"Have you?"

"No; I've tried, though."

"*I've* tried. And I've done it."

"Oh, Edred, you *are* clever. Do say it."

"If I do, do you think the mole will come?"

"Of course it will."

"Well," said Edred slowly, "of course I want to find the treasure and all that. But I *don't* believe in it. It isn't *likely*—that's what I think. Now *is* it likely?"

"Unlikelier things happened in 'The Amulet,'" said Elfrida.

"Ah," said Edred, "that's a story."

"The mole said *we* were in a story. I say, Edred, do say your poetry."

Edred slowly said it—

"'Mole, mole,

Come out of your hole;

I know you're blind,

But *I* don't mind.'"

Elfrida looked eagerly round her. There was the short turf; the castle walls, ivied and grey, rose high above her; pigeons circled overhead, and in the arches of the windows and on the roof of the house they perched, preening their bright feathers or telling each other, "Coo, coo; cooroo, cooroo," whatever that may mean. But there was no mole—not a hint or a dream or idea of a mole.

"Edred," said his sister.

"Well?"

"Did you *really* make that up? Don't be cross, but I do think I've heard something like it before."

"I—I adopted it," said Edred.

"?" said Elfrida.

"Haven't you seen it in books, 'Adopted from the French'? I altered it."

"I don't believe that'll do. How much did you alter? What's the real poetry like?"

"'The mole, the mole,

He lives in a hole.

The mole is blind;

I don't mind,'"

said Edred sulkily. "Auntie told me it the day you went to her with Mrs. Harrison."

"I'm sure you ought to make it up all yourself. You see, the mole doesn't come."

"There isn't any mole," said Edred.

"Let's both think hard. I'm sure I could make poetry—if I knew how to begin."

"If any one's got to make it, it's me," said Edred. "You're not Lord Arden."

"You're very unkind," said Elfrida, and Edred knew she was right.

"I don't mind trying," he said, condescendingly; "you make the poetry and I'll say it."

Elfrida buried her head in her hands and thought till her forehead felt as large as a mangel-wurzel, and her blood throbbed in it like a church clock ticking.

"Got it yet?" he asked, just as she thought she really had got it.

"*Don't!*" said the poet, in agony.

Then there was silence, except for the pigeons and the skylarks, and the mooing of a cow at a distant red-roofed farm.

"Will this do?" she said at last, lifting her head from her hands and her elbows from the grass; there were deep dents and lines on her elbows made by the grass-stalks she had leaned on so long.

"Spit it out," said Edred.

Thus encouraged, Elfrida said, very slowly and carefully, "'Oh, Mouldiwarp'—I think it would rather be called that than mole, don't you?—'Oh, Mouldiwarp, do please come out and show us how to set about it'—that means the treasure. I hope it'll understand."

"That's not poetry," said Edred.

"Yes, it is, if you say it right on—

"'Oh, Mouldiwarp, do please come out

And show us how to set about

It.'"

"There ought to be some more," said Edred—rather impressed, all the same.

"There is," said Elfrida. "Oh, wait a minute—I shall remember directly. It—what I mean is, how to find the treasure and make Edred brave and wise and kind."

"I'm kind enough if it comes to that," said Lord Arden.

"Oh, I *know* you are; but poetry has to rhyme—you know it has. I expect poets often have to say what they don't mean because of that."

"Well, say it straight through," said Edred, and Elfrida said, obediently—

"'Oh, Mouldiwarp, do please come out

And show us how to set about

It. What I mean is how to find

The treasure, and make Edred brave and wise and kind.'

I'll write it down if you've got a pencil."

Edred produced a piece of pink chalk, but he had no paper, so Elfrida had to stretch out her white petticoat, put a big stone on the hem, and hold it out tightly with both hands, while Edred wrote at her dictation.

Then Edred studiously repeated the lines again and again, as he was accustomed to repeat "The Battle of Ivry," till at last he was able to stand up and say—

"'Oh, Mouldiwarp, do please come out

And show me how to set about

It. What I mean is how to find

The treasure, and make me brave and wise——'

If you don't mind," he added.

And instantly there was the white mole.

"What do you want now?" it said very crossly indeed. "And call that poetry?"

"It's the first I ever made," said Elfrida, of the hot ears. "Perhaps it'll be better next time."

"We want you to do what the spell says," said Edred.

"Make *you* brave and wise? That can't be done all in a minute. That's a long job, that is," said the mole viciously.

"Don't be so cross, dear," said Elfrida; "and if it's going to be so long hadn't you better begin?"

"I ain't agoin' to do no more'n my share," said the mole, somewhat softened though, perhaps by the "dear." "You tell me what you want, and p'raps I'll do it."

"I know what I want," said Edred, "but I don't know whether you *can* do it."

"Ha!" laughed the mole contemptuously.

"I got it out of a book Elfrida got on my birthday," Edred said. "The children in it went into the past. I'd like to go into the past—and find that treasure!"

"Choose your period," said the mole wearily.

"Choose——?"

"Your period. What time you'd like to go back to. If you don't choose before I've counted ten it's all off. One, two, three, four——"

It counted ten through a blank silence.

"Nine, ten," it ended. "Oh, very well, den, you'll have to take your luck, that's all."

"Bother!" said Edred. "I couldn't think of anything except all the dates of all the kings of England all at once."

"Lucky to know 'em," said the mole, and so plainly not believing that he did know them that Edred found himself saying under his breath,

"William the First, 1066; William the Second, 1087; Henry the First, 1100."

The mole yawned, which, of course, was very rude of it.

"Don't be cross, dear," said Elfrida again; "you help us your own way."

"Now you're talking," said the mole, which, of course, Elfrida knew. "Well, I'll give you a piece of advice. Don't you be nasty to each other for a whole day, and then——"

"*You* needn't talk," said Edred, still under his breath.

"Very well," said the mole, whose ears were sharper than his eyes. "I won't."

"Oh, don't!" sighed Elfrida; "*what* is it we are to do when we've been nice to each other for a whole day?"

"Well, *when* you've done that," said the mole, "look for the door."

"What door?" asked Elfrida.

"*The* door," said the mole.

"But where is it?" Edred asked.

"In the house it be, of course," said the mole. "Where else to gracious should it be?"

And it ran with mouse-like quickness across the grass and vanished down what looked like a rabbit-hole.

"Now," said Elfrida triumphantly, "you've got to believe in the mole."

"Yes," said Edred, "and you've got to be nice to me for a whole day, or it's no use my believing."

"Aren't I generally nice?" the girl pleaded, and her lips trembled.

"Yes," said her brother. "Yes, Lady Arden; and now I'm going to be nice, too. And where shall we look for the door?"

This problem occupied them till tea-time. After tea they decided to paint—with the new paint-box and the beautiful new brushes. Elfrida wanted to paint Mr. Millar's illustrations in "The Amulet," and Edred wanted to paint them, too. This could not be, as you will see if you have the book. Edred contended that they were his paints. Elfrida reminded him that it was her book. The heated discussion that followed ended quite suddenly and breathlessly.

"*I* wouldn't be a selfish pig," said Edred.

"No more would I," said Elfrida. "Oh, Edred, *is* this being nice to each other for twenty-four hours?"

"Oh," said Edred. "Yes—well—all right. Never mind. We'll begin again to-morrow."

But it is much more difficult than you would think to be really nice to your brother or sister for a whole day. Three days passed before the two Ardens could succeed in this seemingly so simple thing. The days were not dull ones at all. There were beautiful things in them that I wish I had time to tell you about—such as climbings and discoveries and books with pictures, and a bureau with a secret drawer. It had nothing in it but a farthing and a bit of red tape—secret drawers never have—but it was a very nice secret drawer for all that.

And at last a day came when each held its temper with a strong bit. They began by being very polite to each other, and presently it grew to seem like a game.

"Let's call each other Lord and Lady Arden all the time, and pretend that we're no relation," said Elfrida. And really that helped tremendously. It is wonderful how much more polite you can be to outsiders than you can to your relations, who are, when all's said and done, the people you really love.

As the time went on they grew more and more careful. It was like building a house of cards. As hour after hour of blameless politeness was added to the score, they grew almost breathlessly anxious. If, after all this, some natural annoyance should spoil everything!

"I do hope," said Edred, towards tea-time, "that you won't go and do anything tiresome."

"Oh, dear, I do hope I shan't," said Elfrida.

And this was just like them both.

After tea they decided to read, so as to lessen the chances of failure. They both wanted the same book—"Treasure Island" it was—and for a moment the niceness of both hung in the balance. Then, with one accord, each said, "No—you have it!" and the matter ended in each taking a quite different book that it didn't particularly want to read.

At bedtime Edred lighted Elfrida's candle for her, and she picked up the matches for him when he dropped them.

"Bless their hearts," said Mrs. Honeysett, in the passage.

They parted with the heartfelt remark, "We've done it this time."

Now, of course, in the three days when they had not succeeded in being nice to each other they had "looked for the door," but as the mole had not said where it was, nor what kind of a door, their search had not been fruitful. Most of the rooms had several doors, and as there were a good many rooms the doors numbered fifty-seven, counting cupboards. And among these there was none that seemed worthy to rank above all others as *the* door. Many of the doors in the old part of the house looked as though they might be *the* one, but since there *were* many no one could be sure.

"How shall we know?" Edred asked next morning, through his egg and toast.

"I suppose it's like when people fall in love," said Elfrida, through hers. "You see the door and you know at once that it is the only princess in the world, for you—I mean door, of course," she added.

And then, when breakfast was over, they stood up and looked at each other.

"Now," they said together.

"We'll look at every single door. Perhaps there'll be magic writing on *the* door come out in the night, like mushrooms," said the girl.

"More likely that mole was kidding us," said the boy.

"Oh, *no*," said the girl; "and we must look at them on both sides—every one. Oh, I do wonder what's inside the door, don't you?"

"Bluebeard's wives, I shouldn't wonder," said the boy, "with their heads——"

"If you don't stop," said the girl, putting her fingers in her ears, "I won't look for the door at all. No, I don't mean to be aggravating; but please don't. You know I hate it."

"Come on," said Edred, "and don't be a duffer, old chap."

The proudest moments of Elfrida's life were when her brother called her "old chap."

So they went and looked at all the fifty-seven doors, one after the other, on the inside and on the outside; some were painted and some were grained, some were carved and some were plain, some had panels and others had none, but they were all of them doors—just doors, and nothing more. Each was just a door, and none of them had any claim at all to be spoken of as THE door. And when they had looked at all the fifty-seven on the inside and on the outside, there was nothing for it but to look again. So they looked again, very carefully, to see if there were any magic writing that they hadn't happened to notice. And there wasn't. So then they began to tap the walls to try and discover a door with a secret spring. And that was no good either.

"There isn't any old door," said Edred. "I told you that mole was pulling our leg."

"I'm *sure* there is," said Elfrida, sniffing a little from prolonged anxiety. "Look here—let's play it like the willing game. I'll be blindfolded, and you hold my hand and will me to find the door."

"I don't believe in the willing game," said Edred disagreeably.

"No more do I," said Elfrida; "but we must do something, you know. It's no good sitting down and saying there isn't any door."

"There isn't, all the same," said Edred. "Well, come on."

So Elfrida was blindfolded with her best silk scarf—the blue one with the hem-stitched ends—and Edred took her hands. And at once—this happened in the library, where they had found the spell—Elfrida began to walk in a steady and purposeful way. She crossed the hall and went through the green baize door into the other house; went along its corridor and up its dusty stairs—up, and up, and up——

"We've looked everywhere here," said Edred, but Elfrida did not stop for that.

"I know I'm going straight to it," she said. "Oh! do try to believe a little, or we shall never find anything," and went on along the corridor, where the spiders had draped the picture-frames with their grey crape curtains. There were many doors in this corridor, and Elfrida stopped suddenly at one of them—a door just like the others.

"This," she said, putting her hand out till it rested on the panel, all spread out like a pink starfish,—"this is the door."

She felt for the handle, turned it, and went in, still pulling at Edred's hand and with the blue scarf still on her eyes. Edred followed.

"I say!" he said, and then she pulled off the scarf.

The door closed itself very softly behind them.

They were in a long attic room close under the roof—a room that they had certainly, in all their explorings, never found before. There were no windows—the roof sloped down at the sides almost to the floor. There was no ceiling—old worm-eaten roof-beams showed the tiles between—and old tie-beams crossed it so that as you stared up it looked like a great ladder with the rungs very far apart. Here and there through the chinks of the tiles a golden dusty light filtered in, and outside was the "tick, tick" of moving pigeon feet, the rustling of pigeon feathers, the "cooroocoo" of pigeon voices. The long room was almost bare; only along each side, close under the roof, was a row of chests, and no two chests were alike.

"Oh!" said Edred. "I'm kind and wise now. I feel it inside me. So now we've got the treasure. We'll rebuild the castle."

He got to the nearest chest and pushed at the lid, but Elfrida had to push too before he could get the heavy thing up. And when it was up, alas! there was no treasure in the chest—only folded clothes.

So then they tried the next chest.

And in all the chests there was no treasure at all—only clothes. Clothes, and more clothes again.

"Well, never mind," said Elfrida, trying to speak comfortably. "They'll be splendid for dressing up in."

"That's all very well," said Edred, "but I want the treasure."

"Perhaps," said Elfrida, with some want of tact,—"perhaps you're not 'good and wise' yet. Not *quite*, I mean," she hastened to add. "Let's take the things out and look at them. Perhaps the treasure's in the pockets."

But it wasn't—not a bit of it; not even a threepenny-bit.

The clothes in the first chest were full riding cloaks and long boots, short-waisted dresses and embroidered scarves, tight breeches and coats with bright buttons. There were very interesting waistcoats and odd-shaped hats. One, a little green one, looked as though it would fit Edred. He tried it on. And at the same minute Elfrida lifted out a little straw bonnet trimmed with blue ribbons. "Here's one for me," she said, and put it on.

And then it seemed as though the cooing and rustling of the pigeons came right through the roof and crowded round them in a sort of dazzlement and cloud of pigeon noises. The pigeon noises came closer and closer, and garments were drawn out of the chest and put on the children. They did not know how it was done, any more than you do—

but it seemed, somehow, that the pigeon noises were like hands that helped, and presently there the two children stood in clothing such as they had never worn. Elfrida had a short-waisted dress of green-sprigged cotton, with a long and skimpy skirt. Her square-toed brown shoes were gone, and her feet wore flimsy sandals. Her arms were bare, and a muslin handkerchief was folded across her chest. Edred wore very white trousers that came right up under his arms, a blue coat with brass buttons, and a sort of frilly tucker round his neck.

"I say!" they both said, when the pigeon noises had taken themselves away, and they were face to face in the long, empty room.

"That was funny," Edred added; "let's go down and show Mrs. Honeysett."

But when they got out of the door they saw that Mrs. Honeysett, or some one else, must have been very busy while they were on the other side of it, for the floor of the gallery was neatly swept and polished; a strip of carpet, worn, but clean, ran along it, and prints hung straight and square on the cleanly, whitewashed walls, and there was not a cobweb to be seen anywhere. The children opened the gallery doors as they went along, and every room was neat and clean—no dust, no tattered curtains, only perfect neatness and a sort of rather bare comfort showed in all the rooms. Mrs. Honeysett was in none of them. There were no workmen about, yet the baize door was gone, and in its stead was a door of old wood, very shaky and crooked.

The children ran down the passage to the parlour and burst open the door, looking for Mrs. Honeysett.

There sat a very upright old lady and a very upright old gentleman, and their clothes were not the clothes people wear nowadays. They were like the clothes the children themselves had on. The old lady was hemming a fine white frill; the old gentleman was reading what looked like a page from some newspaper.

"Hoity-toity," said the old lady very severely; "we forget our manners, I think. Make your curtsey, miss."

Elfrida made one as well as she could.

"To teach you respect for your elders," said the old gentleman, "you had best get by heart one of Dr. Watts's Divine and Moral Songs. I leave you to see to it, my lady."

"'HOITY-TOITY,' SAID THE OLD LADY VERY SEVERELY; 'WE FORGET OUR MANNERS, I THINK.'"

He laid down the sheet and went out, very straight and dignified, and without quite knowing how it happened the children found themselves sitting on two little stools in a room that was, and was not, the parlour in which they had had that hopeful eggy breakfast, each holding a marbled side of Dr. Watts's Hymns.

"You will commit to memory the whole of the one commencing—

"'Happy the child whose youngest years

Receive instruction well,'

And you will be deprived of pudding with your dinners," remarked the old lady.

"I say!" murmured Edred.

"Oh, *hush*!" said Elfrida, as the old lady carried her cambric frills to the window-seat.

"But I won't stand it," whispered Edred. "I'll tell Aunt Edith—and who's *she* anyhow?" He glowered at the old lady across the speckless carpet.

"Oh, don't you *understand*?" Elfrida whispered back. "We've got turned into somebody else, and she's our grandmamma."

I don't know how it was that Elfrida saw this and Edred didn't. Perhaps because she was a girl, perhaps because she was two years older than he. They looked hopelessly at the bright sunlight outside, and then at the dull, small print of the marble-backed book.

"Edred," said the old lady, "hand me the paper." She pointed at the sheet on the brightly polished table. He got up and carried it across to her, and as he did so he glanced at it and saw:—

THE TIMES.
June 16, 1807.

And then he knew, as well as Elfrida did, exactly where he was, and *when*.

CHAPTER III
IN BONEY'S TIMES

Edred crept back to his stool, and took his corner of the marble-backed book of Dr. Watts with fingers that trembled. If you are inclined to despise him, consider that it was his first real adventure. Even in ordinary life, and in the time he naturally lived in, nothing particularly thrilling had ever happened to happen to him until he became Lord Arden and explored Arden Castle. And now he and Elfrida had not only discovered a disused house and a wonderful garret with chests in it, but had been clothed by mysterious pigeon noises in clothes belonging to another age. But, you will say, pigeon noises can't clothe you in anything, whatever it belongs to. Well, that was just what Edred told himself at the time. And yet it was certain that they did. This sort of thing it was that made the whole business so mysterious. Further, he and his sister had managed somehow to go back a hundred years. He knew this quite well, though he had no evidence but that one sheet of newspaper. He felt it, as they say, in his bones. I don't know how it was, perhaps the air felt a hundred years younger. Shepherds and country people can tell the hour of night by the feel of the air. So perhaps very sensitive people can tell the century by much the same means. These, of course, would be the people to whom adventures in times past or present would be likely to happen. We must always consider what is likely, especially when we are reading stories about unusual things.

"I say," Edred whispered presently, "we've got back to 1807. That paper says so."

"I know," Elfrida whispered. So she must have had more of that like-shepherds-telling-the-time-of-night feeling than even her brother.

"I wish I could remember what was happening in history in 1807," said Elfrida, "but we never get past Edward IV. We always have to go back to the Saxons because of the new girls."

"But we're not in history. We're at Arden," Edred said.

"We *are* in history. It'll be awful not even knowing who's king," said Elfrida; and then the stiff old lady looked up over very large spectacles with thick silver rims, and said—

"Silence!"

Presently she laid down the *Times* and got ink and paper—no envelopes—and began to write. She was finishing a letter, the large sheet was almost covered on one side. When she had covered it quite, she turned it round and began to write across it. She used a white goose-quill pen. The inkstand was of china, with gold scrolls and cupids and wreaths of roses painted on it. On one side was the ink-well, on the other a thing like a china pepper-pot, and in front a tray for the pens and sealing-wax to lie in. Both children now knew their unpleasant poem by heart; so they watched the old lady, who was grandmother to the children she supposed them to be. When she had finished writing she sprinkled some dust out of the pepper-pot over the letter to dry the ink. There was no blotting-paper to be seen. Then she folded the sheet, and sealed it with a silver seal from the pen-tray, and wrote the address on the outside. Then—

"Have you got your task?" she asked.

"Here it is," said Elfrida, holding up the book.

"No impudence, miss!" said the grandmother sternly. "You very well know that I mean, have you got it by rote yet? And you know, too, that you should say 'ma'am' whenever you address me."

"Yes, ma'am," said Elfrida; and this was taken to mean that she knew her task.

"Then come and say it. No, no; you know better than that. Feet in the first position, hands behind you, heads straight, and do not fidget with your feet."

So then first Elfrida and then Edred recited the melancholy verses.

"Now," said the old lady, "you may go and play in the garden."

"Mayn't we take your letter to the post?" Elfrida asked.

"Yes; but you are not to stay in the 'George' bar, mind, not even if Mrs. Skinner should invite you. Just hand her the letter and come out. Shut the door softly, and do not shuffle with your feet."

"Yes, ma'am," said Elfrida; and on that they got out.

"They'll find us out—bound to," said Edred; "we don't know a single thing about anything. I don't know where the 'George' is, or where to get a stamp, or anything."

"We must find some one we can trust, and tell them the truth," said Elfrida.

"There isn't any one," said Edred, "that I'd trust. You can't trust the sort of people who stick this sort of baby flummery round a chap's neck." He crumpled his starched frill with hot, angry fingers.

"Mine prickles all round, too," Elfrida reminded him, "and it's lower, and you get bigger as you go down, so it prickles more of me than yours does you."

"Let's go back to the attic and try and get back into our own time. I expect we just got in to the wrong door, don't you? Let's go now."

"Oh, no," said Elfrida. "How dreadfully dull! Why, we shall see all sorts of things, and be top in history for the rest of our lives. Let's go through with it."

"Do you remember which door it was—the attic, I mean?" Edred suddenly asked. "Was it the third on the left?"

"I don't know. But we can easily find it when we want it."

"I'd like to know *now*," said Edred obstinately. "You never know when you *are* going to want things. Mrs. Honeysett says you ought always to be able to lay your hand on anything you want the moment you *do* want it. I should like to be quite certain about being able to lay our hands on our own clothes. Suppose some one goes and tidies them up. You know what people are."

"All right," said Elfrida, "we'll go and tidy them up ourselves. It won't take a minute."

It would certainly not have taken five—if things had been as the children expected. They raced up the stairs to the corridor where the prints were.

"It's not the first door, I'm certain," said Edred, so they opened the second. But it was not that either. So then they tried all the doors in turn, even opening, at last, the first one of all. And it was not that, even. *It was not any of them.*

"We've come to the wrong corridor," said the boy.

"It's the only one," said the girl. And it was. For though they hunted all over the house, upstairs and downstairs, and tried every door, the door of the attic they could not find again. And what is more, when they came to count up, there were fifty-seven doors without it.

"Fifty-five, fifty-six, fifty-seven," said Elfrida, and ended in a sob,—"the door's gone! We shall have to stay here for ever and ever. Oh, I want auntie—I do, I do!"

She sat down abruptly on a small green mat in front of the last door, which happened to be that of the kitchen.

Edred says he did not cry too. And if what he says is true, Elfrida's crying must have been louder than was usual with her; for the kitchen door opened, and the two children were caught up in two fat arms and hurried into a pleasant kitchen, where bright brass and copper pots hung on the walls, and between a large fire and a large meat screen a leg of mutton turned round and round with nobody to help it.

"Hold your noise," said the owner of the fat arms, who now proved to be a very stout woman in a chocolate-coloured print gown sprigged with blue roses. She had a large linen apron and a cap with flappy frills, and between the frills just such another good, kind, jolly face as Mrs. Honeysett's own. "Here, stop your mouths," she said, "or your granny'll be after you—to say nothing of Boney. Stop your crying, do, and see what cookie's got for you."

She opened a tin canister and picked out two lumps of brown stuff that looked like sand—about the size and shape of prunes they were.

"What's that?" Edred asked.

"Drabbit me," said the cook, "what a child it is! Not know sugar when he sees it! Well, well, Master Edred, what next, I should like to know?"

The children took the lumps and sucked them. They were of sugar, sure enough, but the sugar had a strong, coarse taste behind its sweetness, and if the children had really not been quite extra polite and kind they would have followed the promptings of Nature and——— But, of course, they knew that this would be both disgusting and ungrateful. So they got the sugar down somehow, while cook beamed at them with a wide, kind smile between her cap-frills, and two hands, as big as little beefsteak puddings, on her hips.

"Now, no more crybabying," she said; "run along and play."

"We've got to take granny's letter to post," said Edred, "and we don't——"

"Cook," said Elfrida, on a sudden impulse, "can you keep a secret?"

"Can't I?" said the cook. "Haven't I kept the secret of how furmety's made, and Bakewell pies and all? There's no furmety to hold a candle to mine in this country, as well you know."

"We don't know *anything*," said Elfrida; "that's just it. And we daren't let granny know how much we don't know. Something's happened to us, so that we can't remember anything that happened more than an hour ago."

"Bless me," said the cook, "don't you remember old cookie giving you the baked apple-dumplings when you were sent to bed without your suppers a week come Thursday?"

"No," said Elfrida; "but I'm sure you did. Only what are we to do?"

"You're not deceiving poor cookie, are you now, like you did about the French soldiers being hid in the windmill, upsetting all the village like you did?"

"No; it's true—it's dreadfully true. You'll have to help us. We don't remember *anything*, either of us."

The cook sat down heavily in a polished arm-chair with a patchwork cushion.

"She's overlooked you. There's not a doubt about it. You're bewitched. Oh, my pretty little dears, that ever I should see the day——"

The cook's fat, jolly face twisted and puckered in a way with which each child was familiar in the face of the other.

"Don't cry," they said both together; and Elfrida added, "Who's overlooked what?"

"Old Betty Lovell has—that I'll be bound! She's bewitched you both, sure as eggs is eggs. I knew there'd be some sort of a to-do when my lord had her put in the stocks for stealing sticks in the wood. We've got to get her to take it off, my dears, that's what we've got to do, for sure; without you could find a white Mouldiwarp, and that's not likely."

"A white Mouldiwarp?" said both the children, and again they spoke together like a chorus and looked at each other like conspirators.

"You know the rhyme—oh! but if you've forgotten everything you've forgotten that too."

"Say it, won't you?" said Edred.

"Let's see, how do it go?—

"White Mouldiwarp a spell can make,

White Mouldiwarp a spell can break;

When all be well, let Mouldiwarp be,

When all goes ill, then turn to he."

"Well, all's not gone ill yet," said Elfrida, wriggling her neck in its prickly muslin tucker. "Let's go and see the witch."

"You'd best take her something—a screw of sugar she'd like, and a pinch of tea."

"Why, she'd not say 'Thank you' for it," said Edred, looking at the tiny packets.

"I expect you've forgotten," said cook gently, "that tea's ten shillings a pound and sugar's gone up to three-and-six since the war."

"What war?"

"The French war. You haven't forgotten we're at war with Boney and the French, and the bonfire we had up at the church when the news came of the drubbing we gave them at Trafalgar, and poor dear Lord Nelson and all? And your grandfather reading out about it to them from the 'George' balcony, and all the people waiting to cheer, and him not able to get it out for choking pride and because of Lord Nelson—God bless him!—and the people couldn't get their cheers out neither, for the same cause, and every one blowing their noses and shaking each other's hands like as if it was a mad funeral?"

"How splendid!" said Elfrida. "But we don't remember it."

"Nor you don't remember how you killed all the white butterflies last year because you said they were Frenchies in their white coats? And the birching you got, for cruelty to dumb animals, his lordship said. You howled for an hour together after it, so you did."

"I'm glad we've forgotten *that*, anyhow," said Edred.

"Gracious!" said the cook. "Half after eleven, and my eggs not so much as broke for my pudding. Off you go with your letter. Don't you tell any one else about you forgetting. And then you come home along by Dering's Spinney—and go see old Betty. Speak pretty to her and give her the tea and sugar, and keep your feet crossed under your chair if she asks you to sit down. And I'll give you an old knife-blade apiece to put in your pockets; she can't do nothing if you've got steel on you. And get her to take it off—the ill-wishing, I mean. And don't let her know you've got steel; they don't like to think you've been beforehand with them."

So the children went down across the fields to the "George," and the bean-flowers smelt as sweet, and the skylarks sang as clearly, and the sun and the sky were just as golden and blue as they had been last week. And last week was really a hundred years on in the future. And yet it was last week too—from where they were. Time is a very confusing thing, as the children remarked to each other more than once.

They found the "George" half-way up Arden village, a stately, great house shaped like an E, with many windows and a great porch with a balcony over it. They gave their letter to a lady in a round cap who sat sewing in a pleasant room where there were many bottles and kegs, and rows of bright pewter ale-pots, and little fat mugs to measure other things with, and pewter plates on a brown dresser. There were greyhounds, too, all sprawling, legs and shoulders and tails entangled together like a bunch of dead eels, before the widest hearth the children had ever seen. They hurried away the moment they had given the letter. A coach, top-heavy with luggage, had drawn up in front of the porch, and as they went out they saw the ostlers leading away the six smoking horses. Edred felt that he *must* see the stables, so they followed, and the stables were as big as the house, and there were horses going in and horses going out, and hay and straw, and ostlers with buckets and ostlers with harness, and stalls and loose-boxes beyond counting, and bustle and hurry beyond words.

"How ever many horses have you got?" said Elfrida, addressing a man who had not joined in the kindly chorus of "Hulloa, little 'uns!" that greeted the children. So she judged him to be a new-comer. As he was.

"Two-and-fifty," said the man.

"What for?" Elfrida asked.

"Why, for the coaches, and the post-shays, and the King's messengers, for sure," the man answered. "How else'd us all get about the country, and get to hear the newses, if it wasn't for the stable the 'George' keeps?"

And then the children remembered that this was the time before railways and telegrams and telephones.

It is always difficult to remember exactly where one is when one happens to get into a century that is not one's own.

Edred would have liked to stay all day watching the busyness of every one and the beautifulness of the horses, but Elfrida dragged him away.

They had to find the witch, she reminded him; and in a dreadful tumble-down cottage, with big holes in its roof of rotten thatch, they did find her.

She was exactly like the pictures of witches in story books, only she had not a broomstick or a high-pointed hat. She had instead a dirty cap that had once been white, and a rusty gown that had once been black, and a streaky shawl that might once, perhaps, have been scarlet. But nobody could be sure of that now. There was a black cat sitting on a very dirty wooden settle, and the old woman herself sat on a rickety three-legged stool, her wrinkled face bent over a speckled hen which she was nursing in her lap and holding gently in her yellow, wrinkled hands.

As soon as Edred caught sight of her through the crooked doorway, he stopped. "I'm not going in," he said, "what's the good? We know jolly well she *hasn't* bewitched us. And if we go cheeking her she *may*, and then we shall be in a nice hole."

"There's the tea and sugar," said Elfrida.

"'I'VE BROUGHT YOU SOME TEA AND SUGAR,' SHE SAID."

"You just give it her and come away. I'll wait for you by the stile."

So Elfrida went into the cottage alone, and said "Good morning" in rather a frightened way.

"I've brought you some tea and sugar," she said, and stood waiting for the "Thank you," without which it would not be polite to say "Good morning" and to go away.

The "Thank you" never came. Instead, the witch stopped stroking the hen, and said—

"What for? I've not done you no 'arm."

"No," said Elfrida. "I'm sure you wouldn't."

"Then what have you brought it for?"

"For—oh, just for you," said Elfrida. "I thought you'd like it. It's just a—a love-gift, you know."

This was Aunt Edith's way of calling a present that didn't come just because it was your birthday or Christmas, or you had had a tooth out.

"A love-gift?" said the old woman slowly. "After all this long time?"

Elfrida did not understand. How should she? It's almost impossible for even the most grown up and clever of us to know how women used to be treated—and not so very long ago either—if they were once suspected of being witches. It generally began by the old woman's being cleverer than her neighbours, having more wit to find out what was the matter with sick people, and more still to cure them. Then her extra cleverness would help her to foretell storms and gales and frosts, and to find water by the divining rod—a very mysterious business. And when once you can find out where water is by just carrying a forked hazel twig between your hands and walking across a meadow, you can most likely find out a good many other things that your stupid neighbours would never dream of. And in those long-ago days—which really aren't so very long ago—your being so much cleverer than your neighbours would be quite enough. You would soon be known as the "wise woman"—and from "wise woman" to witch was a very short step indeed.

So Elfrida, not understanding, said, "Yes; is your fowl ill?"

"'Twill mend," said the old woman,—"'twill mend. The healing of my hands has gone into it." She rose, set the hen on the hearth, where it fluttered, squawked, and settled among grey ashes, very much annoying the black cat, and laid her hands suddenly on Elfrida's shoulders.

"And now the healing of my hands is for you," she said. "You have brought me a love-gift. Never a gift have I had these fifty years but was a gift of fear or a payment for help—to buy me to take off a spell or put a spell on. But you have brought me a love-gift, and I tell you you shall have your heart's desire. You shall have love around and about you all your life long. That which is lost shall be found. That which came not shall come again. In this world's goods you shall be blessed, and blessed in the goods of the heart also. I know—I see—and for you I see everything good and fair. Your future shall be clean and sweet as your kind heart."

She took her hands away. Elfrida, very much impressed by these flattering remarks which she felt she did not deserve, stood still, not knowing what to say or do; she rather wanted to cry.

"I only brought it because cook told me," she said.

"Cook didn't give you the kind heart that makes you want to cry for me now," said the witch.

The old woman sank down in a crouching heap, and her voice changed to one of sing-song.

"I know," she said,—"I know many things. All alone the livelong day and the death-long night, I have learned to see. As cats see through the dark, I see through the days that have been and shall be. I know that you are not here, that you are not now. You will return whence you came, and this time that is not yours shall bear no trace of you. And my blessing shall be with you in your own time and your own place, because you brought a love-gift to the poor old wise woman of Arden."

"Is there anything I can do for you?" Elfrida asked, very sorry indeed, for the old woman's voice was very pitiful.

"Kiss me," said the old woman,—"kiss me with your little child's mouth, that has come back a hundred years to do it."

Elfrida did not wish to kiss the wrinkled, grey face, but her heart wished her to be kind, and she obeyed her heart.

"Ah!" said the wise woman, "now I see. Oh, never have I had such a vision. None of them all has ever been like this. I see great globes of light like the sun in the streets of the city, where now are only little oil-lamps and guttering lanterns. I see iron roads, with fiery dragons drawing the coaches, and rich and poor riding up and down on them. Men shall speak in England and their voice be heard in France—more, the voices of men dead shall be kept alive in boxes and speak at the will of those who still live. The handlooms shall cease in the cottages, and the weavers shall work in palaces with a thousand windows lighted as bright as day. The sun shall stoop to make men's portraits more like than any painter can make them. There shall be ships that shall run under the seas like conger-eels, and ships that shall ride over the clouds like great birds. And bread that is now a shilling and ninepence shall be fivepence, and the corn and the beef shall come from overseas to feed us. And every child shall be taught who can learn, and——"

"Peace, prater," cried a stern voice in the doorway. Elfrida turned. There stood the grandfather, Lord Arden, very straight and tall and grey, leaning on his gold-headed cane, and beside him Edred, looking very small and found-out.

The old witch did not seem to see them; her eyes, that rolled and blinked, saw nothing. But she must have heard, for—

"Loss to Arden," she said; "loss and woe to Arden. The hangings of your house shall be given to the spider, and the mice shall eat your carved furnishings. Your gold shall be less and less, and your house go down and down till there is not a field that is yours about your house."

Lord Arden shrugged his shoulders.

"Likely tales," he said, "to frighten babes with. Tell me rather, if you would have me believe, what shall hap to-morrow."

"To-morrow," said the wise woman, "the French shall land in Lymchurch Bay."

Lord Arden laughed.

"And I give you a sign—three signs," said the woman faintly; for it is tiring work seeing into the future, even when you are enlightened with a kiss from some one who has been there. "You shall see the white Mouldiwarp, that is the badge of Arden, on your threshold as you enter."

"That shall be one sign," said the old man mockingly.

"And the second," she said, "shall be again the badge of your house, in your own chair in your own parlour."

"That seems likely," said Lord Arden, sneering.

"And the third," said she, "shall be the badge of your house in the arms of this child."

She turned her back, and picked the hen out of the ashes.

Lord Arden led Edred and Elfrida away, one in each hand, and as he went he was very severe on disobedient children who went straying after wicked witches, and they could not defend themselves without blaming the cook, which, of course, they would not do.

"Bread and water for dinner," he said, "to teach you better ways."

"Oh, grandfather," said Elfrida, catching at his hand, "don't be so unkind! Just think about when *you* were little. I'm sure you liked looking at witches, didn't you, now?"

Lord Arden stared angrily at her, and then he chuckled. "It's a bold girl, so it is," he said. "I own I remember well seeing a witch ducked no further off than Newchurch, and playing truant from my tutor to see it, too."

"There now, you see," said Elfrida coaxingly, "we don't mean to be naughty; we're just like what you were. You won't make it bread and water, will you? Especially if bread's so dear."

Lord Arden chuckled again.

"Why, the little white mouse has found a tongue, and never was I spoken to so bold since the days I wore petticoats myself," he said. "Well, well; we'll say no more about it this time."

And Edred, who had privately considered that Elfrida was behaving like an utter idiot, thought better of it.

So they turned across the summer fields to Arden Castle. There seemed to be more of the castle than when the children had first seen it, and it was tidier, much. And on the doorstep sat a white mole.

"THE MOULDIWARP MADE A LITTLE RUN AND A LITTLE JUMP, AND ELFRIDA CAUGHT IT."

"There now!" said Elfrida. The mole vanished like a streak of white paint that is rubbed out.

"Pooh!" said Lord Arden. "There's plenty white moles in the world."

But when he saw the white mole sitting up in his own carved arm-chair in the parlour, he owned that it was very unusual.

Elfrida stooped and held out her arms. She was extremely glad to see the mole. Because ever since she and her brother had come into this strange time she had felt that it would be the greatest possible comfort to have the mole at hand—the mole, who understood everything, to keep and advise; and, above all, to get them safely back into the century they belonged to.

And the Mouldiwarp made a little run and a little jump, and Elfrida caught it and held it against her waist with both her hands.

"Stay with me," whispered Elfrida to the mole.

"By George!" said Lord Arden to the universe.

"So now you see," said Edred to Lord Arden.

CHAPTER IV
THE LANDING OF THE FRENCH

Then they had dinner. The children had to sit very straight and eat very slowly, and their glasses were filled with beer instead of water; and when they asked for water Lady Arden asked how many more times they would have to be told that water was unwholesome. Lord Arden was very quiet. At quite the beginning of dinner he had told his wife all about the wise woman, and the landing of the French, and the three signs, and she had said, "Law, save us, my lord; you don't say so?" and gone on placidly cutting up her meat. But when the cloth had been drawn, and decanters of wine placed among the dishes of dried plums and preserved pears, Lord Arden brought down his fist on the table and said—

"Not more than three glasses for me to-day, my lady. I am not superstitious, as well you know; but facts are facts. What did you do with that white Mouldiwarp?"

Elfrida had put it in the bottom drawer of the tallboys in her room (cook had told her which room that was), and said so rather timidly.

"It's my belief," said Lady Arden, who seemed to see what was her husband's belief and to make it her own—a very winning quality—"it's my belief that it's a direct warning; in return, perhaps, for the tea and sugar."

"Ah!" said Lord Arden. "Well, whether or no, every man in this village shall be armed and paraded this day, or I'll know the reason why. I'm not going to have the French stepping ashore as cool as cucumbers, without 'With your leave,' or 'By your leave,' and any one to say afterwards, 'Well, Arden, you had fair warning, only you would know best.'"

"No," said Lady Arden, "that *would* be unpleasant."

Lord Arden's decision was made stronger by the arrival of a man on a very hot horse.

"The French are coming," he said, quite out of breath. But he could not say how he knew. "They all say so," was all that could be got out of him, and "They told me to come tell you, my lord, and what's us to do?"

We live so safely now; we have nothing to be afraid of. When we have wars they are not in our own country. The police look after burglars, and even thunder is attended to by lightning-rods. It is not easy for us to understand the frantic terror of those times, when, from day to day, every man, woman, and child trembled in its shoes for fear lest "the French should come"—the French, led by Boney. Boney, to us, is Napoleon Buonaparte, a little person in a cocked hat out of the history books. To those who lived in England when he was a man alive, he was "the Terror that walked by night," making children afraid to go to bed, and causing strong men to sleep in their boots, with sword and pistol by the bed-head, within easy reach of the newly awakened hand.

Edred and Elfrida began to understand a little, when they saw how the foretelling of the wise woman, strengthened by the rumours that began to run about like rats in every house in the village, stirred the people to the wildest activity.

Lord Arden was so busy giving orders, and my lady so busy talking his orders over with the maidservants, that the children were left free to use their eyes and ears. And they went down into the village and saw many strange things. They saw men at the grindstone sharpening old swords, and others who had no swords putting a fine edge on billhooks, hatchets, scythes, and kitchen choppers. They saw other men boarding up their windows and digging holes in their gardens and burying their money and their teaspoons in the holes. No one knew how the rumour had begun, but every one believed it now.

They went in and out of the cottages as they chose. Every one seemed to know them and to be pleased, in an absent sort of way, to see them, but nobody had time to talk to them, so they soon lost the fear they had had at first of being found out to be not the people they were being taken for. They found the women busy brushing and mending old scarlet coats and tight white trousers, and all along the dip of the cliff men were posted, with spy-glasses, looking out to sea. Other men toiled up the slope with great bundles of brown brush-wood and dried furze on their backs, and those bundles were piled high, ready to be lighted the moment it should be certain that the French were coming.

Elfrida wished more than ever that she knew more about the later chapters of the history book. Did Boney land in England on the 17th of June, 1807? She could not remember. There was something, she knew, in the book about a French invasion, but she could not remember what it was an invasion of, nor when it took place. So she and Edred knew as little as any one else what really *was* going to happen. The Mouldiwarp, in the hurried interview she had had with it before dinner, had promised to come if she called it, "With poetry, of course," it added, as it curled up in the corner of the drawer, and this comforted her a good deal when, going up to get her bonnet, she found the bottom drawer empty. So, though she was as interested as Edred in all that was going on, it was only with half her mind. The other half was busy trying to make up a piece of poetry, so that any emergency which might suddenly arise would not find her powerless because poetry-less.

So for once Edred was more observant than she, and when he noticed that the men built a bonfire not at all on the spot which Lord Arden had pointed out as most convenient, he wondered why.

And presently, seeing a man going by that very spot, he asked him why. To his surprise, the man at once poked him in the ribs with a very hard finger, and said—

"Ah, you're a little wag, you are! But you're a little gentleman, too, and so's the little lady, bless her. You never gave us away to the Preventives—for all you found out."

"Of course," said Elfrida cautiously, "we should never give any one away."

"Want to come along down now?" the man asked. He was a brown-faced, sturdy, sailor-looking man, with a short pigtail sticking out from the back of his head like the china handle of a Japanese teapot.

"Oh, yes," said Elfrida, and Edred did not say "Oh, no."

"Then just you wait till I'm out of sight, and then come down the way you see me go. Go long same as if you was after butterflies or the like—a bit this way and a bit that—see?" said the man. And they obeyed.

Alas! too few children in those uninteresting times of ours have ever been in a smuggler's cave. To Edred and to Elfrida it was as great a novelty as it would be to you or to me.

When they came up with the brown man he was crouching in the middle of a patch of furze.

"Jump they outside bushes," he said. And they jumped, and wound their way among the furze-bushes by little narrow rabbit-paths till they stood by his side.

Then he lifted a great heap of furze and bramble that looked as if it had lived and died exactly where it was. And there was a hole—with steps going down.

It was dark below, but Elfrida did not hesitate to do as she was told and to go forward. And if Edred hesitated it was only for a minute.

The children went down some half a dozen steps. Then the brown man came into the hole too, and drew the furze after him. And he lighted a lantern; there was a tallow candle in it, and it smelt very nasty indeed. But what are smells, even those of hot tallow and hot iron, compared with the splendid exploring of a smuggler's cave? It was everything the children had ever dreamed of—and more.

There was the slow descent with the yellowness of the lantern flame casting golden lights and inky shadows on the smooth whiteness of the passage's chalk walls. There were steps, there was a rude heavy door, fastened by a great lock and a key to open it—as big as a church key. And when the door had creaked open there was the great cave. It was so high that you could not see the roof—only darkness. Out of an opening in the chalk at the upper end a stream of water fell, slid along a smooth channel down the middle of the cave and ran along down a steep incline, rather like a small railway cutting, and disappeared under a low arch.

"So there'd always be water if you had to stand a siege," said Edred.

On both sides of the great cave barrels and bales were heaped on a sanded floor. There were a table and benches cut out of solid chalk, and an irregular opening partly blocked by a mass of fallen cliff, through which you saw the mysterious twilit sea, with stars coming out over it.

You saw this, and you felt—quite suddenly, too—a wild wind that pressed itself against you like a wrestler trying a fall, and whistled in your ears and drove you back to the big cave, out of breath and panting.

"There'll be half a gale to-night," said the smuggler; for such, no doubt, he was.

"Do you think the French *will* land to-morrow in Lymchurch Bay?" Edred asked.

"'DO YOU THINK THE FRENCH WILL LAND TO-MORROW IN LYMCHURCH BAY?' EDRED ASKED."

By the light of the lantern the smuggler solemnly winked.

"You two can keep a secret, I know," he said. "The French won't land; it's us what'll land, and we'll land here and not in bay; and what we'll land is a good drop of the real thing, and a yard or two of silk or lace maybe. I don't know who 'twas put it about as the French was a-coming, but you may lay to it they aren't no friends of the Revenue."

"Oh, I see," said Elfrida. "And did——"

"The worst of it'll be the look-out they'll keep. Lucky for us it's all our men as has volunteered for duty. And we know our friends."

"But do you mean," said Edred, "that you can be friends with a Frenchman, when we're at war with them?"

"It's like this, little man," said the smuggler, sitting down on a keg that stood handily on its head ready for a seat. "We ain't no quarrel with the free-trade men—neither here nor there. A man's got his living to get, hasn't he now? So you see a man's trade comes first—what he gets his bread by. So you see these chaps as meet us mid-channel and hand us the stuff—they're free traders first and Frenchies after—the same like we're merchants before all. We ain't no quarrel with them. It's the French soldiers we're at war with, not the honest French traders that's in the same boat as us ourselves."

"Then somebody's just made up about Boney coming, so as to keep people busy in the bay while you're smuggling here?" said Edred.

"I wouldn't go so far as that, sir," said the man, "but if it did happen that way it 'ud be a sort of special dispensation for us free-trade men that get our living by honest work and honest danger; that's all I say, knowing by what's gone before that you two are safe as any old salt afloat."

The two children would have given a good deal to know what it was that had "gone before." But they never did know. And sometimes, even now, they wonder what it was that the Edred and Elfrida of those days had done to win the confidence of this swaggering smuggler. They both think, and I daresay they are right, that it must have been something rather fine.

Having seen all the ins and outs of the cave, the children were not sorry to get back to Arden Castle, for it was now dark, and long past their proper bedtime, and it really had been rather a wearing day.

They were put to bed, rather severely, by Lady Arden's own maid, whom they had not met before and did not want to meet again—so shrivelled and dry and harsh was she. And they slept like happy little tops, in the coarse homespun linen sheets scented with lavender grown in the castle garden, that were spread over soft, fat, pincushion-beds, filled with the feathers of geese eaten at the castle table.

Only Elfrida woke once and found the room filled with red light, and, looking out of the window, saw that one of the beacon bonfires was alight and that the flames and smoke were streaming across the dark summer sky—driven by the wind that shouted and yelled and shook the windows, and was by this time, she felt sure, at least three-quarters of a gale. The beacon was lighted; therefore the French were coming. And Elfrida yawned and went back to bed. She was too sleepy to believe in Boney. But at that time, a hundred years ago, hundreds of little children shivered and cried in their beds, being quite sure that now at last all the dreadful prophecies of mothers and nurses would come true, and that Boney, in all his mysterious, unknown horror, would really now, at last, "have them."

It was grey morning when the wind, wearied of the silly resistance of the leaded window, suddenly put forth his strength, tore the window from its hinges, drove it across the window frame, and swept through the room, flapping the bedclothes like wet sails, and wakening the children most thoroughly, far beyond any hope of "one more snooze." They got up and dressed. No one was about in the house, but the front door was open. It was quite calm on that side, but as soon as the children left the shelter of the castle wall the wind caught at them, hit, slapped, drove, worried, beat them, till they had hard work to stand upright, and getting along was very slow and difficult. Yet they made their way somehow to the cliff, where a thick, black crowd stood—a crowd that was not really black when you got quite close and could look at it in the grey dawn-light, but rather brilliantly red, white, and blue, like the Union Jack, because they were the armed men in their make-shift uniforms whom old Lord Arden had drilled and paraded the evening before. And they were all looking out to sea.

The sea was like the inside of an oyster-shell, barred with ridges of cold silver, the sky above was grey as a gull's wing, and between sea and sky a ship was driving straight on to the rocks a hundred feet below.

"'Tis a French ship, by her rig," some one said.

"The first of the fleet—a scout," said another, "and Heaven has sent a storm to destroy them like it destroyed the accursed Armada in Queen Bess's time."

And still the ship came nearer.

"'Tis the *Bonne Esperance*," said the low voice of the smuggler friend close to Elfrida's ear, and she could only just hear him through the whistling of the gale. "'Tis true what old Betty said; the French will land here to-day—but they'll land dead corpses. And all our little cargo—they've missed our boat in the gale—it'll all be smashed to bits afore our eyes. It's poor work being a honest merchant."

The men in their queer uniforms, carrying their queer weapons, huddled closer together, and all eyes were fixed on the ship as it came on and on.

"Is it *sure* to be wrecked?" whispered Elfrida, catching at old Lord Arden's hand.

"No hope, my child. Get you home to bed," he said.

It did not make any difference that all this had happened a hundred years ago. There was the cold, furious sea lashing the rocks far down below the cliff. Elfrida could not bear to stay and see that ship smash on the rocks as her carved work-box had smashed when she dropped it on the kitchen bricks. She could not even bear to think of seeing it. Poetry was difficult, but to stay here and see a ship wrecked—a ship that had men aboard—was more difficult still.

"Oh, Mouldiwarp, do come to me;

I cannot bear it, do you see,"

was not, perhaps, fine poetry, but it expressed her feelings exactly, and, anyhow, it did what it was meant to do. The white mole rubbed against her ankles even as she spoke. She caught it up.

"Oh, what are we to do?"

"Go home," it said, "to the castle—you'll find the door now."

And they turned to go. And as they turned they heard a grinding crunch, mixed with the noise of the waves and winds, enormously louder, but yet just the sort of noise a dog makes when he is eating the bones of the chicken you had for dinner and gets the chicken's ribs all at once into his mouth. Then there was a sort of sighing moan from the crowd on the cliff, who had been there all night for the French to land, and then Lord Arden's voice—

"The French have landed. She spoke the truth. The French have landed—Heaven help them!"

And as the children ran towards the house they knew that every man in that crowd would now be ready to risk his life to save from the sea those Frenchies whom they had sat up all night to kill with swords and scythes and bills and meat-choppers. Men are queer creatures!

To get out of it—back to the safe quiet of a life without shipwrecks and witches—that was all Elfrida wanted. Holding the mole in one hand and dragging Edred by the other, she got back to the castle and in at the open front door, up the stairs, and straight to a door—she knew it would be the right one, and it was.

There was the large attic with the beams, and the long, wonderful row of chests under the sloping roof. And the moment the door was shut, the raging noise of the winds ceased, as the flaring noise of gas ceases when you turn it off. And now once more the golden light filtered through the chinks of the tiles, and outside was the "tick, tick" of moving pigeon feet, the rustling of pigeon feathers, and the cooroocoo of pigeon voices.

On the ground lay their own clothes. "Change," said the white mole, a little out of breath because it had been held very tight and carried very fast.

And the moment they began to put on their own clothes it seemed that the pigeon noises came closer and closer, and somehow helped them out of the prickly clothes of 1807 and back into the comfortable sailor suits of 1907.

"Did ye find the treasure?" the mole asked, and the children answered—

"Why no; we never thought of it."

"It don't make no odds," said the mole. ""Twaren't dere."

"There?" said Elfrida. "Then we're *here*? We're *now* again, I mean? We're not then?"

"Oh, you're *now*, sure enough," said the mole, "and won't you catch it! Dame Honeysett's been raising the countryside arter ye. Next time ye go gallivantin' into old ancient days you'd best set the clock back. Young folks don't know everything. Get along down and take your scolding.

"What must be must.

If you can't get crumb, you must put up with crust.

Good-bye."

It ran under one of the chests, and Edred and Elfrida were left looking at each other in the attic between the rows of chests.

"Do you *like* adventures?" said Edred slowly.

"Yes," said Elfrida firmly; "and so do you. Come along down."

CHAPTER V
THE HIGHWAYMAN AND THE ——

They both meant what they said. And yet, of course, it is nonsense to promise that you will never do anything again, because, of course, you must do *something*, if it's only simple subtraction or eating poached eggs and sausages. You will, of course, understand that what they meant was that they would never again do anything to cause Mrs. Honeysett a moment's uneasiness, and in order to make this possible the first thing to do was, of course, to find out how to set the clock back. Slowly munching sausage, and feeling, as she always did when she ate slowly, that she was doing something very virtuous and ought to have a prize or a medal for it, Elfrida asked her mind to be kind enough to get some poetry ready by the time she had finished breakfast. And sure enough, her mind, in its own secret backyard, as it were, did get something ready. And while this was happening Elfrida, in what corresponded to her mind's front garden, was wishing that she had been born a poet.

"Like the one who did the piece about the favourite gold-fish drowned in a tub of cats," she said pensively.

"Yes, or even Shakespeare," said Edred; "only he's so long always."

"I wonder," said the girl, "where the clock is that we've got to set back?"

"Oh, Mouldiwarp'll tell us," said the boy.

But Mouldiwarp didn't.

When breakfast was over they went out into the grassy space round which the ruined walls of the castle rose up so grey and stately, with the wallflowers and toad-flax growing out of them, and sat down among the round-faced, white-frilled daisies and told each other what they had thought, or what they thought they had thought, while they were back in those times when people were afraid of Boney.

And the castle's sward was very green, and the daisies were very white, and the sun shone on everything very grand and golden.

And as they sat there it came over Elfrida suddenly how good a place it was and how lucky they were to be there at home at Arden, rather than in the house with the pale, smooth brass door-knocker that stood in the street with the red pavement, and the lodgers who kept all on ringing their bells—so that she said, quite without knowing she was going to say anything—

"Arden, Arden, Arden,

Lawn and castle and garden;

Daisies and grass and wallflowers gold—

Mouldiwarp, come out of the mould."

"That's more like poetry, that is," said the Mouldiwarp, sitting on the green grass between the children; "more lik'n anything I've heard ye say yet—so 'tis. An' now den, what is it for you dis fine day an' all?"

It seemed in such a good temper that Elfrida asked a question that had long tried to get itself asked.

"Why," was the question, and it was spoken to the white mole,—"why do you talk like the country people do?"

"Sussex barn an' bred," said the mole, "but I know other talk. Sussex talks what they call 'racy of the soil'—means 'smells of the earth' where I live. I can talk all sorts, though. I used to spit French once on a time, young Fitz-le-seigneur."

"You must know lots and lots," said Edred.

"I do," said the mole.

"How old are you?" Edred asked, in spite of Elfrida's warning "Hush! it's rude."

"'S old as my tongue an' a little older'n me teeth," said the mole, showing them.

"Ah, don't be cross," said Elfrida, "and such a beautiful day, too, and just when we wanted you to show us how to put back the clock and all."

"That's a deed, that is," said the mole, "but you've not quarrelled this three days, so you can go where you please and do what you will. Only you're in the way here if you want to stop the clock. Get up into the gate tower and look out, and when you see the great clock face, come down at once and sit on the second hand. That'll stop it, if anything will."

Looking out through the breezy arch among the swinging ends of ivy and the rustle and whir of pigeon wings, the children saw a very curious sight.

The green and white of grass and daisies began to swim, as it were, before their eyes. The lawn within the castle walls was all uneven because the grass had not been laid there by careful gardeners, with spirit-levels and rollers, who wanted to make a lawn, but by Nature herself, who wanted just to cover up bits of broken crockery and stone, and old birds' nests, and all sorts of odd rubbish. And now it began to stretch itself, as though it were a live carpet, and to straighten and tighten itself till it lay perfectly flat.

And the grass seemed to be getting greener in places. And in other places there were patches of white thicker and purer than before.

"Look! look!" cried Edred; "look! the daisies are walking about!"

They were. Stiffly and steadily, like well-drilled little soldiers, the daisies were forming into twos, into fours, into companies. Looking down from the window of the gate tower it was like watching thousands of little white beads sort themselves out from among green ones.

"What *are* they going to do?" Edred asked, but naturally Elfrida was not able to answer.

The daisies marched very steadily, like little people who knew their business very well. They massed themselves together in regiments, in armies. On certain parts of the smooth grass certain companies of them stopped and stayed.

"They're making a sort of pattern," said Edred. "Look! there's a big ring all round—a sort of pattern."

"I should think they were!" cried Elfrida. "Look! look! It's the clock."

It was. On the pure green face of the lawn was an enormous circle marked by a thick line of closely packed white daisies. Within it were the figures that are on the face of a clock—all twelve of them. The hands were of white daisies, too, both the minute hand and the hand that marks the hours, and between the VI and the centre was a smaller circle, also white and of daisies—round which they could see a second hand move—a white second hand formed of daisies wheeling with a precision that would have made the haughtiest general in the land shed tears of pure admiration.

With one accord the two children blundered down the dark, dusty, cobwebby, twisty stairs of the gate tower and rushed across the lawn. In the very centre of the clock-face sat the Mouldiwarp, looking conscious and a little conceited.

"How *did* you do it?" Elfrida gasped.

"The daisies did it. Poor little things! They can't invent at all. But they do carry out other people's ideas quite nicely. All the white things have to obey me, of course," it added carelessly.

"THEY SAT DOWN ON THE CLOSE, WHITE LINE OF DAISIES."

"And this is The Clock?"

The Mouldiwarp giggled. "My child, what presumption! The clock is much too big for you to see ever—all at once. The sun's the centre of it. This is just a pretending clock. It'll do for what we want, of course, or I wouldn't have had it made for you. Sit down on the second hand—oh no, it won't hurt the daisies. Count a hundred—yes, that's right."

They sat down on the close, white line of daisies and began to count earnestly.

"And now," the Mouldiwarp said, when the hundred was counted, "it's just the same time as it was when you began! So now you understand."

They said they did, and I am sure I hope *you* do.

"But if we sit here," said Elfrida, "how can we ever be anywhere else?"

"You can't," said the Mouldiwarp. "So one of you will have to stay and the other to go."

"You go, Elfie," said Edred. "I'll stay till you come back."

"That's very dear of you," said Elfrida, "but I'd rather we went together. Can't you manage it?" she asked the mole.

"I *could*, of course," it said; "but . . . he's afraid to go without you," it said suddenly.

"He isn't, and he's two years younger than me, anyway," Elfrida said hotly.

"Well, go without him," said the mole. "You understand perfectly, don't you, that when he has stopped the clock your going is the same as your not going, and your being here is the same as not being, and—— What I mean," it added, hastily returning to Sussex talk, "you needn't be so turble put out. He won't know you've gone nor yet 'e won't believe you've come back. Be off with 'e, my gell."

Elfrida hesitated. Then, "Oh, Edred," she said, "I *have* had such a time! Did it seem very long? I know it was horrid of me, but it was so interesting I *couldn't* come back before."

"Nonsense," said Edred. "Well, go if you like; I don't mind."

"I've *been*, I tell you," said Elfrida, dragging him off the second hand of the daisy clock, whose soldiers instantly resumed their wheeling march.

"So now you see," said the mole. "Tell you what—next time you wanter stop de clock we'll just wheel de barrer on to it. Now you go along and play. You've had enough Arden magic for this 'ere Fursday, so you 'ave, bless yer hearts an' all."

And they went.

That was how Edred perceived the adventure of "The Highwayman and the ———." But I will not anticipate. The way the adventure seemed to Elfrida was rather different.

After the mole said "my gell" she hesitated, and then went slowly towards the castle where the red roof of the house showed between the old, ivy-grown grey buttresses. She looked back, to see Edred and the Mouldiwarp close together on the face of the wonderful green and white clock. They were very still. She made her mind up—ran indoors and up the stairs and straight to The Door—she found it at once—shut the door, and opened the second chest to the right.

"You change your clothes and the times change too—

Change, that is what you've got to do;

Cooroo, cooroo, cooroo, cooroo,"

said the pigeons or the silence or Elfrida.

"I wonder," she said, slipping on a quilted green satin petticoat with pink rosebuds embroidered on it, "whether Shakespeare began being a poet like that—just little odd lines coming into his head without him meaning them to." And her mind as she put on a pink-and-white brocaded dress, was busy with such words as "Our great poet, Miss Elfrida Arden," or "Miss Arden, the female Milton of nowadays."

She tied a white, soft little cap with pink ribbons under her chin and ran to open the door. She was not a bit afraid. It was like going into a dream. Nothing would be real there. Yet as she ran through the attic door and the lace of her sleeve caught on a big rusty nail and tore with a harsh hissing noise, she felt very sorry. In a thing that was only a dream that lace felt very real, and was very beautiful.

But she had only half the first half of a thought to give to the lace—for the door opened, not on the quiet corridor with the old prints at Arden Castle, but on a quite strange panelled room, full of a most extraordinary disorder of stuffs—feathers, dresses, cloaks, bonnet-boxes, parcels, rolls, packets, lace, scarves, hats, gloves, and finery of all sorts. There were a good many people there: serving-maids—she knew they were serving-maids—a gentleman in knee-breeches showing some fine china on a lacquered tray, and in the middle a very pretty, languishing-looking young lady with whom Elfrida at once fell deeply in love. All the women wore enormous crinolines—or hoops.

"What! Hid in the closet all the while, cousin?" said the young lady. "Oh, but it's the slyest chit! Come, see how the new scarf becomes thy Bet. Is it not vastly modish?"

"Yes," said Elfrida, not knowing in the least what to say.

Everything gave a sort of tremble and twist, like the glass, bits in a kaleidoscope give just before they settle into a pattern. Then, as with the bits of glass, everything *was* settled, and Elfrida, instead of feeling that she was looking at a picture, felt that she was alive, with live people.

Some extraordinary accident had fixed in Elfrida's mind the fact that Queen Anne began to reign in 1702. I don't know how it was. These accidents do sometimes occur. And she knew that in Queen Anne's day ladies wore hoops. Also, since they had gone back a hundred years to Boney's time, perhaps this second venture had taken her back two hundred years. If so——

"'COME, SEE HOW THE NEW SCARF BECOMES THY BET.
IS IT NOT VASTLY MODISH?'"

"Please," she said, very quickly, "is this 1707, and is Queen Anne dead?"

"Heaven forbid," said every one in the room; and Bet added, "La, child, don't delay us with your prattle. The coach will be here at ten, and we must lie at Tonbridge to-night."

So Elfrida, all eyes and ears, squeezed into a corner between a band-box and a roll of thick, pink-flowered silk and looked and listened.

Bet, she gathered, was her cousin—an Arden, too. She and Bet and the maids, and an escort of she couldn't quite make out how many men, were to go down to Arden together. The many men were because of the Arden jewels, that had been reset in the newest mode, and the collar of pearls and other presents Uncle Arden had given to Bet; and the highwaymen, who, she learned, were growing so bold that they would attack a coach in St. Paul's Churchyard in broad daylight. Bet, it seemed, had undertaken commissions for all her girl friends near Arden, and had put off most of them till the last moment. She had carefully spent her own pin-money during her stay in town, and was now hastily spending theirs. The room was crowded with tradesmen and women actually pushing each other to get near the lady who had money to spend. One woman with a basket of china was offering it in exchange for old clothes or shoes, just as old women do now at back doors. And Cousin Bet's maid had a very good bargain, she considered, in a china teapot and two dishes, in exchange for a worn, blue lutestring dress and a hooped petticoat of violet quilted satin. Then there was a hasty meal of cakes and hot chocolate, and, Elfrida being wrapped up in long-skirted coat and scarves almost beyond bearing, it was announced that the coach was at the door. It was a very tight fit when at last they were all packed into the carriage, for though the carriage was large there was a great deal to fill it up, what with Cousin Bet and her great hoops, and the maids, and the band-boxes and packages of different sizes and shapes, and the horrid little pet dog that yapped and yahed, and tried to bite every one, from the footmen to Elfrida. The streets were narrow and very dirty, and smelt very nasty in the hot June sun.

And it was very hot and stuffy inside the carriage, and more bumpety than you would think possible—more bumpety even than a wagon going across a furrowed corn-field. Elfrida felt rather headachy, as you do when you go out in a small boat and every one says it is not at all rough. By the time the carriage got to Lewisham Elfrida's bones were quite sore, and she felt as though she had been beaten. There were no springs to the carriage, and it reminded her of a bathing-machine more than anything else—you know the way it bumps on the shingly part of the shore when they are drawing you up at the beach, and you tumble about and can't go on dressing, and all your things slide off the seats. The maids were cross and looked it. Cousin Bet had danced till nigh midnight, and been up with the lark, so she said. And, having said it, went to sleep in a corner of the carriage looking crosser than the maids. Elfrida began to feel that empty, uninterested sensation which makes you wish you hadn't come. The carriage plunged and rattled on through the green country, the wheels bounding in and out of the most dreadful ruts. More than once the wheel got into a rut so deep that it took all the men to heave it out again. Cousin Bet woke up to say that it was vastly annoying, and instantly went to sleep again.

Elfrida, being the smallest person in the carriage except Amour, the dog, was constantly being thrown into somebody's lap—to the annoyance of both parties. It was very much the most uncomfortable ride she had ever had. She thought of the smooth, swift rush of the train—even the carrier's cart was luxury compared to this. "The roads aren't like roads at all," she told herself, "they're like ploughed fields with celery trenches in them"—she had a friend a market gardener, so she knew.

Long before the carriage drew up in front of the "Bull" at Tonbridge, Elfrida felt that if she only had a piece of poetry ready she would say it, and ask the Mouldiwarp to take her back to her own times, where, at any rate, carriages had springs and roads *were* roads. And when the carriage did stop she was so stiff she could hardly stand.

"Come along in," said a stout, pleasant-faced lady in a frilled cap; "come in, my poppet. There's a fine supper, though it's me says it, and a bed that you won't beat in Kent for soft and clean, you may lay to that."

There was a great bustle of shouting ostlers and stablemen; the horses were taken out before the travellers were free of the carriage. Supper was laid in a big, low, upper room, with shining furniture and windows at both ends, one set looking on the road where the sign of the "Bull" creaked and swung, and the other looking on a very neat green garden, with clipped box hedges and yew arbours. Getting all the luggage into the house seemed likely to be a long business. Elfrida saw that she would not be missed, and she slipped down the twisty-cornery back-stairs and through the back kitchen into the green garden. It was pleasant to stretch one's legs, and not to be cramped and buffeted and shaken. But she walked down the grass-path rather demurely, for she was very stiff indeed.

And it was there, in a yew arbour, that she came suddenly on the grandest and handsomest gentleman that she had ever seen. He wore a white wig, very full at the sides and covered with powder, and a full-skirted coat of dark-blue silk, and under it a long waistcoat with the loveliest roses and forget-me-nots tied in bunches with gold ribbons, embroidered on silk. He had lace ruffles and a jewelled brooch, and the jolliest blue eyes in the world. He looked at Elfrida very kindly with his jolly eyes.

"A lady of quality, I'll be bound," he said, "and travelling with her suite."

"I'm Miss Arden of Arden," said Elfrida.

"Your servant, madam," said he, springing to his feet and waving his hat in a very flourishing sort of bow.

Elfrida's little curtsey was not at all the right kind of curtsey, but it had to do.

"And what can I do to please Miss Arden of Arden?" he asked. "Would she like a ride on my black mare?"

"Oh, *no*, thank you," said Elfrida, so earnestly that he laughed as he said—

"Sure I should not have thought fear lived with those eyes."

"I'm not afraid," said Elfrida contemptuously; "only I've been riding in a horrible carriage all day, and I feel as though I never wanted to ride on anything any more."

He laughed again.

"Well, well," he said, "come and sit by me and tell me all the town news."

Elfrida smiled to think what news she *could* tell him, and then frowned in the effort to think of any news that wouldn't seem nonsense.

She told him all that she knew of Cousin Bet and the journey. He was quite politely interested. She told of Cousin Bet's purchases—the collar of pearls and the gold pomander studded with corals, the little gold watch, and the family jewels that had been reset.

"And you have all to-night to rest in from that cruel coach?" he said.

"Yes," said Elfrida, "we don't go on again till after breakfast to-morrow. It's very dull—and oh, so slow! Don't you think you'd like to have a carriage drawn by a fiery iron horse that went sixty miles an hour?"

"You have an ingenious wit," said the beautiful gentleman, "such as I should admire in my wife. Will you marry me when you shall be grown a great girl?"

"No," said Elfrida; "you'd be too old—even if you were to be able to stop alive till I was grown up, you'd be much too old."

"How old do you suppose I shall be when you're seventeen?"

"I should have to do sums," said Elfrida, who was rather good at these exercises. She broke a twig from a currant bush and scratched in the dust.

"I don't know," she said, raising a flushed face, and trampling out her "sum" with little shoes that had red heels, "but I *think* you'll be two hundred and thirty."

On that he laughed more than ever and vowed she was the lady for him. "Your ciphering would double my income ten times over," he said.

He was very kind indeed—would have her taste his wine, which she didn't like, and the little cakes on the red and blue plate, which she did.

"And what's *your* name?" she asked.

"My name," said he, "is a secret. Can you keep a secret?"

"Yes," said Elfrida.

"So can I," said he.

And then a flouncing, angry maid came suddenly sweeping down between the box hedges and dragged Elfrida away before she could curtsey properly and say, "Thank you for being so kind."

"Farewell," said the beautiful gentleman, "doubt not but we shall meet again. And next time 'tis I shall carry thee off and shut thee in a tower for two hundred years till thou art seventeen and hast learned to cipher."

Elfrida was slapped by the maid, which nearly choked her with fury, and set down to supper in the big upstairs room. The maid indignantly told where she had found Elfrida "talking with a strange gentleman," and when Cousin Betty had heard all about it Elfrida told her tale.

"And he was a great dear," she said.

"A——?"

"A very beautiful gentleman. I wish you'd been there, Cousin Betty. *You'd* have liked him too."

Then Cousin Bet also slapped her. And Elfrida wished more than ever that she had some poetry ready for the Mouldiwarp.

The next day's journey was as bumpety as the first, and Elfrida got very tired of the whole business. "Oh, I wish something would happen!" she said.

It was a very much longer day too, and the dusk had fallen while still they were on the road. The sun had set red behind black trees, and brown twilight was thickening all about, when at a cross-roads, a man in a cloak and mask on a big black horse suddenly leaped from a hedge, stooped from his saddle, opened the carriage door, caught Elfrida with one hand by the gathers of her full travelling coat (he must have been frightfully strong, and so must the gathers), set her very neatly and quite comfortably on the saddle before him, and said—

"Hand up your valuables, please—or I shoot the horses. And keep your barkers low, for if you aim at me you shoot the child. And if you shoot my horse, the child and I fall together."

"IF YOU AIM AT ME YOU SHOOT THE CHILD."

But even as he spoke through his black mask, he wheeled the horse so that his body was a shield between her and the pistols of the serving-men.

"What do you want?" Cousin Bet's voice was quite squeaky. "We have no valuables; we are plain country people, travelling home to our farm."

"I want the collar of pearls," said he, "and the pomander, and the little gold watch, and the jewels that have been reset."

Then Elfrida knew who he was.

"Oh," she cried, "you *are* mean!"

"Trade's trade," said he, but he held her quite gently and kindly. "Now, my fair madam——"

The men were hesitating, fingering their pistols. The horses, frightened by the sudden check, were dancing and prancing all across the road: the maidservants were shouting that it was true; he had the child, and better lose a few jewels than all their lives, and Cousin Bet was sobbing and wailing inside the dark coach.

Well, the jewels were handed out—that was how it ended—handed out slowly and grudgingly, and the hand that reached for them through the dusk was very white, Cousin Bet said afterwards.

Elfrida, held by the highwayman's arm, kept very still. Suddenly he stooped and whispered in her ear.

"Are you afraid that I shall do you any harm?"

"No," whispered Elfrida. And to this day she does not know why she was not afraid.

"Then——" said he. "Oh, the brave little lady——"

And on that suddenly set spurs to his horse, leapt the low hedge, and reined up sharply.

"Go on home, my brave fellows," he shouted, "and keep your mouths shut on this night's work. I shall be at Arden before you——"

"The child!" shrieked the maids; "oh, the child!" and even Cousin Bet interrupted her hysterics, now quite strong and overwhelming, to say, "The child——"

"Shall I order supper for you at Arden?" he shouted back mockingly, and rode on across country, with Elfrida, breathlessly frightened and consciously brave, leaning back against his shoulder. It is a very wonderful feeling, riding on a great strong, dark horse, through a deepening night in a strange country, held fast by an arm you can trust, and with the muscles of a horse's great shoulder rippling against your legs as they hang helplessly down. Elfrida ceased to think of Mouldiwarps or try to be a poet.

And quite soon they were at the top of Arden Hill, and the lights of the castle gleamed and blinked below them.

"Now, sweetheart," said the highwayman, "I shall set you down in sight of the door and wait till the door opens. You can tell them all that has chanced, save this that I tell you now. You will see me again. They will not know me, but you will. Keep a still tongue till to-morrow, and I swear Miss Arden shall have all her jewels again, and you shall have a gold locket to put your true love's hair in when you're seventeen and I'm two hundred and thirty. And leave the parlour window open. And when I tap, come to it. Is it a bargain?"

"Then you're not really a highwayman?"

"What should you say," he asked, "if I told you that I was the third James, the rightful King of England, come to claim my own?"

"Oh!" said Elfrida, and he set her down, and she walked to the door of the castle and thumped on it with her fists.

Her tale had been told to the servants, and again to Cousin Bet and the maids, and the chorus of lament and astonishment was settling down to a desire to have something to eat; anyhow, the servants had gone to the kitchen to hurry the supper. Cousin Bet and Elfrida were alone in the parlour, where Elfrida had dutifully set the window ajar.

The laurel that was trained all up that side of the house stirred in the breeze and tapped at the window. Elfrida crossed to the window-seat. No, it was only the laurel. But next moment a hand tapped—a hand with rings on it, and a white square showed in the window—a letter.

"For Miss Betty Arden," said a whispering voice.

Elfrida carried the letter to where her cousin sat, and laid it on her flowered silk lap.

"For me, child? Where did you get it?"

"Read it," said Elfrida, "it's from a gentleman."

"Lud!" said Cousin Bet. "What a day!—a highwayman and the jewels lost, and now a love-letter."

She opened it, read it—read it again and let her hand flutter out with it in a helpless sort of way towards Elfrida, who, very brisk and businesslike, took it and read it. It was clearly and beautifully written.

"The Chevalier St. George," it said, "visiting his kingdom in secret on pressing affairs of State, asks housing and hiding beneath the roof of the loyal Ardens."

"Now, don't scream," said Elfrida sharply; "who's the Chevalier St. George?"

"Our King," said Betty in a whisper—"our King over the water—King James the Third. Oh, why isn't my uncle at home? They'll kill the King if they find him. What shall I do? What shall I do?"

"Do?" said Elfrida. "Why don't be so silly. That's what you've got to do. Why, it's a glorious chance. Think how every one will say how brave you were. Is he Bonnie Prince Charlie? Will he be King some day?"

"No, not Charles—James; uncle wants him to be King."

"Then let's help him," said Elfrida, "and perhaps it'll be your doing that he is King." Her history had never got beyond Edward the Fourth on account of having to go back to 1066 on account of new girls, and she had only heard of Prince Charlie in ballads and story books. "And when he's King he'll make you dowager-duchess of somewhere and give you his portrait set in diamonds. Now don't scream. He's outside. I'll call him in. Where can we hide him?"

CHAPTER VI
THE SECRET PANEL

"Where shall we hide him?" Elfrida asked impatiently.

Cousin Bet, fired by Elfrida's enthusiasm, jumped up and began to finger the carved flowers above the chimneypiece.

"The secret room," she said; "but slip the bolt to and turn the key in the lock."

Elfrida locked the room door, and turned to see the carved mantelpiece open like a cupboard.

Then Elfrida flew to the window and set back the casement very wide, and in climbed the beautiful gentleman and stood there, very handsome and tall, bowing to Miss Betty, who sank on her knees and kissed the white, jewelled hand he held out.

"Quick!" said Elfrida. "Get into the hole."

"There are stairs," said Betty, snatching a candle in its silver candlestick and holding it high.

The Chevalier St. George sprang to a chair, got his knee on the mantelpiece, and went into the hole, just as Alice goes through the looking-glass in Mr. Tenniel's picture. Betty handed him the candle, which his white hand reached down to take. Then Elfrida jumped on the chair and shut the panel, leaped down, and opened the room door just as the maid reached its other side with the supper-tray.

When the cousins were alone Bet threw her arms round Elfrida.

"BETTY HANDED HIM THE CANDLE."

"Don't be afraid, little cousin," she whispered, "your Cousin Bet will see that no harm comes to you from this adventure."

"Well, I do think!" said Elfrida getting out of the embrace most promptly, "when it was me let him in, and you'd have screamed the house down, if I hadn't stopped you——"

"Stop chattering, child," said Bet, drawing a distracted hand over her pretty forehead, "and let me set my wits to work how I may serve my King."

"*I*," said Elfrida scornfully, "should give him something to eat and see that his bed's aired; but I suppose that would be too vulgar and common for you."

The two looked at each other across the untasted supper.

"Impertinent chit!" said Bet.

"Chit yourself," said Elfrida.

Then she laughed.

"Come, Cousin Bet," she said, "your uncle's away and you're grown up. I'll tell you what to do. You just be wise and splendid, so that your portrait'll be in the illustrated Christmas numbers in white satin and an anxious expression. 'The saviour of her King'—that's what it'll say."

"Don't wander in your speech, child," said Cousin Bet, pressing her hand to her brow, "I've enough to distract me without that. And if you desire to ask my pardon, do so."

"Oh, well, I beg your pardon—there!" said Elfrida, with extreme irritation. "*Now* perhaps you'll give your King something to eat."

"Climb into that hole—with a tray? And the servants, perhaps, coming in any minute? What would you say to them if they did?"

"All right, then, *I'll* go," said Elfrida, only too glad of the chance.

Bet touched the secret spring, and when Elfrida had climbed into the dark hole—which she did quite easily—handed her the supper-tray.

"Oh, bother," said Elfrida, setting it down at her feet with great promptness. "It's too heavy. He'll have to come down and fetch it. Give me a candle and shut the panel, and tell me which way to go."

"To the right and up the steps. Be sure you kneel and kiss his hand before you say a word."

Elfrida reached down for the candle in its silver candlestick, the panel clicked into place, and she stood there among the cobwebby shadows of the secret passage, the light in her hand and the tray at her feet.

"It's only a Mouldiwarp magic adventure," she said, to hearten herself, turned to the right, and went up the stairs. They were steep and narrow. At the top she saw the long, light-line of a slightly opened door. To knock seemed unwise. Instead she spoke softly, her lips against the line of light.

"It's me," she said, and instantly the door opened, and the beautiful gentleman stood before her.

The secret room had a little furniture—a couch, a table, chairs—all old-fashioned, and their shapes showed beautiful, even in the dim light of the two candles.

"Your supper," said Elfrida, "is at the bottom of the stairs. The tray was too heavy for me. Do you mind fetching it up?"

"If you'll show me a light," he said, and went.

"You'll stay and eat with me?" said he, when she had lighted him back to the secret room, and he had set the tray on the table.

"I mustn't," said Elfrida. "Cousin Bet's such a muff; she wouldn't know where to say I was if the servants came in. Oh, I say! I'm so sorry I forgot. She told me to kneel and kiss your hand before I said anything about supper. I'll do it now."

"Nay," said he, "I'll kiss thy cheek, little lady, and drink a health to him who shall have thy lips when thou'rt seventeen and I am—what was it—five hundred?"

"Two hundred and thirty," said Elfrida, returning his kiss cordially. "You are nice, you know. I wish you were real. I'd better go back to Bet now."

"Real?" he said.

"Oh, I'm talking nonsense, I know," said Elfrida. "I'll go now."

"The absent tray will betray you," said he, taking food and wine from it and setting them on the table. "Now I will carry this down again. You have all the courage, but not quite the cunning of a conspirator."

"How long are you going to stay here?" Elfrida asked. "I suppose you're escaping from some one or something, like in history?"

"I shall not stay long," he said. "If any one should ask you if you have seen the King, what would you say?"

"I should say 'no,'" said Elfrida boldly. "You see, I can't possibly know that you're the King. You just say so, that's all. Perhaps really you aren't."

"Exquisite!" said he. "So you don't believe me?"

"Oh, yes, I do!" said Elfrida; "but I needn't, you know."

"S'life!" he said. "But I wish I were. There'd be a coronet for somebody."

"You wish you were——"

"Safely away, my little lady. And as for coronets, the jewels are safe. See, I have set them in the cupboard in the corner."

And he had.

Then he carried down the tray, and Elfrida, who was very hungry, tried to persuade Bet that she must eat, if only to keep up her strength for the deeds of daring that might want doing at any moment.

But Bet declared that she could not eat; the least morsel would choke her. And as for going to bed, she was assuring her cousin that she knew her duty to her King better than that, and that she would defend her Sovereign with her life, if need were, when her loyal ecstasies were suddenly interrupted.

For the quiet of the night was broken by a great knocking at the castle door and the heavy voice of a man crying—

"Open, in the Queen's name!"

"They've come for him! All is lost! We are betrayed! What shall we do?"

"*Eat*," said Elfrida,—"eat for your life."

She pushed Bet into a chair and thrust a plate before her, put a chunk of meat-pie on her plate and another on her own.

"Get your mouth full," she whispered, filling her own as she spoke—"so full you can't speak—it'll give you time to think."

"'NOW,' SAID A DOZEN VOICES, 'THE TRUTH, LITTLE MISS.'"

And then the door opened, and in a moment the room was full of gentlemen in riding dress, with very stern faces. And they all had swords.

Betty, with her mouth quite full, was trying not to look towards the panel.

Elfrida, whose mouth was equally full, looked at the gentleman who seemed to be leading the others, and remarked—

"This is a nice time of night to come knocking people up!"

"All hours are alike to a loyal subject," said a round, fat, blue-eyed gentleman in a green suit. "Have you any strangers under your roof to-night?"

"Oh!" cried Bet, "all is lost!"

The gentlemen exchanged glances and crowded round her. Elfrida shrugged the shoulders of her mind—if a mind has shoulders—and told herself that it didn't matter. History knew best, no doubt, and whatever seemed to be happening now was only history.

"You *have* a stranger here?" they asked; and, "Where is he? You cannot refuse to give him up."

"My heart told me so," cried Bet. "I knew it was he you were seeking," and with that she fainted elegantly into the arms of the nearest gentleman, who was dressed in plum-colour, and seemed to be struggling with some emotion which made him look as if he were laughing.

"Ask the child—children and fools speak the truth," said the fat, blue-eyed gentleman.

Elfrida found herself suddenly lifted on to the table, from which she could see over the heads of the gentlemen who stood all round her. She could see Bet reclining on the sofa, and the open door with servants crowding in it, all eyes and ears.

"Now," said a dozen voices, "the truth, little miss."

"What do you want to know?" she asked; and, in a much lower tone, "I shan't tell you anything unless you send the servants away."

The door was closed and the truth was asked for again.

"If you'll only tell me what you want to know," she said again.

"Does any stranger lie here to-night?"

"No," said Elfrida. She knew that the beautiful gentleman in the secret chamber was not lying down, but sitting to his supper.

"But Miss Arden said 'All is lost,' and she knew 'twas he whom we sought."

"Well," Elfrida carefully explained, "it's like this. You see, we were robbed by a highwayman to-day, and I think that upset my cousin. She's rather easily upset, I'm afraid."

"Very easily," several voices agreed, and some one added that it was a hare-brained business.

"The shortest way's the best," said the plum-coloured gentleman. "Is Sir Edward Talbot here?"

"No, he isn't," said Elfrida downrightly, "and I don't believe you've got any business coming into people's houses and frightening other people into fits, and I shall tell Lord Arden when he comes home. So now you know."

"Zooks!" some one cried, "the child's got a spirit; and she's right, too, strike me if she isn't."

"But, snails!" exclaimed another, "we do but protect Lord Arden's house in his absence."

"If," said Elfrida, "you think your Talbot's playing hide-and-seek here, and if he's done anything wrong, you can look for him if you like. But I don't believe Lord Arden will be pleased. That's all. I should like to get down on to the floor, if you please!"

I don't know whether Elfrida would have had the courage to say all this if she had not remembered that this was history-times, and not now-times. But the gentlemen seemed delighted with her bravery.

They lifted her gently down, and with many apologies for having discommoded the ladies, they went out of the room and out of the castle. Through the window Elfrida heard the laughing voices and clatter and stamp of their horses' hoofs as they mounted and rode off. They all seemed to be laughing. And she felt that she moved in the midst of mysteries.

She could not bear to go back into her own time without seeing the end of the adventure. So she went to bed in a large four-poster, with Cousin Bet for company. The fainting fit lasted exactly as long as the strange gentlemen were in the house and no longer, which was very convenient.

Elfrida got up extremely early in the morning and went down into the parlour. She had meant to go and see how the King was, and whether he wanted his shaving-water first thing, as her daddy used to do. But it was so very, very early that she decided that it would be better to wait a little. The King might be sleepy, and sleepy people were not always grateful, she knew, for early shaving-water.

So she went out into the fields where the dew was grey on the grass, and up on to Arden Knoll. And she stood there and heard the skylarks, and looked at the castle and thought how new the mortar looked in the parts about the living house. And presently she saw two figures coming across the fields from where the spire of Arden Church rose out of the tops of trees as round and green as the best double-curled parsley. And one of the gentlemen wore a green coat and the other a purple coat, and she thought to herself how convenient it was to recognise people half a mile away by the colour of their clothes.

Quite plainly they were going to the castle—so she went down, too, and met them at the gate with a civil "Good morning."

"You are no lie-abed at least," said the green gentleman. "And so no stranger lay at Arden last night, eh?"

Elfrida found this difficult to answer. No doubt the King had lain—was probably still lying—in the secret chamber. But was he a stranger? No, of course he wasn't. So—

"No," she said.

And then through the open window of the parlour came, very unexpectedly and suddenly, a leg in a riding-boot, then another leg, and the whole of the beautiful gentleman stood in front of them.

"So-ho!" he said. "Speak softly, for the servants are not yet about."

"They *are*," said Elfrida, "only they're at the back. Creep along under the wall; you will get away without their seeing you then."

"Always a wonderful counsellor," said the beautiful gentleman, bowing gracefully. "Come with us, little maid. I have no secrets from thee."

So they all crept along close to the castle wall to that corner from which, between two shoulders of down, you can see the sea. There they stopped.

"And the wager's mine," said the beautiful gentleman, "for all you tried to spoil it. That was not in the bond, Fitzgerald, entering Arden at night at nine of the clock, to ferret me out like a pack of hounds after Reynard."

"There was nothing barred," said the green gentleman. "We tried waylaying you on the road, but you were an hour early."

"Ah," said the beautiful gentleman, "putting back clocks is easy work. And the ostler at the 'Bull' loves a handsome wager nigh as well as he loves a guinea."

"I do *wish* you'd explain," said Elfrida, almost stamping with curiosity and impatience.

"And so I will, my pretty," said he, laughing.

"Aren't you the King? You said you were."

"Nay, nay—not so fast. I asked thee what thou wouldst say if I told you I was King James."

"Then who *are* you?" she asked.

"Plain Edward Talbot, Baronet, at your ladyship's service," he said, with another of his fine bows.

"But I don't *understand*," she said, "*do* tell me all about it from the beginning." So he told her, and the other gentlemen stood by, laughing.

"The other night I was dining with Mr. Fitzgerald here, and the talk turned on highway robbery, and on Arden Castle here, with other matters. And these gentlemen, with others of the party, laid me a wager—five hundred guineas it was—that I would not rob a coach. I took the wager. And I wagered beside that I would rob a coach of the Arden jewels, and that I would lie a night at Arden beside, and no one should know my name there. And I have done all three and won my wager. I am but newly come home from foreign parts, so your cousin could not know my face. But zounds, child! had it not been for thee I had lost my wager. I counted on Miss Arden's help—and a pale-faced, fainting, useless fine lady I should have found her. But thou—thou'rt a girl in a thousand. And I'll buy thee the finest fairing I can find next time I go to London. We are all friends. Tell pretty miss to hold that tongue of hers, and none shall hear the tale from us."

"But all these gentlemen coming last night. All the servants know."

"The gentlemen came, no doubt, to protect Miss Arden, in case the villainous highwayman should have hidden behind the window curtain. Oh, but the wise child it is—has a care for every weak point in our armour!"

Then he told his friends the whole of the adventure, and they laughed very merrily, for all they had lost their wager, and went home to breakfast across the dewy fields.

"It's nice of him to think me brave and all that," Elfrida told herself, "but I *do* wish he'd *really* been the King."

When she had told Betty what had happened everything seemed suddenly to be not worth while; she did not feel as though she cared to stay any longer in that part of the past—so she ran upstairs, through the attic and the pigeon noises, back into her own times, and went down and found Edred sitting on the second hand of the daisy-clock; and he did not believe that she had been away at all. For all the time she had been away seemed no time to him, because he had been sitting on that second hand.

So when the Mouldiwarp told them to go along in, they went; and the way they went was not in, but out, and round under the castle wall to the corner from which you could see the sea. And there they lay on the warm grass, and Elfrida told Edred the whole story, and at first he did not believe a word of it.

"But it's true, I tell you," said she. "You don't suppose I should make up a whole tale like that, do you?"

"No," said Edred. "Of course, you're not clever enough. But you might have read it in a book."

"Well, I didn't," said Elfrida,—"so there!"

"If it was really true, you might have come back for me. You know how I've always wanted to meet a highwayman—you know you do."

"How could I come back? How was I to get off the horse and run home and get in among the chests and the pigeon noises and come out here and take you back? The highwayman—Talbot, I mean—would have been gone long before we got back."

"No, he wouldn't," said Edred obstinately. "You forget I was sitting on the clock and stopping it. There wasn't any time while you were gone—if you *were* gone."

"There was with *me*," said Elfrida. "Don't you see——"

"There wouldn't have been if you'd come back where I was," Edred interrupted.

"How can you be so aggravating?" Elfrida found suddenly that she was losing her temper. "You *can't* be as stupid as that, really."

"Oh, can't I?" said Edred. "I can though, if I like. And stupider—*much* stupider," he added darkly. "You wait."

"Edred," said his sister slowly and fervently, "sometimes I feel as if I *must* shake you."

"You daren't!" said Edred.

"Do you dare me to?"

"*Yes*," said Edred fiercely.

Of course, you are aware that after that, by all family laws, Elfrida was obliged to shake him. She did, and burst into tears. He looked at her for a moment and—but no—tears are unmanly. I would not betray the weakness of my hero. Let us draw a veil, or take a turn round the castle and come back to them presently.

It is just as well that we went away when we did, for we really turned our backs on a most unpleasant scene. And now that we come back to them, though crying is still going on, Elfrida is saying that she is very sorry, and is trying to find her handkerchief to lend to Edred, whose own is unexpectedly mislaid.

"Oh, all right," he says, "I'm sorry too. There! But us saying we're sorry won't make us unquarrel. That's the worst of it. We shan't be able to find The Door for three days now. I do wish we hadn't. It *is* sickening."

"Never mind," said Elfrida; "we didn't have a real I'll-never-speak-to-you-again-you-see-if-I-do quarrel, did we?"

"I don't suppose it matters what sort of quarrel you had," said the boy in gloom. "Look here—I'll tell you what—you tell me all about it over again and I'll try to believe you. I really will, on the honour of an Arden."

So she told him all over again.

"ELFRIDA WAS OBLIGED TO SHAKE HIM."

"And where," said Edred, when she had quite finished,—"where did you put the jewels?"

"I—they—he put them in the corner cupboard in the secret room," said Elfrida.

"If you'd taken me and not been in such a hurry—no, I'm not quarrelling, I'm only reasoning with you like Aunt Edith—if *I'd* been there I should have buried those jewels somewhere and then come back for me, and we'd have dug them up, and been rich beyond the dreams of—what do they call it?"

"But I never told Betty where they were. Perhaps they're there now. Let's go and look."

"If they are," said he, "I'll believe everything you've been telling me without trying at all."

"You'll have to do that—if there's a secret room, won't you?"

"P'r'aps," said Edred; "let's go and see. I expect I shall have got a headache presently. You didn't ought to have shaken me. Mrs. Honeysett says it's very bad for people to be shaken—it mixes up their brains inside their heads so that they ache, and you're stupid. I expect that's what made you say I was stupid."

"Oh, dear," said Elfrida despairingly. "You know that was before I shook you, and I did say I was sorry."

"I know it was, but it comes to the same thing. Come on—let's have a squint at your old secret room."

But, unfortunately it was now dinner-time. If you do happen to know the secret of a carved panel with a staircase hidden away behind it, you don't want to tell that secret lightly—as though it were the day of the week, or the date of the Battle of Waterloo, or what nine times seven is—not even to a grown-up so justly liked as Mrs. Honeysett. And, besides, a hot beefsteak pudding and greens do not seem to go well with the romances of old days. To have looked for the spring of that panel while that dinner smoked on the board would have been as unseemly as to try on a new gold crown over curl-papers. Elfrida felt this. And Edred did not more than half believe in the secret, anyway. And besides he was very hungry.

"Wait till afterwards," was what they said to each other in whispers, while Mrs. Honeysett was changing the plates.

"You do do beautiful cooking," Edred remarked, as the gooseberry-pie was cut open and revealed its chrysoprase-coloured contents.

"You do the beautiful eating then," said Mrs. Honeysett, "and you be quick about it. You ain't got into no mischief this morning, have you? You look as though butter wouldn't melt in either of your mouths, and that's always a sign of something being up with most children."

"No, *indeed* we haven't," said Elfrida earnestly, "and we don't mean to either. And our looking like that's only because we brushed our hairs with wet brushes, most likely. It does make you look good, somehow; I've often noticed it."

"I've been flying round this morning," Mrs. Honeysett went on, "so as to get down to my sister's for a bit this afternoon. She's not so well again, poor old dear, and I might be kept late. But my niece Emily's coming up to take charge. She's a nice lively young girl; she'll get you your teas, and look after you as nice as nice. Now don't you go doing anything what you wouldn't if I was behind of you, will you? That's dears."

Nothing could have happened better. Both children felt that Emily, being a young girl, would be more easy to manage than Mrs. Honeysett. As soon as they were alone they talked it over comfortably, and decided that the best thing would be to ask Emily if she would go down to the station and see if there was a parcel there for Master Arden or Miss Arden.

"And if there isn't," Elfrida giggled, "we'll say she'd better wait till it comes. We'll run down and fetch her as soon as we've explored the secret chamber."

"I say," Edred remarked thoughtfully, "we haven't bothered much about finding the treasure, have we? I thought that was what we were going into history for."

"Now, Edred," said his sister, "you know Very well we didn't go into history on purpose."

"No; but," said Edred, "we ought to have. Suppose the treasure is really those jewels. We'd sell them and rebuild Arden Castle like it used to be, wouldn't we?"

"We'd give Auntie Edith a few jewels, I think, wouldn't we? She is such a dear, you know."

"Yes; she should have first choice. I do believe we're on the brink, and I feel just exactly like as if something real was going to happen—not in history, but here at Arden—Now-Arden."

"I *do* hope we find the jewels," said Elfrida. "Oh, I do! And I do hope we manage the lively young girl all right."

Mrs. Honeysett's best dress was a nice bright red—the kind of colour you can see a long way off. They watched it till it disappeared round a shoulder of the downs, and then set about the task of managing Emily.

The lively young girl proved quite easy to manage. The idea of "popping on her hat" and running down to the station was naturally much pleasanter to her than the idea of washing the plates that had been used for beefsteak pudding and gooseberry-pie, and then giving the kitchen a thorough scrub out—which was the way Mrs. Honeysett had meant her to spend the afternoon.

Her best dress—she had slipped the skirt over her print gown so as to look smart as she came up through the village—was a vivid violet, another good distance colour. It also was watched till it dipped into the lane.

"And now," cried Elfrida, "we're all alone, and we can explore the great secret!"

"But suppose somebody comes," said Edred, "and interrupts, and finds it out, and grabs the jewels, and all is lost. There's tramps, you know, and gipsy-women with baskets."

"Yes—or drink of water, or to ask the time. I'll tell you what—we'll lock up the doors, back and front."

They did. But even this did not satisfy the suddenly cautious Edred.

"The parlour door, too," he said.

So they locked the parlour door, and Elfrida put the key in a safe place, "for fear of accidents," she said. I do not at all know what she meant, and when she came to think it over she did not know either. But it seemed all right at the time.

They had provided themselves with a box of matches and a candle—and now the decisive moment had come, as they say about battles.

Elfrida fumbled for the secret spring.

"How does it open?" asked the boy.

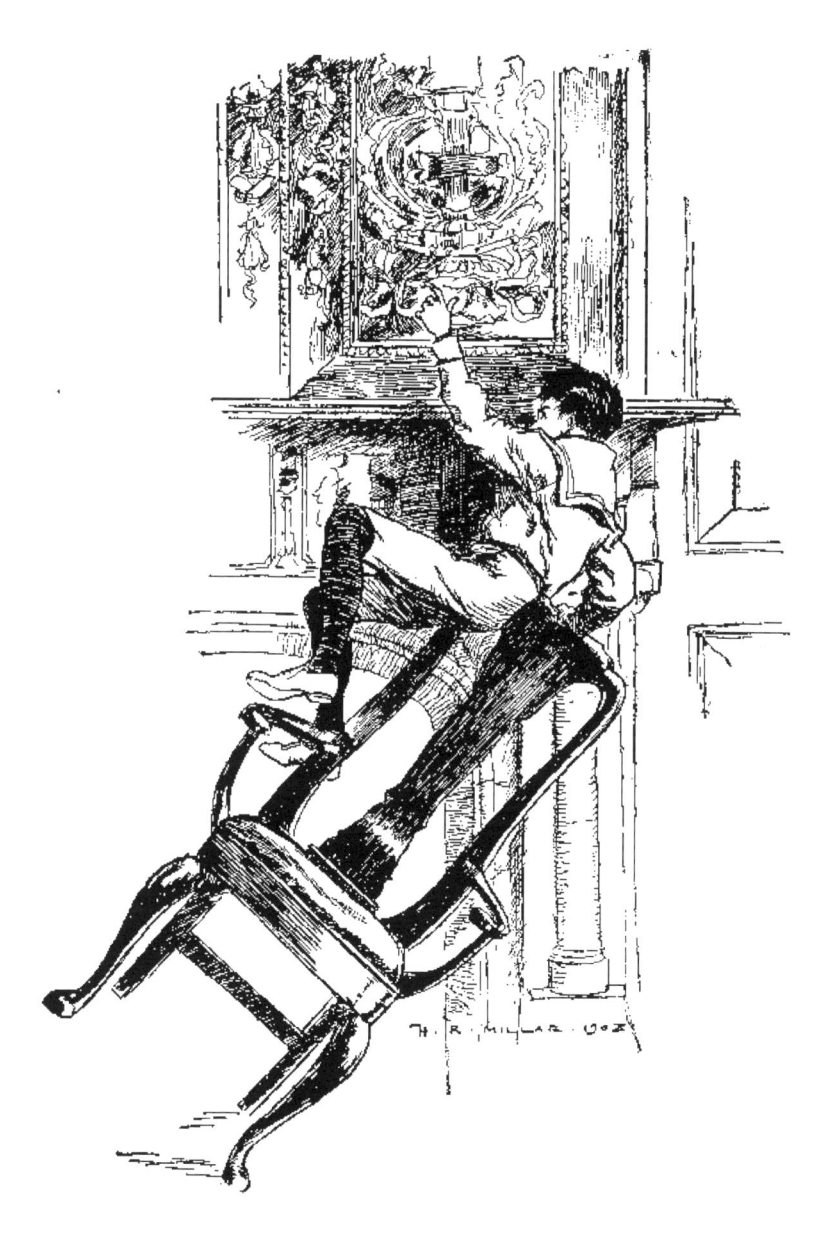

"EDRED AND THE BIG CHAIR FELL TO THE FLOOR."

"I'll show you presently," said the girl. She could not show him then, because, in point of fact, she did not know. She only knew there *was* a secret spring, and she was feeling for it with both hands among the carved wreaths of the panels, as she stood with one foot on each of the arms of a very high chair—the only chair in the room high enough for her to be able to reach all round the panel. Suddenly something clicked and the secret door flew open—she just had time to jump to the floor, or it would have knocked her down.

Then she climbed up again and got into the hole, and Edred handed her the candle.

"Where's the matches?" she asked.

"In my pocket," said he firmly. "I'm not going to have you starting off without me—*again*."

"Well, come on, then," said Elfrida, ignoring the injustice of this speech.

"All right," said Edred, climbing on the chair. "How does it open?"

He had half closed the door, and was feeling among the carved leaves, as he had seen her do.

"Oh, come on," said Elfrida, "oh, look out!"

Well might she request her careless brother to look out. As he reached up to touch the carving, the chair tilted, he was jerked forward, caught at the carving to save himself, missed it, and fell forward with all his weight against the half-open door. It shut with a loud bang. Then a resounding crash echoed through the quiet house as Edred and the big chair fell to the floor in, so to speak, each other's arms.

There was a stricken pause. Then Elfrida from the other side of the panel beat upon it with her fists and shouted—

"Open the door! You aren't hurt, are you?"

"Yes, I am—very much," said Edred, from the outside of the secret door, and also from the hearthrug. "I've twisted my leg in the knickerbocker part, and I've got a great bump on my head, and I think I'm going to be very poorly."

"Well, open the panel first," said Elfrida rather unfeelingly. But then she was alone in the dark on the other side of the panel.

"I don't know how to," said Edred, and Elfrida heard the sound of some one picking himself up from among disordered furniture.

"Feel among the leaves, like I did," she said. "It's quite easy. You'll soon find it."

Silence.

CHAPTER VII
THE KEY OF THE PARLOUR

Elfrida was behind the secret panel, and the panel had shut with a spring. She had come there hoping to find the jewels that had been hidden two hundred years ago by Sir Edward Talbot, when he was pretending to be the Chevalier St. George. She had not had time even to look for the jewels before the panel closed, and now that she was alone in the dusty dark, with the door shut between her and the bright, light parlour where her brother was, the jewels hardly seemed to matter at all, and what did so dreadfully and very much matter was that closed panel. Edred had tried to open it, and he had fallen off the chair. Well, there had been plenty of time for him to get up again.

"Why don't you open the door?" she called impatiently. And there was no answer. Behind that panel silence seemed a thousand times more silent than it ever had before. And it was so dark. And Edred had the matches in his pocket.

"Edred! Edred!" she called suddenly and very loud, "why don't you open the door?"

And this time he answered.

"Because I can't reach," he said.

I feel that I ought to make that the end of the chapter, and leave you to wonder till the next how Elfrida got out, and how she liked the not getting out, which certainly looked as though it were going to last longer than any one could possibly be expected to find pleasant.

But that would make the chapter too short—and there are other reasons. So I will not disguise from you that when Elfrida put her hand to her pocket and felt something there—something hard and heavy—and remembered that she had put the key of the parlour there because it was such a nice safe place, where it couldn't possibly be lost, she uttered what is known as a hollow groan.

"Aha! you see now," said Edred outside. "You see I'm not so stupid after all."

Elfrida was thinking.

"I say," she called through the panel, "it's no use my standing here. I shall try to feel my way up to the secret chamber. I wish I could remember whether there's a window there or not. If I were you I should just take a book and read till something happens. Mrs. Honeysett's sure to come back some time."

"I can't hear half you say," said Edred. "You do whiffle so."

"Take a book!" shouted his sister. "Read! Mrs.—Honeysett—will—come—back—some—time."

So Edred got down a book called "Red Cotton Nightcap Country," which he thought looked interesting; but I don't advise you to try it. And Elfrida, her heart beating rather heavily, put out her hands and felt her way along the passage to the stairs.

"It's all very well," she told herself, "the secret panel is there all right, like it was when I went into the past, but suppose the stairs are gone, or weren't really ever there at all? Or suppose I walked straight into a wall or something? Or perhaps not a *wall*—a *well*," she suggested to herself with a sudden thrill of terror; and after that she felt very carefully with each foot in turn before she ventured to put it down in a fresh step.

The boards were soft to tread on, as though they had been carpeted with velvet, and so were the stairs. For there *were* stairs, sure enough. She went up them very slowly and carefully, reaching her hands before her. And at last her hands came against something that seemed like a door. She stroked it gently, feeling for the latch, which she presently found. The door had not been opened for such a very long time that it was not at all inclined to open now. Elfrida had to shove with shoulder and knee, and with all the strength she had. The door gave way—out of politeness, I should think, for Elfrida's knee and shoulder and strength were all quite small—and there was the room just as she had seen it when the Chevalier St. George stood in it bowing and smiling by the light of one candle in a silver candlestick. Only now Elfrida was alone, and the light was a sort of green twilight that came from a little window over the mantelpiece, that was hung outside with a thick curtain of ivy. If Elfrida had come out of the sunlight she would have called this a green darkness. But she had been so long in the dark that this shadowy dusk seemed quite light to her. All the same she made haste, when she had shut the door, to drag a chair in front of the fireplace and to get the window open. It opened inwards, and it did not want to open at all. But it, also, was polite enough to yield to her wishes, and when it had suddenly given way she reached out and broke the ivy-leaves off one by one, making more and more daylight in the secret room. She did not let the leaves fall outside, but on the hearthstone, "for," said she, "we don't want outside people to get to know all about the Ardens' secret hiding-place. I'm glad I thought of that. I really *am* rather like a detective in a book."

When all the leaves were plucked from the window's square, and only the brown ivy boughs left, she turned back to the room. The furniture was all powdered heavily with dust, and what had made the floor so soft to walk upon was the thick carpet of dust that lay there. There was the table on which the Chevalier St. George—no, Sir Edward Talbot—had set the tray. There were the chairs, and there, sure enough, was the corner cupboard in which he had put the jewels. Elfrida got its door open with I don't know what of mingled hopes and fears. It had three shelves, but the jewels were on none of them. In fact there was nothing on any of them. But on the inside of the door her hand, as she held it open, felt something rough. And when she looked it was a name carved, and when she swung the door well back so that the light fell full on it she saw that the name was "E. Talbot." So then she knew that all she had seen in that room before must have really happened two hundred years before, and was not just a piece of magic Mouldiwarpiness.

She climbed up on the chair again and looked out through the little window. She could see nothing of the Castle walls—only the distant shoulder of the downs and the path that cut across it towards the station. She would have liked to see a red figure or a violet one coming along that path. But there was no figure on it at all.

What do you usually do when you are shut up in a secret room, with no chance of getting out for hours? As for me, I always say poetry to myself. It is one of the uses of poetry—one says it to oneself in distressing circumstances of that kind, or when one has to wait at railway stations, or when one cannot get to sleep at night. You will find poetry most useful for this purpose. So learn plenty of it, and be sure it is the best kind, because this is most useful as well as most agreeable.

Elfrida began with "Ruin seize thee, ruthless King!" but there were parts of that which she liked best when there were other people about—so she stopped it, and began "Horatius and the Bridge." This lasts a long time. Then came the Favourite Cat drowned in a tub of Gold-fish—and in the middle of that, quite suddenly, and I don't know why, she thought of the Mouldiwarp.

"We didn't quite quarrel," she told herself. "At least not really, truly quarrelling. I might try anyhow."

So she set to work to make a piece of poetry to call up the Mouldiwarp with.

"SHE SAW THAT THE NAME WAS 'E. TALBOT.'"

This was how, after a long time, the first piece came out—

> "'The Mouldiwarp of Arden
>
> By the nine gods it swore
>
> That Elfrida of Arden
>
> Should be shut up no more.
>
> By the nine gods it swore it
>
> And named a convenient time, no doubt,
>
> And bade its messengers ride forth
>
> East and West, South and North,
>
> To let Elfrida out.'"

But when she said it aloud nothing happened. "I wonder," said Elfrida, "whether it's because we quarrelled, or because it just says he let me out and doesn't ask him to, or because I had to say *El*frida, to make it sound right, or because it's such dreadful nonsense. I'll try again."

She tried again. This time she got—

> "'Behind the secret panel's lines
>
> The pensive *El*frida, reclines
>
> And wishes she was at home.
>
> At least I am at home, of course,

But things are getting worse and worse.

Dear Mole, come, come, come, come!'"

She said it aloud, and when she came to the last words there was the white Mouldiwarp sitting on the floor at her feet and looking up at her with eyes that blinked.

"You *are* good to come," Elfrida said.

"Well, what do you want now?" said the Mole.

"I—I ought to tell you that I oughtn't to ask you to do anything, but I didn't think you'd come if it really counted as a quarrel. It was only a little one, and we were both sorry quite directly."

"You have a straightforward nature," said the Mouldiwarp. "Well, well, I must say you've got yourself into a nice hole!"

"It would be a *very* nice hole," said Elfrida eagerly, "if only the panel were open. I wouldn't mind how long I stayed here then. That's funny, isn't it?"

"Yes," said the Mole. "Well, if you hadn't quarrelled I could get you into another time—some time when the panel was open—and you could just walk out. You shouldn't quarrel. It makes everything different. It puts dust into the works. It stops the wheels of the clock."

"The clock!" said Elfrida slowly. "Couldn't that work backwards?"

"I don't know what you mean," said the Mole.

"I don't know that I quite know myself," Elfrida explained; "but the daisy-clock. You sit on the second hand and there isn't any time—and yet there's lots where you're not sitting. If I could sit on the daisy-clock the time wouldn't be anything before some one comes to let me out. But

I can't get to the daisy-clock, even if you'd make it for me. So *that's* no good."

"You are a very clever little girl," said the Mouldiwarp, "and all the clocks in the world aren't made of daisies. Move the tables and chairs back against the wall; we'll see what we can do for you."

While Elfrida was carrying out this order—the white Mole stood on its hind feet and called out softly in a language she did not understand. Others understood it though, it seemed, for a white pigeon fluttered in through the window, and then another and another, till the room seemed full of circling wings and gentle cooings, and a shower of soft, white feathers fell like snow.

Then the Mole was silent, and one by one the white pigeons sailed back through the window into the blue and gold world of out-of-doors.

"Get up on a chair and keep out of the way," said the Mouldiwarp. And Elfrida did.

And then a soft wind blew through the little room—a wind like the wind that breathes softly in walled gardens and shakes down the rose-leaves on sparkling summer mornings. And the white feathers on the floor were stirred by the sweet wind, and drifted into little heaps and lines and curves till they made on the dusty floor the circle of a clock-face, with all its figures and its long hand and its short hand and its second hand. And the white Mole stood in the middle.

"All white things obey me," it said. "Come, sit down on the minute hand, and you'll be there in no time."

"Where?" asked Elfrida, getting off the chair.

"Why, at the time when they open the panel. Let me get out of the clock first. And give me the key of the parlour door. It'll save time in the end."

"THE ROOM SEEMED FULL OF CIRCLING WINGS."

So Elfrida sat down on the minute hand, and instantly it began to move round—faster than you can possibly imagine. And it was very soft to sit on—like a cloud would be if the laws of nature ever permitted you to sit on clouds. And it spun round so that it seemed no time at all before she found herself sitting on the floor and heard voices, and knew that the secret panel was open.

"I see," she said wisely, "it does work backwards, doesn't it?"

But there was no one to answer her, for the Mouldiwarp was gone. And the white pigeons' feathers were in heaps on the floor. She saw them, as she stood up. And there wasn't any clock-face any more.

. . . . .

Edred soon got tired of "Red Cotton Nightcap Country," which really is not half such good fun as it sounds, even for grown-ups, and he tried several other books. But reading did not seem amusing, somehow. And the house was so much too quiet, and the clock outside ticked so much too loud—and Elfrida was shut up, and there were bars to the windows, and the door was locked. He walked about, and sat in each of the chairs in turn, but no one of them was comfortable. And his thoughts were not comfortable either. Suppose no one ever came to let them out! Supposing the years rolled on and found him still a prisoner, when he was a white-haired old man, like people in the Bastille, or in Iron Masks? His eyes filled with tears at the thought. Fortunately it did not occur to him that unless some one came pretty soon he would be unlikely to live to a great age, since people cannot live long without eating. If he had thought of this he would have been even more unhappy than he was—and he was quite unhappy enough. Then he began to wonder if "anything had happened" to Elfrida. She was dreadfully quiet inside there behind the panel. He wished he had not quarrelled with her. Everything was very miserable. He went to the window and looked out, as Elfrida had done, to see if he could see a red dress or a violet dress coming over the downs. But there was nothing. And the time got longer and longer, drawing itself out like a putty snake, when you rub it between your warm hands—and at last, what with misery, and having cried a good deal, and its being long past tea-time, he fell asleep on the window-seat.

He was roused by a hand on his shoulder and a voice calling his name.

Next moment he was in the arms of Aunt Edith, or as much in her arms as he could be with the window-bars between them.

When he had told her where Elfrida was, and where the room-key was, which took some time, he began to cry again—for he did not quite see, even now, how he was to be got out.

"Now don't be a dear silly," said Aunt Edith. "If we can't get you out any other way I'll run and fetch a locksmith. But look what I found right in the middle of the path as I came up from the station."

It was a key. And tied to it was an ivory label, and on the label were written the words, "Parlour door, Arden."

"You might try it," she said.

He did try it. And it fitted. And he unlocked the parlour door and then the front door, so that Aunt Edith could come in.

And together they got the kitchen steps and found the secret spring and opened the panel, and got out the dusty Elfrida. And then Aunt Edith lighted the kitchen fire and boiled the kettle; they had tea, which every one wanted very badly indeed. And Aunt Edith had brought little cakes for tea with pink icing on them, very soft inside with apricot jam. And she had come to stay over Sunday.

She was as much excited as the children over the secret panel, and after tea (when Edred had fetched Emily back from the wild-goose chase for a parcel at the station, on which she was still engaged), the aunt and the niece and the nephew explored the secret stair and the secret chamber thoroughly.

"What a wonderful lot of pigeons' feathers!" said Aunt Edith; "they must have been piling up here for years and years."

"It was lucky, you finding that key," said Edred. "I wonder who dropped it. Where's the other one, Elf?"

"I don't know," said Elfrida truthfully, "it isn't in my pocket now."

And though Edred and Aunt Edith searched every corner of the secret hiding-place they never found that key.

Elfrida alone knows that she gave it to the Mouldiwarp. And as Mrs. Honeysett declared that there had never been a parlour key with a label on it in *her* time it certainly does seem as though the Mole must have put the key he got from Elfrida on the path for Aunt Edith to find, after carefully labelling it to prevent mistakes. How the Mole got the label is another question, but I really think that finding a label for a key is quite a simple thing to do—I have done it myself. Whereas making a clock-face of white pigeon feathers is very difficult indeed—and a thing that I have never been able to do. And as for making that clock-face the means of persuading time to go fast or slow, just as one wishes—well, I don't suppose even *you* could do that.

Elfrida found it rather a relief to go back to the ordinary world, where magic moles did not upset the clock—a world made pleasant by nice aunts and the old delightful games that delight ordinary people. Games such as "Hunt the thimble," "What is my thought like," and "Proverbs." The three had a delightful weekend, and Aunt Edith told them all about the lodgers and the seaside house, which already seemed very long ago and far away. On Sunday evening, as they walked home from Arden Church, where they had tried to attend to the service, and not to look *too* much at the tombs and monuments of dead-and-gone Ardens that lined the chancel, the three sat down on Arden Knoll, and Aunt Edith explained things a little to them. She told them much more than they could understand about wills, and trustees, and incomes, but they were honoured by her confidence, and pleased by the fact that she seemed to think they *could* understand such grown-up kind of things. And the thing that remained on their minds after the talk, like a ship cast up by a high tide, was this: that Arden Castle was theirs, and that there was very little money to "keep it up" with. So that every one must be very careful, and no one must be at all extravagant. And Aunt Edith was going back to the world of lawyers, and wills, and trustees, early on Monday morning, and they must be very good children, and not bother Mrs. Honeysett, and never, never lock themselves in and hide the key in safe places.

All this remained, as the lasting result of the pleasant talk on the downs in the softly lessening light.

And another thing remained, which Edred put into words as the two children walked back from the station, where they had seen Aunt Edith into the train and waved their goodbyes to her.

"It is very important indeed," he said, "for us to find the treasure. Then we could 'keep up' the Castle without any bother. We must have it *built* up again first, of course, and then we'll *keep* it up. And we won't have any old clocks and not keeping together, this time. We'll both of us go and find the attic the minute our quarrel's three days old, and we'll ask the Mouldiwarp to send us to a time when we can really *see* the treasure with our own eyes. I do think that's a good idea, don't you?" he asked, with modest pride.

"Very," Elfrida said. "And I say, Edred, I don't mean to quarrel any more if I can help it. It is such waste of time," she added in her best grown-up manner, "and it does delay everything so. Delays are dangerous. It says so in the 'proverb' game. Suppose there really was a chance of *getting* the treasure and we had to wait three days because of quarrelling. But I'll tell you one thing I found out: you can get the Mole to come and help you, even if you have quarrelled a little. Because *I* did." And she told him how.

"But, I expect," she added. "It would only come if I were in the most awful trouble and all human aid despaired of."

"Well, we're not that now," said Edred, knocking the head off a poppy with his stick, "and I'm jolly glad we're not."

"I wonder," said Elfrida, "who lives in that cottage where the witch was. I know exactly where it is. I expect it's been pulled down, though. Let's go round that way. It'll be something to do."

So they went round that way, and the way was quite easy to find. But when they got to the place where the tumbledown cottage had been in Boney's time, there was only a little slate-roofed house with a blue bill pasted up on its yellow-brick face saying that somebody's A1 ginger-beer and up-to-date minerals were sold there. The house was dull to look at, and they did not happen to have any spare money for ginger-beer, so they turned round to go home and suddenly found themselves face to face with a woman. She wore a red-and-black plaid blouse and a bought ready-made black skirt, and on her head was a man's peaked cap such as women in the country wear now instead of the pretty sun bonnets that they used to wear when I was a little girl.

"So they've pulled the old cottage down," she said. "This new house'll be fine and dry inside, I lay. The rain comes in through the roof of the old one so's you might a'most as well be laying in the open medder."

The children listened politely, and both were wondering where they had seen this woman before, for her face was strangely familiar to them, and yet they didn't seem really to know her either.

"Most of the cottages 'bout here is just as bad as they always was," she went on. "When Arden has the handling of the treasure he'll see to it that poor folks lie warm and dry, won't he now?"

And then all in a minute the children both knew, and she knew that they knew.

"Why," said Edred, "you're the——"

"Yes," she said, "I'm the witch come from old ancient times. If you can go back I can go forth, because then and now's the same if I know how to make a clock."

"Can you make clocks?" said Elfrida. "I thought it was only——"

"So it be," said the witch. "I can't make 'em, but I know them as can. And I've come 'ere to find you, 'cause you brought me the tea and sugar. I've got the wise eye, I have. I can see back and forth. I looked forrard and I saw ye, and I looked back and I saw what you're seeking, and I know where the treasure is and——"

"But where did you get those clothes?" Edred asked; and it was a question he was afterwards to have reason to regret.

"Oh, clothes is easy come by," said the witch. "If it was only clothes I could be a crowned queen this very minute."

The children had a fleeting impression of seeing against the criss-cross fence of the potato patch a lady in crimson and ermine with a gold crown. They blinked, startled, and saw that there was no crimson and gold, only the dull clothes of the witch against the background of potato patch.

"And how did you get here?" Edred asked.

"That speckled hen of mine's a-settin' on the clock-face now," she said. "I quieted her with a chalk-line drawn from her beak's end straight out into the world of wonders. If she rouses up, then I'm back there, and I can't never come back here, my dears, nor more than once, I can't. So let's make haste down to the Castle, and I'll show you where my great granny see them put the treasure when she was a little gell."

The three hurried down the steep-banked lane.

"Many's the time," the witch went on, "my granny pointed it out to me. It's just alongside where———"

And then the witch was not there any more. Edred and Elfrida were alone in the lane. The speckled hen must have recovered from her "quieting," and got off the clock.

"She's gone right enough," said Edred, "and now we'll never know. And just when she was going to tell us where it was. I do think it's too jolly stupid for anything."

"It's *you* that's too jolly stupid for anything," said Elfrida hotly. "What did you want to go asking her about her silly clothes for? It was *that* did it. She'd have told us where it was before now if you hadn't taken her time up with clothes. As if *clothes* mattered! I do wish to goodness you'd *sometimes* try to behave as if you'd got some sense."

"Go it!" said Edred bitterly. "As if everything wasn't tiresome enough. Now there's another three days to wait, because of your nagging. Oh, it's just exactly like a girl, so it is!"

"I'm—I'm sorry," said Elfrida, awestricken. "Let's do something good to make up. I'll give you that note-book of mine with the lead-pointed mother-of-pearl pencil, and we'll go round to all the cottages and find out which are leaky, so as to be ready to patch them up when we've got the treasure."

"A LADY IN CRIMSON AND ERMINE WITH A GOLD CROWN."

"I don't *want* to be good," said Edred bitterly. "*I* haven't quarrelled and put everything back, but I'm going to now," he said, with determination. "I don't see why everything should be smashed up and me not said any of the things I want to say."

"Oh, *don't!*" cried Elfrida; "it's bad enough to quarrel when you don't want to, but to *set out* to quarrel! Don't!"

Edred didn't. He kicked the dust up with his boots, and the two went back to the Castle in gloomy silence.

At the gate Edred paused. "I'll make it up now if you like," he said. "I've only just thought of it—but perhaps it's three days from the *end* of the quarrel."

"I see," said Elfrida; "so the longer we keep it up——"

"Yes," said Edred; "so let's call it Pax and not waste any *more* time."

CHAPTER VIII
GUY FAWKES

Three days, because there had been a quarrel. But days pass quickly when the sun shines, and it is holiday-time, and you have a big ruined castle to explore and examine—a castle that is your own, or your brother's.

"After all," said Elfrida sensibly, "we might quite likely find the treasure ourselves, without any magic Mouldiwarpiness at all. We'll look thoroughly. We won't leave a stone unturned."

"We shall have to leave a good many stones unturned," said Edred, looking at the great grey mass of the keep that towered tall and frowning above them.

"Well, you know what I mean," said Elfrida. "Come on!" and they went.

They climbed the steep, worn stairs that wound round and round in the darkness—stairs littered with dead leaves and mould and dropped feathers, and the dry, deserted nests of owls and jackdaws; stairs that ended suddenly in daylight and a steep last step, and the top of a broad ivy-grown wall from which you could look down, down, down; past the holes in the walls where the big beams used to be, past the old fireplaces still black with the smoke of fires long since burnt out, past the doors and windows of rooms whose floors fell away long ago; down, down, to where ferns and grass and brambles grew green at the very bottom of the tower.

Then there were arched doors that led to colonnades with strong little pillars and narrow windows, wonderful little unexpected chambers and corners—the best place in the whole wide world for serious and energetic hide-and-seek.

"How glorious," said Elfrida, as they rested, scarlet and panting, after a thrilling game of "I spy,"—"if all these broken bits were mended, so that you couldn't see where the new bits were stuck on! And if it could all be exactly like it was when it was brand-new."

"There wasn't the house when it was brand-new—the house like it is now, I mean," said Edred. "I don't suppose there was any attic with chests in when the castle was new."

"There couldn't be, not with *all* the chests," said Elfrida; "of course not, because some of the clothes in the chest weren't made till long after the castle was built. I believe grown-ups can tell what a broken thing was like when it was new. I know they can with bones—mastodons and things. And they made out what Hercules was like out of one foot of him that they found, I believe," she added hazily.

"I've got an idea," said Edred, "if we could get back to where the castle was all perfect like a model and draw pictures of every part. Then when we found the treasure we should know exactly what to build it up like, shouldn't we?"

"Yes," said Elfrida very gently. "We certainly should. But then we should have to know how to draw first, shouldn't we?"

"Of course we should," Edred agreed, "but that wouldn't take long if we really tried. I never do try at school. I don't like it. But it's jolly easy. I know that. Burslem mi. always takes the drawing prize, and you know what a duffer *he* is. We might begin to learn now, don't you think?"

Elfrida sat down on a fallen stone in the middle of the castle yard, and looked at the intricate wonderful arches and pillars, the crenulated battlements of the towers, the splendid stoutness of the walls, and she sighed.

"Yes," she said, "let's begin now——"

"And you'll have to lend me one of your pencils," said he, "because I broke mine all to bits trying to get the parlour door open the day you'd got the key in your pocket. Quite a long one it was. You'll have to lend me a long one, Elf. I can't draw with those little endy-bits that get inside your hand and prick you with the other end."

"I don't mind," said she, "so long as you don't put it in your mouth."

So they got large sheets of writing-paper, and brown calf-bound books for the paper to lie flat on, and they started to draw Arden Castle. And as Elfrida tried to draw everything she knew was there, as well as everything she could see, her drawing soon became almost entirely covered with black-lead.

They had no indiarubber, and if you drew anything wrong it had to stay drawn. When you first begin to draw, you draw a good many things wrong, don't you? I assure you that nobody would have known that the black and grey muddle on Elfrida's paper was meant to be a picture of a castle. Edred's was much more easily recognised, even before he printed "Arden Castle" under it in large, uneven letters. He never once raised his eyes from his paper, and just drew what he thought the front of the castle looked like from the outside. Also he sucked his pencil earnestly— Elfrida's pencil, I mean—and this made the lines of his drawing very black.

"There!" he said at last, "it's ever so much liker than yours."

"Yes," said Elfrida, "but there's more *in* mine."

"It doesn't matter how much there is in a picture if you can't tell what it's meant for," said Edred, with some truth. "Now, in mine you can see the towers, and the big gate, and the windows, and the twiddly in-and-outness on top."

"Yes," said Elfrida, "but . . . well, let's do something else. I don't believe we should either of us learn to draw well enough to rebuild Arden by; not before we've found the treasure, I mean. Perhaps we might meet a real artist, like the one we saw drawing the castle yesterday—in the past I mean—and get him to draw it for us, and bring the picture back with us, and——"

"Oh," cried Edred, jumping up and dropping his masterpiece, and the calf-bound volume and the pencil. "*I* know. The Brownie!"

"The Brownie?"

"Yes—take it with us. Then we could photograph the castle all perfect."

"But we can't take it with us."

"Can't we?" said Edred; "that's all *you* know. Now I'll tell you something. That first time—a bit of plaster was in my shoe when we changed, and it was in my shoe when we got there, and I took it out when we were learning about 'dog's delight.' And I flipped it out of the window. And when we got back, and I'd changed and everything, there was that bit of plaster in my own shoe. If we can take plaster we can take photographs—cameras, I mean." This close and intelligent reasoning commanded Elfrida's respect, and she wished she had thought of it herself. But then she had not had any plaster in her shoe. So she said—

"You're getting quite clever, aren't you?"

"Aha," said Edred, "you'd like to have thought of that yourself, wouldn't you? I can be clever sometimes, same as you can."

It is very annoying to have our thoughts read. Elfrida said swiftly, "Not often you can't," and then stopped short. For a moment the children stood looking at each other with a very peculiar expression. Then a sigh of relief broke from each.

"Fielded!" said Edred.

"Just in time!" said Elfrida. "It wasn't a quarrel; nobody could say it was a quarrel. Come on, let's go and look at the cottages, like the witch told us to."

They went. They made a tour of inspection that day and the next and the next. And they saw a great many things that a grown-up inspector would never have seen. Poor people are very friendly and kind to you when you are a child. They will let you come into their houses and talk to you and show you things in a way that they would never condescend to do with your grown-up relations. This is, of course, if you are a really nice child, and treat them in a respectful and friendly way. Edred and Elfrida very soon knew more about the insides of the cottages round Arden than any grown-up could have learned in a year. They knew what wages the master of the house got, what there was for dinner, and what, oftener, there wasn't, how many children were still living, and how many had failed to live. They knew exactly where the rain came through the rotten thatch in bad weather, and where the boards didn't fit and so let the draughts in, and how some of the doors wouldn't shut, some wouldn't open, and how the bedroom windows were, as often as not, not made to open at all.

And when they weren't visiting the cottages or exploring the castle they found a joyous way of passing the time in the reading aloud of the history of Arden. They took it in turns to read aloud. Elfrida looked carefully for some mention of Sir Edward Talbot and his pretending to be the Chevalier St. George. There was none, but a Sir Edward Talbot had been accused, with the Lord Arden of the time, of plotting against His Most Christian Majesty King James I.

"I wonder if he was like my Edward Talbot?" said Elfrida. "I would like to see him again. I wish I'd told him about us having been born so many years after he died. But it would have been difficult to explain, wouldn't it? Let's look in Green's History Book and see what they looked like when it was His Most Christian Majesty King James the First."

Perhaps it was this which decided the children, when the three days were over, to put on the clothes which most resembled the ones in the pictures of James I.'s time in Green's History.

Edred had full breeches, puffed out like balloons, and a steeple-crowned hat, and a sort of tunic of crimson velvet, and a big starched ruff round his little neck more uncomfortable even than your Eton collar is after you've been wearing flannels for days and days. And Elfrida had long, tight stays with a large, flat-shaped piece of wood down the front, and very full, long skirts over a very abrupt hoop.

When the three days were over the door of the attic, which, as usual after a quarrel, had been quite invisible and impossible to find, had become as plain as the nose on the face of the plainest person you know, and the children had walked in, and looked in the chests till they found what they wanted.

And now they put on ruffs and all the rest of it to the accompaniment, or, as it always seemed, with the help, of soft pigeon noises.

While they were dressing Elfrida held the Brownie camera tightly, in one hand or the other. This made dressing rather slow and difficult, but the children had agreed that if it were not done the Brownie would be, as Edred put it, "liable to vanish," as everything else belonging to their own time always did—except their clothes. I can't explain to you just now how it was that their clothes *didn't* vanish. It would take too long. But it was all part of the magic of white feathers which are, as you know, the clothes of white pigeons.

"THE WALLS SEEMED TO TREMBLE AND SHAKE AND GO CROOKED."

And now a very odd thing happened. As Edred put on his second shoe—which was the last touch to their united toilets—the walls seemed to tremble and shake and go crooked, like a house of cards at the very instant before it topples down. The floor slanted to that degree that standing on it was so difficult as to be at last impossible. The rafters all seemed to get crooked and mixed, like a box of matches when you spill them on the floor. The tiled roof that showed blue daylight through seemed to spin like a top, and you could not tell at all which way up you were. All this happened with dreadful suddenness, but almost as soon as it had begun it stopped with a jerk like that of a clockwork engine that has gone wrong. And the attic was gone—and the chests, and the blue-chinked tiles of the roof, and the walls and the rafters. And the room had shrunk to less than half its old size. And it was higher, and it was not an attic any more, but a round room with narrow windows, and just such a fireplace, with a stone hood, as the ones the children had seen when they looked down from the tops of the towers. You must have often heard of events that take people's breath away. This sudden change did really take away the breaths of Edred and Elfrida, so that for a few moments they could only stare at each other "like Guy Fawkes masks," as Elfrida later said.

"*I* see," said Edred, when breath enough for speech had returned to him. "This is the place where the attic was after the tower fell to pieces."

"But there isn't any attic really," said Elfrida. "You know we can't find it if we quarrelled, and Mrs. Honeysett doesn't ever find it. It isn't anywhere."

"Yes, it is," said Edred. "We couldn't find it if it wasn't."

"Well," said Elfrida gloomily, "I only hope we *may* find it, that's all. I suppose we may as well go out. It's no use sticking in this horrid little room." Her hand was on the door, but even as she fumbled with the latch, which was of iron and of a shape to which she was wholly unaccustomed, something else happened, even more disconcerting than the turn-over-change in which the attic and the chests had disappeared. It is very difficult to describe. Perhaps you happen to dislike travelling in trains with your back to the engine? If you do dislike it, you dislike it very much indeed. It makes your head ache, and gives you a queer feeling at the back of your neck, and makes you turn so pale that the grown-up people with whom you are travelling will ask you what is the matter, and sometimes heartlessly insist that the buns you had at the junction, or the chocolate creams pressed into your hand at the parting hour by Uncle Fred or Aunt Imogen, are the cause of your sufferings. The worst feeling of all is that terrible sensation, as though your heart and lungs and the front part of your waistcoat were being drawn slowly but surely through your backbone, and taken a very long way off.

The sensations which now held Edred and Elfrida were exactly like those which—if you don't like travelling backwards—you know only too well—and the sensations were so acute that both children shut their eyes. The whirling feeling, and the withdrawing-waistcoat feeling, and the headache, and the back-of-the-neck feeling stopped as suddenly as they had begun, and the two children opened their eyes in a room which Edred at least had never seen before. To Elfrida it seemed strange yet familiar. The shape of the room, the position of doors and windows, the mantelpiece with its curious carvings—these she knew. And some of the furniture, too. Yet the room seemed bare—barer than it should have been. But why should it look bare—barer than it should have been—unless she knew how much less bare it once was? Unless, in fact, she had seen it before?

"Oh, I know," she cried, standing in her stiff skirts and heavy shoes in the middle of the room. "I know. This is Lord Arden's town house. This is where I was with Cousin Betty. Only there aren't such nice chairs and things, and it was full of people then."

Edred remained silent, his mouth half open and his eyes half shut in a sort of trance of astonishment. This was very different from the last adventure in which he had taken part. For then he had only gone to the house in Arden Castle as it was in Boney's time, and he had gone to it by the simple means of walking down a staircase with which he was already familiar. But now he had been transported in a most violent and unpleasing manner, not only from his own times to times much earlier, but also from Arden Castle, which he knew, to Arden House, which he did not know. So he was silent, and when he did speak it was with discontent verging on disgust.

"I don't like it," he began. "Let's go back. I don't like it. And we didn't take the photograph. And I don't like it. And my clothes are horrid. I feel something between a balloon and a Bluecoat boy. And you've no idea how silly you look—like Mrs. Noah out of the Ark, only tubby. And I don't know who we're supposed to be. And I don't suppose this is Arden House. And if it is, you don't know *when*. Suppose it's Inquisition times, and they put us on the stake? Let's go back; I don't like it," he ended.

"Now you just listen," said Elfrida, knitting her brows under the queer cap she wore. "I know inside me what I mean, but *you* won't unless you jolly well attend."

"Fire ahead."

"Well, then, even if it was Inquisition times it would be all right—for us."

"How do you know?"

"I don't know how I know, but I know I *do* know," said Elfrida firmly. "You see, *I've* been here before. It's not real, you see."

"It *is*," said Edred, kicking the leg of the table.

"Yes, of course . . . but . . . look here! You remember the water-shoot at Earl's Court, and you were so frightened."

"I wasn't."

"Yes, you were; and I didn't half like it myself. I wished we hadn't, rather. And when it started, and we knew we'd *got* to go on with it. Oh, horrible! And when it was over we wanted to go again, and we did, and it's been so jolly to remember. This is like that. See?"

"I don't," said Edred, "understand a single word you say. This isn't a bit like the water-shoot or anything. Now, is it?"

Elfrida frowned. Afterwards she was glad that she had done no more than frown. It is dangerous, as you know, to quarrel in a boat, but far more dangerous to quarrel in a century that is not your own. She frowned and opened her mouth. And just as her mouth opened the door of the room followed its example, and a short, dark, cross-looking woman in a brown skirt and strange cap came hurrying in.

"So it's here you've hidden yourselves!" she cried. "And I looking high and low to change your dress."

"What for?" said Edred, for it was his arm which she had quite ungently caught.

"For what?" she said, as she dragged him out of the room. "Why, to attend my lord your father and your lady mother at the masque at Whitehall. Had you forgot already? And thou so desirous to attend them in thy new white velvet broidered with the orange-tawny, and thy lady mother's diamond buckles, and the silken cloak, and the shoe-roses, and the cobweb-lawn starched ruff, and the little sword and all."

The woman had dragged Edred out of the room and by the stairs by this time. Elfrida, following, decided that her speech was the harshest part of her.

"'THOU'RT A FINE PAGE, INDEED, MY DEAR SON,' SAID THE LADY. 'STAND ASIDE AND TAKE MY TRAIN.'"

"If she was really horrid," thought the girl, "she wouldn't try to cheer him up with velvet and swords and diamond buckles."

"Can't *I* go?" she said aloud.

The woman turned and slapped her—not hard, but smartly. "I told thee how it would be if thou wouldst not hold that dunning tongue. No; thou can't go. Little ladies stay at home and sew their samplers. Thou'll go to Court soon enough, I warrant."

So Elfrida sat and watched while Edred was partially washed—the soap got in his eyes just as it gets in yours nowadays—and dressed in the beautiful white page's dress, white velvet, diamond buckles, little sword, and all.

"You are splendid," she said. "Oh, I do wish I was a boy!" she added, for perhaps the two thousand and thirty-second time in her short life.

"It's not that thou'll be wishing when *thy* time comes to go to Court," said the woman. "There, my little lord, give thy old nurse a kiss and stand very cautious and perfect, not to soil thy fine feathers. And when thou hearest thy mother's robes on the stairs go out and make thy bow like thy tutor taught thee."

It was not Edred's tutor who had taught him to bow. But when a rustling of silks sounded on the stairs he was able to go out and make a very creditable obeisance to the stately magnificence that swept down towards him. Elfrida thought it best to curtsey beside her brother. Aunt Edith had taught them to dance the minuet, and somehow the bow and curtsey which belong to that dance seemed the right thing now. And the lady on the stairs smiled, well pleased. She was a wonderfully dressed lady. Her bodice was of yellow satin, richly embroidered; her petticoat of gold tissue with stripes; her robe of red velvet, lined with yellow muslin with stripes of pure gold. She had a point lace apron and a collar of white satin under a delicately worked ruff. And she was a blaze of beautiful jewels.

"Thou'rt a fine page, indeed, my dear son," said the lady. "Stand aside and take my train as I pass. And thou, dear daughter, so soon as thou'rt of an age for it, thou shalt have a train and a page to carry it for thee."

She swept on, and the children followed. Lord Arden was in the hall, hardly less splendid than his wife, and they all went off in a coach that was very grand, if rather clumsy. Its shape reminded Elfrida of the coach which the fairy-godmother made for Cinderella out of the pumpkin, and she herself, as she peeped through the crowd of liveried servants to see it start, felt as much like Cinderella as any one need wish to feel, and perhaps a little more. But she consoled herself by encouraging a secret feeling she had that something was bound to happen; and sure enough something did. And that is what I am going to tell you about. I own that I should like to tell you also what happened to Edred, but his part of the adventure was not really an adventure at all—though it was a thing that he will never forget as long as he remembers any magic happenings.

"We went to the King's house," he told Elfrida later. "Whitehall is the name. I should like to call my house Whitehall—if it wasn't called Arden Castle, you know. And there were thousands of servants, I should think, all much finer than you could dream of, and lords and ladies, and lots of things to eat, and bear-baiting and cock-fighting in the garden."

"Cruel!" said Elfrida. "I hope you didn't look."

"A little I did," said Edred. "Boys have to be brave to bear sights of blood and horror, you know, in case of them growing up to be soldiers. But I liked the masque best. The Queen acted in it. There wasn't any talking, you know, only dressing up and dancing. It was something like the pantomime, but not so sparkly. And there was a sea with waves that moved all silvery, and panelled scenes, and dolphins and fishy things, and a great shell that opened, and the Queen and the ladies came out and danced, and I had a lot to eat, such rummy things, and then I fell asleep, and when I woke up the King himself was looking at me and saying I had a bonny face. Bonny means pretty. You'd think a King would know better, wouldn't you?"

This was all that Edred could find to tell. I could have told more, but one can't tell everything, and there is Elfrida's adventure to be told about.

When the coach had disappeared in the mist and the mud—for the weather was anything but summer weather—Elfrida went upstairs again to the room where she had left the old nurse. She did not know where else to go.

"Sit thee down," said the nurse, "and sew on thy sampler."

There was the sampler, very fine indeed, in a large polished wood frame.

"I wish I needn't," said Elfrida, looking anxiously at the fine silks.

"Tut, tut," said the nurse, "how'll thee grow to be a lady if thou doesn't mind thy needle?"

"I'd much rather talk to you," said Elfrida coaxingly.

"Thou canst chatter as well as sew," the nurse said, "as well I know to my cost. Would that thy needle flew so fast as thy tongue! Sit thee down, and if the little tree be done by dinner-time thou shalt have leave to see thy Cousin Richard."

"I suppose," thought Elfrida, taking up the needle, "that I am fond of my Cousin Richard."

The sewing was difficult, and hurt her eyes, but she persevered. Presently some one called the nurse, and Elfrida was left alone. Then she stopped persevering. "Whatever *is* the good," she asked herself, "of working at a sampler that you haven't time to finish, and that would be worn out, anyhow, years and years before you were born? The Elfrida who's doing that sampler is the same age as me, and born the same day," she reflected. And then she wondered what the date was, and what was the year. She was still wondering, and sticking the needle idly in and out of one hole, without letting it take the silk with it, when there was a sort of clatter on the stairs, the door burst open, and in came a jolly boy of about her own age.

"Thy task done?" he cried. "Mine too. Old Parrot-nose kept me hard at it, but I thought of thee, and for once I did all his biddings. So now we are free. Come, play ball in the garden." This, Elfrida concluded, must be Cousin Dick, and she decided at once that she *was* fond of him.

There was a big and beautiful garden behind the house. The children played ball there, and they ran in the box alleys, and played hide-and-seek among the cut trees and stone seats, and statues and fountains.

Old Parrot-nose, who was Cousin Richard's tutor, and was dressed in black, and looked as though he had been eating lemons and vinegar, sat on a seat and watched them, or walked up and down the flagged terrace with his thumb in a dull-looking book.

When they stopped their game to rest on a stone step, leaning against a stone seat, old Parrot-nose walked very softly up behind the seat, and stood there where they could not see him and listened. Listening is very dishonourable, as we all know, but in those days tutors did not always think it necessary to behave honourably to their pupils.

I always have thought, and I always shall think, that it was the eavesdropping of that tiresome old tutor, Mr. Parados—or Parrot-nose—which caused all the mischief. But Elfrida has always believed, and always will believe, that the disaster was caused by her knowing too much history. That is why she is so careful to make sure that no misfortune shall ever happen on *that* account, any way. That is one of the reasons why she never takes a history prize at school. "You never know," she says. And, in fact, when it comes to a question in an historical examination, she never *does* know.

This was how it happened. Elfrida, now that she was no longer running about in the garden, remembered the question that she had been asking herself over the embroidery frame, and it now seemed sensible to ask the question of some one who could answer it. So she said—

"I say, Cousin Richard, what day is it?"

Elfrida understood him to say that it was the fifth of November.

"Is it really?" she said. "Then it's Guy Fawkes day. Do you have fireworks?" And in pure lightness of heart began to hum—

"Please to remember

The Fifth of November

The gunpowder treason and plot.

I see no reason

Why gunpowder treason

Should ever be forgot."

"'Tis not a merry song, cousin," said Cousin Richard, "nor a safe one. 'Tis best not to sing of treason."

"But it didn't come off, you know, and he's always burnt in the end," said Elfrida.

"Are there more verses?" Cousin Dick asked.

"No."

"I wonder what treason the ballad deals with?" said the boy.

"Don't you know?" It was then that Elfrida made the mistake of showing off her historical knowledge. "*I* know. And I know some of the names of the conspirators, too, and who they wanted to kill, and everything."

"Tell me," said Cousin Richard idly.

"The King hadn't been fair to the Catholics, you know," said Elfrida, full of importance, "so a lot of them decided to kill him and the Houses of Parliament. They made a plot—there were a whole lot of them in it. They said Lord Arden was, but he wasn't, and some of them were to pretend to be hunting, and to seize the Princess Elizabeth and proclaim her Queen, and the rest were to blow the Houses of Parliament up when the King went to open them."

"I never heard this tale from my tutor," said Cousin Richard laughing. "Proceed, cousin."

"Well, Mr. Piercy took a house next the Parliament House, and they dug a secret passage to the vaults under the Parliament Houses; and they put three dozen casks of gunpowder there and covered them with faggots. And they would have been all blown up, only Mr. Tresham wrote to his relation, Lord Monteagle, that they were going to blow up the King and——"

"What King?" said Cousin Richard.

"King James the First," said Elfrida. "Why—what——" for Cousin Richard had sprung to his feet, and old Parrot-nose had Elfrida by the wrist.

"OLD PARROT-NOSE HAD ELFRIDA BY THE WRIST."

He sat down on the seat and drew her gently till she stood in front of him—gently, but it was like the hand of iron in the velvet glove (of which, no doubt, you have often read).

"Now, Mistress Arden," he said softly, "tell me over again this romance that you tell your cousin."

Elfrida told it.

"And where did you hear this pretty story?" he asked.

"Where are we now?" gasped Elfrida, who was beginning to understand.

"Here in the garden—where else?" said Cousin Richard, who seemed to understand nothing of the matter.

"Here—in my custody," said the tutor, who thought he understood everything. "Now tell me all—every name, every particular—or it will be the worse for thee and thy father."

"Come, sir," said Cousin Richard, "you frighten my cousin. It is but a tale she told. She is always merry, and full of many inventions."

"It is a tale she shall tell again before those of higher power than I," said the tutor, in a thoroughly disagreeable way, and his hand tightened on Elfrida's wrist.

"But—but—it's *history*," cried Elfrida, in despair. "It's in all the books."

"Which books?" he asked keenly.

"I don't know—all of them," she sullenly answered; sullenly, because she now really did understand just the sort of adventure in which her unusual knowledge of history, and, to do her justice, her almost equally unusual desire to show off, had landed her.

"Now," said the hateful tutor, for such Elfrida felt him to be, "tell me the names of the conspirators."

"It *can't* do any harm," Elfrida told herself. "This is James the First's time, and I'm in it. But it's three hundred years ago all the same, and it all *has* happened, and it can't make any difference what I say, so I'd better tell all the names I know."

The hateful tutor shook her.

"Yes, all right," she said; and to herself she added, "It's only a sort of dream; I may as well tell." Yet when she opened her mouth to tell all the names she could remember of the conspirators of the poor old Gunpowder Plot that didn't come off, all those years ago, she found herself not telling those names at all. Instead, she found herself saying—

"I'm not going to tell. I don't care what you do to me. I'm sorry I said anything about it. It's all nonsense—I mean, it's only history, and you ought to be ashamed of yourself, listening behind doors—I mean, *out* of doors behind stone seats, when people are talking nonsense to their own cousins."

Elfrida does not remember very exactly what happened after this. She was furiously angry, and when you are furiously angry things get mixed and tangled up in a sort of dreadful red mist. She only remembers that the tutor was very horrid, and twisted her wrists to make her tell, and she screamed and tried to kick him; that Cousin Richard, who did not scream, did, on the other hand, succeed in kicking the tutor; that she was dragged indoors and shut up in a room without a window, so that it was quite dark.

"If only I'd got Edred here," she said to herself, with tears of rage and mortification, "I'd try to make some poetry and get the Mouldiwarp to come and fetch us away. But it's no use till he comes home."

When he did come home—after the bear-baiting and the cock-fighting and the banquet and the masque—Lord and Lady Arden came with him, of course. And they found their house occupied by an armed guard, and in the dark little room a pale child exhausted with weeping, who assured them again and again that it was all nonsense, it was only history, and she hadn't meant to tell—indeed she hadn't. Lady Arden took her in her arms and held her close and tenderly, in spite of the grand red velvet and the jewels.

"Thou'st done no harm," said Lord Arden; "a pack of silly tales. To-morrow I'll see my Lord Salisbury and prick this silly bubble. Go thou to bed, sweetheart," he said to his wife, "and let the little maid lie with thee—she is all a-tremble with tears and terrors. To-morrow, my Lord Secretary shall teach these popinjays their place, and Arden House shall be empty of them, and we shall laugh at this fine piece of work that a solemn marplot has made out of a name or two and a young child's fancies. By to-morrow night all will be well, and we shall lie down in peace."

But when to-morrow night came it had, as all nights have, the day's work behind it. Lord Arden and his lady and the little children lay, not in Arden House in Soho, not in Arden Castle on the downs by the sea, but in the Tower of London, charged with high treason and awaiting their trial.

For my Lord Salisbury had gone to those vaults under the Houses of Parliament, and had found that bold soldier of fortune, Guy Fawkes, with his dark eyes, his dark lantern, and his dark intent; and the names of those in the conspiracy had been given up, and King James was saved, and the Parliaments—but the Catholic gentlemen whom he had deceived, and who had turned against him and his deceits, were face to face with the rack and the scaffold.

"THEY FOUND THEIR HOUSE OCCUPIED BY AN ARMED GUARD."

And I can't explain it at all—because, of course, Elfrida knew as well as I do that it all happened three hundred years ago—or, if you prefer to put it that way, that it had never happened, and that anyway, it was Mr. Tresham's letter to Lord Monteagle, and not Elfrida's singing of that silly rhyme, that had brought the Ardens and all these other gentlemen to the Tower and to the shadow of death. And yet she felt that it was *she* who had betrayed them. She felt also that if she had betrayed a base plot, she ought to be glad, and she was not glad. She felt—and called herself—a sneak. She had taken advantage of having been born so much later than all these people, and of having been rather good at history to give away the lives of all these nobles and gentlemen. That they were traitors to King and Parliament made no manner of difference. It was she, as she felt but too bitterly, who was the traitor. And in the thick-walled room in the Tower, where the name of Raleigh was still fresh in its carving, Elfrida lay awake, long after Lady Arden and Edred were sleeping peacefully, and hated herself, calling herself a Traitor, a Coward, and an Utter Duffer.

CHAPTER IX
THE PRISONERS IN THE TOWER

Imprisoned in the Tower of London, accused of high treason, and having confessed to a too intimate knowledge of the Gunpowder Plot, Elfrida could not help feeling that it would be nice to be back again in her own time, and at Arden, where, if you left events alone, and didn't interfere with them by any sort of magic mouldiwarpiness, nothing dangerous, romantic or thrilling would ever happen. And yet, when she *was* there, as you know, she never could let events alone. She and Edred could not be content with that castle and that house which, even as they stood, would have made you and me so perfectly happy. They wanted the treasure, and they—Elfrida especially—wanted adventures. Well, now they had got an adventure, both of them. There was no knowing how it would turn out either, and that, after all, is the essence of adventures. Edred was lodged with Lord Arden and several other gentlemen in the White Tower, and Elfrida and Lady Arden were in quite a different part of the building. And the children were not allowed to meet. This, of course, made it impossible for either of them to try to get back to their own times. For though they sometimes quarrelled, as you know, they were really fond of each other, and most of us would hesitate to leave even a person we were *not* very fond of alone a prisoner in the Tower in the time of James I. and the Gunpowder Plot.

Elfrida had to wait on her mother and to sew at the sampler, which had been thoughtfully brought by the old nurse with her lady's clothes, and the clothes Elfrida wore. But there were no games, and the only out-of-doors Elfrida could get was on a very narrow terrace where dead flower-stalks stuck up out of a still narrower border, beside a flagged pathway where there was just room for *one* to walk, and not for two. From this terrace you could see the fat, queer-looking ships in the river, and the spire of St. Paul's.

Edred was more fortunate. He was allowed to play in the garden of the Lieutenant of the Tower. But he did not feel much like playing. He wanted to find Elfrida and get back to Arden. Every one was very kind to him, but he had to be very much quieter than he was used to being, and to say Sir and Madam, and not to speak till he was spoken to. You have no idea how tiresome it is not to speak till you are spoken to, with the world full, as it is, of a thousand interesting things that you want to ask questions about.

One day—for they were there quite a number of days—Edred met some one who seemed to like answering questions, and this made more difference than perhaps you would think.

Edred was walking one bright winter morning in the private garden of the Lieutenant of the Tower, and he saw coming towards him a very handsome old gentleman dressed in very handsome clothes, and, what is more, the clothes blazed with jewels. Now, most of the gentlemen who were prisoners in the Tower at that time thought that their very oldest clothes were good enough to be in prison in, so this splendour that was coming across the garden was very unusual as well as very dazzling, and before Edred could remember the rules about not speaking till you're spoken to, he found that he had suddenly bowed and said—

"Your servant, sir;" adding, "you do look ripping!"

"I do not take your meaning," said the gentleman, but he smiled kindly.

"I mean, how splendid you look!"

The old gentleman looked pleased.

"I am happy to command your admiration," he said.

"I mean your clothes;" said Edred, and then feeling with a shock that this was not the way to behave, he added, "Your face is splendid too—

only I've been taught manners, and I know you mustn't tell people they're handsome in their faces. 'Praise to the face is open disgrace,'—Mrs. Honeysett says so."

"Praise to *my* face isn't open disgrace," said the gentleman, "it is a pleasant novelty in these walls."

"Is it your birthday or anything?" Edred asked.

"It is not my birthday," said the gentleman smiling. "But why the question?"

"Because you're so grand," said Edred. "I suppose you're a prince then?"

"No, not a prince—a prisoner."

"Oh, I see," said Edred, as people so often do when they don't; "and you're going to be let out to-day, and you've put on your best things to go home in. I *am* so glad. At least, I'm sorry you're going, but I'm glad on your account."

"Thou'rt a fine, bold boy," said the gentleman. "But no. I am a prisoner, and like to remain so. And for these gauds," he swelled out his chest so that his diamond buttons and ruby earrings and gem-set collar flashed in the winter sun,—"for these gauds, never shall it be said that Walter Raleigh let the shadow of his prison tarnish his pride in the proper arraying of a body that has been honoured to kneel before the Virgin Queen." He took off his hat at the last words and swept it, with a flourish, nearly to the ground.

"*Oh!*" cried Edred, "are you really Sir Walter Raleigh? Oh, how splendid! And now you'll tell me all about the golden South Americas, and sea-fights, and the Armada and the Spaniards, and what you used to play at when you were a little boy."

"Ay," said Sir Walter, "I'll tell thee tales enow. They'll not let me from speaking with thee, I warrant. I would," he said, looking round impatiently, "that I could see the river again. From my late chamber I saw it, and the goodly ships coming in and out—the ships that go down into the great waters." He sighed, was silent a moment, then spoke. "And so thou didst not know thine old friend Raleigh? He was all forgot, all forgot! And yet thou hast rid astride my sword ere now, and I have played with thee in the courtyard at Arden. When England forgets so soon, who can expect more from a child?"

"I'm sorry," said Edred humbly.

"Nay," said Sir Walter, pinching his ear gently, "'tis two years agone, and short years have short memories. Thou shall come with me to my chamber and I will show thee a chart and a map of Windargocoa, that Her Dear Glorious Majesty permitted me to rename Virginia, after her great and gracious self."

So Edred, very glad and proud, went hand in hand with Sir Walter Raleigh to his apartments, and saw many strange things from overseas—dresses of feathers from Mexico, and strange images in gold from strange islands, and the tip of a narwhal's horn from Greenland, and many other things. And Sir Walter told him of his voyages and his fights, and of how he and Humphrey Gilbert, and Adrian Gilbert, and little Jack Davis used to sail their toy boats in the Long Stream, and how they used to row in and out among the big ships down at the Port, and look at the great figure-heads, standing out high above the water, and wonder about them and about the strange lands they came from.

"And often," said Sir Walter, "we found a sea-captain that would tell us lads travellers' tales like these I have told thee. And we sailed our little ships, and then we sailed our big ships—and here I lie in dock, and shall never sail again. But it's oh! to see the Devon moors, and the clear reaches of the Long Stream again! And that I never shall." And with that he leaned his arm on the window-sill, and if he had not been the great

Sir Walter Raleigh, who is in all the history books, Edred would have thought he was crying.

"Oh, do cheer up—do!" said Edred awkwardly. "I don't know whether they'll let you go to Devonshire—but I know they'll let you go back to America some day. With twelve ships. I read about it only yesterday; and your ship will be called the *Destiny*, and you'll sail from the Thames, and Lord Arden will see you off and kiss you for farewell, and give you a medal for a keepsake. Your son will go with you. I *know* it's true. It's all in the book?"

"The book?" Sir Walter asked. "A prophecy, belike?"

"You can call it that if you want to," said Edred cautiously; "but, anyhow, it's true."

He had read it all in the History of Arden.

"If it should be true," said Sir Walter, and the smile came back to his merry eyes, "and if I ever sail to the Golden West again, shrew me but I will sack a Spanish town, and bring thee a collar of gold and pieces of eight—a big bag-full."

"Thank you, very much," said Edred, "it is very kind of you: but I shall not be there."

And all Sir Walter's questions did not make him say how he knew this, or what he meant by it.

After this he met Sir Walter every day in the lieutenant's garden, and the two prisoners comforted each other. At least Edred was comforted, and Sir Walter *seemed* to be. But no one could be sure if it was more than seeming. This was one of the questions that always puzzled the children—and they used to talk it over together till their heads seemed to be spinning round. The question of course was: Did their being in past times make any difference to the other people in past times? In other words, when you were taking part in historical scenes, did it matter what you said or did? Of course, it seemed to matter extremely—at the time. But then if this going into the past was only a sort of dream, then, of course, the people in the past would know nothing about it, unless they had dreamed the same sort of dream—which, as Elfrida often pointed out, was quite likely, especially if time didn't count, or could be cheated by white clocks. On the other hand, if they *really* went into the *real* past—well, then, of course, what they did must count for real too, as Edred so often said. And yet how could it, since they took with them into the past all that they learned here? And with that knowledge they could have revealed plots, shown the issue of wars and the fate of kings, and, as Elfrida put it, "made history turn out quite different." You see the difficulties, don't you? And Betty Lovell's having said that they could leave no trace on times past did not seem to make much difference somehow, one way or the other.

However, just now Elfrida and Edred were in the Tower, and not able to see each other, so they could not discuss that or any other question. And they always hoped that they would meet, but they never did.

But by and by the Queen thought of Lady Arden, and decided that she and her son Edred ought to be let out of the Tower, and she told the King so, and he told Lord Somebody or other, who told the Lieutenant of the Tower, and behold Lady Arden and Edred were abruptly sent home in their own coach, which had been suddenly sent for from Arden House; but Elfrida was left in charge of the wife of the Lieutenant of the Tower, who was a very kind lady. So now Elfrida was in the Tower, and Edred was at Arden House in Soho, and they had not been able to speak to each other or arrange any plan for getting back to 1908 and Arden Castle by the sea.

Of course Elfrida was kept in the Tower because she had sung the rhyme about—

"Please to remember

The fifth of November—

The Gunpowder Treason and Plot,"

and this made people think—or seem to think—that she knew all about the Gunpowder Plot. And so of course she did, though it would have been very difficult for her to show any one at that time *how* she knew it, without being a traitor.

She was now allowed to see Lord Arden every day, and she grew very fond of him. He was curiously like her own daddy, who had gone away to South America with Uncle Jim, and had never come back to his little girl. Lord Arden also seemed to grow fonder of her every day. "Thou'rt a bold piece," he'd tell her, "and thou growest bolder with each day. Hast thou no fear that thy daddy will have thee whipped for answering him so pert?"

"No!" Elfrida would say, hugging him as well as she could for his ruff. "*I* know you wouldn't beat your girl, don't I, daddy?" And as she hugged him it felt *almost* like hugging her own daddy, who would never come home from America.

So she was almost contented. She knew that Lord Arden was not one of those to suffer for the Gunpowder Plot. She knew from the History of Arden that he would just be banished from the Court, and end his days happily at Arden, and she was almost tempted just to go on and let what would happen, and stay with this new daddy who had lived three hundred years before, and pet him and be petted by him. Only she felt that she must do something because of Edred. The worst of it was that she could not think of anything to do. She did not know at all what was happening to Edred—whether he was being happy or unhappy.

As it happened he was being, if not unhappy, at least uncomfortable. Mr. Parados, the tutor, who was as nasty a man as you will find in any seaside academy for young gentlemen, still remained at Arden House, and taught the boys—Edred and his cousin Richard. Mr. Parados was in high favour with the King, because he had listened to what wasn't meant for him, reported it where it would do most mischief—a thing always very pleasing to King James the First—and Lady Arden dared not dismiss him. Besides, she was ill with trouble and anxiety, which Edred could not at all soothe by saying again and again, "Father *won't* be found guilty of treason—he *won't* be executed. He'll just be sent to Arden, and live there quietly with you. I saw it all in a book."

But Lady Arden only cried and cried.

Mr. Parados was very severe, and rapped Edred's knuckles almost continuously during lesson-time, and out of it; said Cousin Richard, "He is for ever bent on spying and browbeating of us."

"He's always messing about—nasty sneak," said Edred. "I should like to be even with him before I go. And I will too."

"Before you go? Go whither?" Cousin Richard asked.

"Elfrida and I are going away," Edred began, and then felt how useless it was to go on, since even when the 1908 Edred—who he was—had gone, the 1605 Elfrida and Edred would of course still be there—that is if . . . He checked the old questions, which he had now no time to consider, and said, in a firm tone which was new to him, and which Elfrida would have been astonished and delighted to hear—

"Yes, I've got two things to do: to be even with old Parrot-nose—to be revenged on him, I mean—and to get Elfrida out of the Tower. And I'll do that first, because she'll like to help with the other."

The boys were on the leads, their backs to a chimney and their faces towards the trap-door, which was the only way of getting on to the roof. It was very cold, and the north wind was blowing, but they had come there because it was one of the few places where Mr. Parrot-nose could not possibly come creeping up behind them to listen to what they were saying.

"Get her out of the Tower?" Dick laughed and then was sad. "I would we could!" he said.

"We *can*," said Edred earnestly. "I've been thinking about it all the time, ever since we came out of the Tower, and I know the way. I shall want you to help me, Dick. You and one grown-up." He spoke in the same grim, self-reliant tone that was so new to him.

"One grown-up?" Dick asked.

"Yes. *I* think Nurse would do it. And I'm going to find out if we can trust her."

"Trust her?" said Dick. "Why, she'd die for any of us Ardens. Ay, and die on the rack before she would betray the lightest word of any of us."

"Then *that's* all right," said Edred.

"What is thy plot?" Dick asked; and he did not laugh, though he might well have wanted to. You see, Edred looked so very small and weak and the Tower was so very big and strong.

"I'm going to get Elfrida out," said Edred, "and I'm going to do it like Lady Nithsdale got her husband out. It will be quite easy. It all depends on knowing when the guard is changed, and I *do* know that."

"But how did my Lady Nithsdale get my Lord Nithsdale out—and from what?" Dick asked.

"Why, out of the Tower, you know," Edred was beginning, when he remembered that Dick did *not* know and couldn't know, because Lord Nithsdale hadn't yet been taken out of the Tower, hadn't even been put in—perhaps, for anything Edred knew, wasn't even born yet. So he said—

"Never mind. I'll tell you all about Lady Nithsdale," and proceeded to tell Dick, vaguely yet inspiringly, the story of that wise and brave lady. *I haven't time to tell you the story, but any grown-up who knows history will be only too pleased to tell it.*

Dick listened with most flattering interest, though it was getting dusk and colder than ever. The lights were lighted in the house and the trap-door had become a yellow square. A shadow in this yellow square warned Dick, and he pinched Edred's arm.

"Come," he said, "and let us apply ourselves to our books. Virtuous youths always act in their preceptors' absence as they would if their preceptors were present. I feel as though mine *were* present. Therefore, I take it, I am a virtuous youth."

On which the shadow disappeared very suddenly, and the two boys, laughing in a choking inside sort of way, went down to learn their lessons by the light of two guttering tallow candles in solid silver candlesticks.

The next day Edred got the old nurse to take him to the Court, and because the Queen was very fond of Lady Arden he actually managed to see her Majesty and, what is more, to get permission to visit his father and sister in the Tower. The permission was written by the Queen's own hand and bade the Lieutenant of the Tower to admit Master Edred Arden and Master Richard Arden and an attendant. Then the nurse became very busy with sewing, and two days went by, and Mr. Parados rapped the boys' fingers and scolded them and scowled at them and wondered why they bore it all so patiently. Then came The Day, and it was bitterly cold, and as the afternoon got older snow began to fall.

"So much the better," said the old nurse, "so much the better."

It was at dusk that the guard was changed at the Tower Gate, and a quarter of an hour before dusk Lord Arden's carriage stopped at the Tower Gate and an old nurse in ruff and cap and red cloak got out of it and lifted out two little gentlemen, one in black with a cloak trimmed with squirrel fur, which was Edred, and another, which was Richard, in grey velvet and marten's fur. And the lieutenant was called, and he read the Queen's order and nodded kindly to Edred, and they all went in. And as they went across the yard to the White Tower, where Lord Arden's lodging was, the snow fell thick on their cloaks and furs and froze to the stuff, for it was bitter cold.

And again, "So much the better," the nurse said, "so much the better."

Elfrida was with Lord Arden, sitting on his knee, when the visitors came in. She jumped up and greeted Edred with a glad cry and a very close hug.

"Go with Nurse," he whispered through the hug. "Do exactly what she tells you."

"But I've made a piece of poetry," Elfrida whispered, "and now you're here."

"*Do what you're told*," whispered Edred in a tone she had never heard from him before and so fiercely that she said no more about poetry. "We must get you out of this," Edred went on. "Don't be a duffer—think of Lady Nithsdale."

Then Elfrida understood. Her arms fell from round Edred's neck and she ran back to Lord Arden and put her arms round *his* neck and kissed him over and over again.

"There, there, my maid, there, there!" he said, patting her shoulder softly, for she was crying.

"Come with me to thy chamber," said the nurse. "I would take thy measure for a new gown and petticoat."

But Elfrida clung closer. "She does not want to leave her dad," said Lord Arden—"dost thou, my maid?"

"No, no," said Elfrida quite wildly, "I don't want to leave my daddy!"

"Come," said Lord Arden, "'tis but for a measuring time. Thou'lt come back, sock lamb as thou art. Go now to return the more quickly."

"Goodbye, dear, dear, *dear* daddy!" said Elfrida, suddenly standing up. "Oh, my dear daddy, goodbye!"

"Why, what a piece of work about a new frock!" said the nurse crossly. "I've no patience with the child," and she caught Elfrida's hand and dragged her into the next room.

"Now," she whispered, already on her knees undoing Elfrida's gown, "not a moment to lose. Hold thy handkerchief to thy face and seem to weep as we go out. Why, thou'rt weeping already! So much the better!"

From under her wide hoop and petticoat the nurse drew out the clothes that were hidden there, a little suit of black exactly like Edred's—cap, cloak, stockings, shoes—all like Edred's to a hair.

And Elfrida before she had finished crying stood up the exact image of her brother—except her face—and that would be hidden by the handkerchief. Then very quickly the nurse went to the door of the apartment and spoke to the guard there.

"Good luck, good gentleman," she said, "my little master is ill—he is too frail to bear these sad meetings and sadder partings. Convey us, I pray you, to the outer gate, that I may find our coach and take him home, and afterwards I will return for my other charge, his noble cousin."

"Is it so?" said the guard kindly. "Poor child! Well, such is life, mistress, and we all have tears to weep."

But he could not leave his post at Lord Arden's door to conduct them to the gates. But he told them the way, and they crossed the courtyard alone, and as they went the snow fell on their cloaks and froze there.

So that the guard at the gate, who had seen an old nurse and two little boys go in through the snow, now saw an old nurse and one little boy go out, all snow-covered, and the little boy appeared to be crying bitterly, and no wonder, the nurse explained, seeing his dear father and sister thus.

"I will convey him to our coach, good masters," she said to the guard, "and return for my other charge, young Master Richard Arden."

And on that she got Elfrida in her boy's clothes out at the gate and into the waiting carriage. The coachman, by previous arrangement with the old nurse, was asleep on the box, and the footman, also by previous arrangement, was refreshing himself at a tavern near by.

"Under the seat," said the old nurse, and thrusting Elfrida in, shut the coach door and left her. And there was Elfrida, dressed like a boy, huddled up among the straw at the bottom of the coach.

"'I WILL CONVEY HIM TO OUR COACH, GOOD MASTERS,'
SHE SAID TO THE GUARD."

So far, so good. But the most dangerous part of the adventure still remained. The nurse got in again easily enough; she was let in by the guard who had seen her come out. And as she went slowly across the snowy courtyard she heard ring under the gateway the stamping feet of the men who had come to relieve guard, and to be themselves the new guard. So far, again, so good. The danger lay with the guard at the door of Lord Arden's rooms, and in the chance that some of the old guard might be lingering about the gateway when she came out, not with *one* little boy as they would expect, but with *two*. But this had to be risked. The nurse waited as long as she dared so as to lessen the chance of meeting any of the old guard as she went out with her charges. She waited quietly in a corner while Lord Arden talked with the boys. And when at last she said, "The time is done, my Lord," she already knew that the guard at the room door had been changed.

"So now for it," said Edred, as he and Richard followed the nurse down the narrow steps and across the snowy courtyard.

The new guard saw the woman and two boys, and the captain of the guard read the Queen's paper, which the old nurse had taken care to get back from the lieutenant. And as plainly Master Edred Arden and Master Richard Arden, with their attendant, had passed in, so now they were permitted to pass out, and two minutes later a great coach was lumbering along the snowy streets, and inside it four people were embracing in rapture at the success of their stratagem.

"But it was Edred thought of it," said Richard, as in honour bound, "and he arranged everything and carried it out."

"How splendid of him!" said Elfrida warmly; and I think it was rather splendid of *her* not to spoil his pride and pleasure in this, the first adventure he had ever planned and executed entirely on his own account. She could very easily have spoiled it, you know, by pointing out to him that the whole thing was quite unnecessary, and that they could have got away much more easily by going into a corner in the Tower and saying poetry to the Mouldiwarp.

So they came to Arden House.

The coachman was apparently asleep again, and the footman went round and did something to the harness after he had got the front door opened, and it was quite easy for the nurse to send the footman who opened the door to order a meal to be served at once for Mr. Arden and Mr. Richard. So that no one saw that instead of the two little boys who had left Arden House in the afternoon three came back to it in the evening.

Then the nurse took them into the parlour and shut the door.

"Now," she said, "Master Richard will go take off his fine suit, and Miss Arden will go into the little room and change her raiment. And for you, Master Edred, you wait here with me."

When the others had obediently gone, the nurse stood looking at Edred with eyes that grew larger and different, and he stood looking at her with eyes that grew rounder and rounder.

"Why," he said at last, "you're the witch—the witch we took the tea and things to."

"And if I am?" said she. "Do you think you're the only people who can come back into other times? You're not all the world yet, Master Arden of Arden. But you've got the makings of a fine boy and a fine man, and I think you've learned something in these old ancient times."

He had, there is no doubt of it. Whether it was being thought important enough to be imprisoned in the Tower, or whether it was the long talks he had with Sir Walter Raleigh, that fine genius and great gentleman, or whether it was Mr. Parados's knuckle-rappings and scowlings, I do not know. But it is certain that this adventure was the beginning of the change in Edred which ended in his being "brave and kind and wise" as the old rhyme had told him to be.

"And now," said the nurse, as Elfrida appeared in her girl's clothes, "there is not a moment to lose. Already at the Tower they have found out our trick. You must go back to your own times."

"She's the witch," Edred briefly answered the open amazement in Elfrida's eyes.

"There is no time to lose," the nurse repeated.

"I *must* be even with old Parados first," said Edred; and so he was, and it took exactly twenty minutes, and I will tell you all about it afterwards.

When he *was* even with old Parados the old nurse sent Richard to bed; and then Elfrida made haste to say, "I did make some poetry to call the Mouldiwarp, but it's all about the Tower, and we're not there now. It's no use saying—

"'Oh, Mouldiwarp, you have the power

To get us out of this beastly Tower,'

when we're not *in* the Tower, and I can't think of anything else, and . . ."

But the nurse interrupted her.

"Never mind about poetry," she said; "poetry's all very well for children, but I know a trick worth two of that."

"'YOU'VE NO MANNERS,' IT SAID TO THE NURSE."

She led them into the dining-room, where the sideboard stood covered with silver, set down the candle, lifted down the great salver with the arms of Arden engraved upon it, and put it on the table.

She breathed on the salver and traced triangles and a circle on the drilled surface; and as the mistiness of her breath faded and the silver shone out again undimmed, there, suddenly, in the middle of the salver, was the live white Mouldiwarp of Arden, looking extremely cross!

"You've no manners," it said to the nurse, "bringing me here in that offhand, rude way, without 'With your leave,' or 'By your leave'! Elfrida could easily have made some poetry. You know well enough," it added angrily, "that it's positively painful to me to be summoned by your triangles and things. Poetry's so easy and simple."

"Poetry's too slow for this night's work," said the nurse shortly. "Come, take the children away, I have done with it."

"You make everything so difficult," said the Mouldiwarp, more crossly than ever. "That's the worst of people who think they know a lot and really only know a little, and pretend they know everything. If I'd come the easy poetry way, I could have taken them back as easily. But now—— Well, it can't be helped. I'll take them back, of course, but it'll be a way they won't like. They'll have to go on to the top of the roof and jump off."

"I don't believe that is necessary," said the witch nurse.

"All right," said the Mouldiwarp, "get them away yourself then," and it actually began to disappear.

"No, no!" said Elfrida, "we'll do anything you say."

"There's a foot of snow on the roof," said the witch nurse.

"So much the better," said the Mouldiwarp, "so much the better. You ought to know that."

"You think yourself very clever," said the nurse.

"Not half so clever as I *am*," said the Mouldiwarp, rather unreasonably Elfrida thought. "There!" it added sharply as a great hammering at the front door shattered the quiet of the night. "There, to the roof for your lives! And I'm not at all sure that it's not too late."

The knocking was growing louder and louder.

CHAPTER X
WHITE WINGS AND A BROWNIE

Perhaps I had better begin this chapter by telling you exactly how Edred "got even with old Parrot-nose," as he put it. You will remember that Master Parados was the Ardens' tutor in the time of King James I., and that it was through his eavesdropping and tale-bearing that Edred and Elfrida were imprisoned in the Tower of London. There was very little time in which to get even with any one, and, of course, getting even with people is not really at all a proper thing to do. Yet Edred did it.

Edred had got Elfrida out of the Tower just as Lady Nithsdale got her lord out, and now he and she and Cousin Richard were at Arden House, in Soho, and the old nurse, who was also, astonishingly, the old witch, had said that there was no time to be lost.

"But I *must* be even with old Parrot-nose," said Edred. He was feeling awfully brave and splendid inside, because of the way he had planned and carried out the Nithsdale rescue of Elfrida; and also he felt that he could not bear to go back to his own times without somehow marking his feelings about Mr. Parados.

As to how it was to be done. Cousin Richard was not to have anything to do with it, because while they would be whisked away by some white road that the Mouldiwarp would find for them when they called it to their help by spoken poetry, he would be left behind to bear the blame of everything. This Edred and Elfrida decided in a quick-whispered conference, but Cousin Dick wanted to know what they were talking about, and why he wasn't to help in what he had wanted to do these four years.

"If we tell you," said Elfrida, "you won't believe us."

"You might at least make the trial," said Cousin Richard.

So they told him, and though they were as quick as possible, the story took some time to tell. Richard Arden listened intently. When the tale was told he said nothing.

"You don't believe it," said Edred; "I knew you wouldn't. Well, it doesn't matter. What can we do to pay out old Parrot-nose?"

"I don't like it," said Richard suddenly; "it's never been like this before. It makes it seem not real. It's only a dream really, I suppose. And I always believed so that it wasn't."

"I don't understand a word you're saying," said Edred, "but what we've been saying's true anyhow. Look here." He darted to the dark corner of the parlour, where he had hidden the camera behind a curtain. "Look here, I bet you haven't got anything like this. It comes from *our* times, ever so far on in history—out of the times where *we* come from—the times that haven't happened yet—at least *now* we're *here* they haven't happened yet. You don't know what it is. It's a machine for the sun to make pictures with."

"Oh, stow that," said Richard wearily. "I know now it's all a silly dream. But it's not worth while trying to dream that I don't know a Kodak when I see it. That's a Brownie!"

There was a pause, full of speechless amazement.

Then—"If you've dreamed about our times," said Elfrida, "you might believe in us dreaming about yours. Did you dream of anything except Brownies? Did you ever dream of fine carriages, fine boats, and——"

"Don't talk as if I were a baby," Richard interrupted. "I know all about railways and steamboats, and the Hippodrome and the Crystal Palace. I know Kent made 615 against Derbyshire last Thursday. Now, then—"

"But I say. Do tell us——"

"I sha'n't tell you anything more. But I'll help you to get even with Parrot-nose. I don't care if I am left here after you go," said Richard. "Let's shovel all the snow off the roof into his room, and take our chance."

Edred and Elfrida would have liked something more subtle, but there was no time to think of anything.

"I know where there are shovels," said Richard, "if they've not got mixed up in the dream."

"I say," said Edred slowly, "I'd like to write that down about Kent, and see if it's right afterwards."

There was a quill sticking out of the pewter inkstand on the table where they were used to do their lessons. But no paper.

"Here, hurry up," said Cousin Richard, and pulled a paper out of the front of his doublet. "I'll write it, shall I?"

He wrote, and gave the thing screwed up to Edred, who put it in the front of *his* doublet.

Then the three went up on to the roof, groped among the snow till they found the edge of the skylight that was the tutor's window—for learning was lodged in the attic at Arden House. They broke the thick glass with the edges of their spades, and shovelled in the thick, white snow—shovelled all the harder for the shouts and angry words that presently sounded below them. Then, when Mr. Parados came angrily up on to the roof, shivering and stumbling among the snow, they slipped behind the chimney-stack, and so got back to the trap-door before he did, and shut it and bolted it, and said "A-ha!" underneath it, and went away—locking his room door as they passed, and leaving him to stand there on the roof and shout for help from the street below, or else to drop through his broken skylight into the heaped snow in his room. He was quite free, and could do whichever he chose.

They never knew which he *did* choose, and you will never know either.

And then Richard was sent to bed by the old witch-nurse, and went.

And the Mouldiwarp was summoned, and insisted that the only way back to their own times was by jumping off the roof. And, of course, Mr. Parados was on the roof, which made all the difference. And the soldiers of the guard were knocking at the front door with the butts of their pistols.

"But we can't go on to the roof," said Edred, and explained about Mr. Parados.

"Humph," said the Mouldiwarp, "that's terr'ble unfortunate, that is. Well, the top landing window will have to do, that's all. Where's the other child?"

"Gone to bed," said the witch-nurse shortly.

"Te-he!" chuckled the Mouldiwarp. "Some people's too clever by half. Think of you not having found *that* out, and you a witch too. Te-he!"

And all the time the soldiers were hammering away like mad at the front door.

Elfrida caught the Mouldiwarp and the nurse caught Edred's hand, and the four raced up the stairs to the very top landing, where there was a little window at the very end. The air was keen and cold. The window opened difficultly, and when it was opened the air was much colder than before.

"Now, then, out with you—ladies first," cried the Mouldiwarp.

"You don't really mean," said Elfrida,—"you *can't* mean that we're to jump out into—into nothing?"

"I mean you're to jump out right enough," said the Mouldiwarp. "What you're to jump into's any pair of shoes—and it's my look-out, anyway."

"It's ours a little too, isn't it?" said Elfrida timidly, and her teeth were chattering; she always said afterwards that it was with cold.

"Then get along home your way," said the Mouldiwarp, beginning to vanish.

"Oh, *don't!* Don't go!" Elfrida cried, and the pounding on the door downstairs got louder and louder.

"If I don't then you must," said the Mouldiwarp testily. But it stopped vanishing.

"Put me down," it said. "Put me down and jump, for goodness' sake!"

She put it down.

Suddenly the nurse caught Elfrida in her arms and kissed her many times.

"Farewell, my honey love," she said. "All partings are not for ever, else I could scarce let thee go. Now, climb up; set thy foot here on the beam, now thy knee on the sill. So—jump!"

Elfrida crouched on the window-ledge, where the snow lay thick and crisp. It was very, very cold. Have you ever had to jump out of a top-floor window into the dark when it was snowing heavily? If so, you will remember how much courage it needed. Elfrida set her teeth, looking down into black nothing dotted with snowflakes. Then she looked back into a black passage, lighted only by the rush-light the nurse carried.

"Edred'll be all right?" she asked. "You're sure he'll jump all right?"

"Of course I shall," said Edred, in his new voice. "Here, let me go first, to show you I'm not a coward."

Of course, Elfrida instantly jumped. And next moment Edred jumped too.

It was a horrible moment because, however much you trusted the Mouldiwarp, you could not in an instant forget what you had been taught all your life—that if you jumped out of top-floor windows you would certainly be smashed to pieces on the stones below. To remember this and, remembering it, to jump clear, is a very brave deed. And brave deeds, sooner or later, have their reward.

The brave deed of Edred and Elfrida received its reward sooner. As Elfrida jumped she saw the snowflakes gather and thicken into a cloud beneath her. The cloud was not the sort that lets you through, either. It was solid and soft as piled eiderdown feathers; she knew this as it rose up and caught her, or as she fell on it—she never knew which. Next moment Edred was beside her, and the white, downy softness was shaping itself round and under them into the form of a seat—a back, arms, and place for the feet to rest.

"It's—what's that in your hand?" Elfrida asked.

"Reins," said Edred, with certainty. "White reins. It's a carriage."

It was—a carriage made of white snowflakes—the snowflakes that were warm and soft as feathers. There were white, soft carriage-rugs that curled round and tucked themselves in entirely of their own accord. The reins were of snowflakes, joined together by some magic weaving, and warm and soft as white velvet. And the horses!

"There aren't any horses; they're swans—white swans!" cried Elfrida, and the voice of the Mouldiwarp, behind and above, cried softly, "All white things obey me."

Edred knew how to drive. And now he could not resist the temptation to drive the six white swans round to the front of the house and to swoop down, passing just over the heads of the soldiers of the guard who were still earnestly pounding at the door of Arden House, and yelled to them, "Ha, ha! Sold again!" Which seemed to startle them very much. Then he wheeled the swans round and drove quickly through the air along the way which he knew quite well, without being told, to be the right way. And as the snow-carriage wheeled, both Edred and Elfrida had a strange, sudden vision of another smaller snow-carriage, drawn by two swans only, that circled above theirs and vanished in the deep dark of the sky, giving them an odd, tantalising glimpse of a face they knew and yet couldn't remember distinctly enough to give a name to the owner of it.

Then the swans spread their white, mighty wings to the air, and strained with their long, strong necks against their collars, and the snow equipage streamed out of London like a slender white scarf driven along in the wind. And London was left behind, and the snowstorm, and soon the dark blue of the sky was over them, jewelled with the quiet silver of watchful stars, and the deeper dark of the Kentish county lay below, jewelled with the quiet gold from the windows of farms already half-asleep, and the air that rushed past their faces as they went was no longer cold, but soft as June air is, and Elfrida always declared afterwards that she could smell white lilies all the way.

So across the darkened counties they went, and the ride was more wonderful than any ride they had ever had before or would ever have again.

All too soon the swans hung, poised on long, level wings, outside the window of a tower in Arden Castle—a tower they did not know.

But though they did not know the tower, it was quite plain that they were meant to get in at the window of it.

"Dear swans," said Elfrida, who had been thinking as she sat clutching her Brownie, "can't we stay in your carriage till it's light? We do so want to take a photograph of the castle."

The swans shook their white, flat, snake-like heads, just as though they understood. And there was the open window, evidently waiting to welcome the children.

So they got out—very much against their wills. And there they were in the dark room of the tower, and it was very cold.

But before they had time to begin to understand how cold it was, and how uncomfortable they were likely to be for the rest of the night, six swan's heads appeared at the window and said something.

"Oh," said Elfrida, "I do wish we'd learned Swanish instead of French at school!"

But it did not matter. The next moment the swans' heads ducked and reappeared, holding in their beaks the soft, fluffy, white rugs that had kept the children so warm in the snow-carriage. The swans pushed the rugs through the window with their strong, white wings, and made some more remarks in swan language.

"Oh, thank you!" said the children. "Goodbye, goodbye."

Then there was the rush of wide-going wings, and the children, tired out, cuddled on the floor, wrapped in the soft rugs.

The happiest kind of dreams were tucked up in that coverlet, and it seemed hardly any time at all before the children woke to find the winter sunshine looking in at them through the narrow windows of the tower.

Elfrida jumped up and threw off the silver-white, downy-soft coverlet. It instantly tore itself into five pieces of different shapes and sizes, and these screwed themselves up, and drew themselves in, and blew themselves out, and turned before her very eyes into a silver basin of warm water, a piece of lily-scented soap, a towel, a silver comb, and an ivory tooth-brush.

"Well!" said Elfrida. When she had finished her simple toilet, the basin, soap, towel, tooth-brush, and comb ran together like globules of quicksilver, made a curious tousled lump of themselves, and straightened out into the fluffy coverlet again.

"Well!" said Elfrida, again. Then she woke Edred, and his coverlet played the same clever and pretty trick for him.

And when the children started to go down with the Brownie and take the photographs of the castle, the shining coverlets jumped up into two white furry coats, such as the very affluent might wear when they went a-motoring—if the very affluent ever thought of anything so pretty. And one of the coats came politely to the side of each child, holding out its arms as if it were saying—

"Do, please, oblige me by putting me on."

Which, of course, both the children did.

They crept down the corkscrew stairs, and through a heavy door that opened under the arch of the great gateway. The great gate was open, and on the step of the door opposite to the one by which they had come out a soldier sat. He held his helmet between his knees, and was scouring it with sand and whistling as he scoured. He touched his forehead with his sandy hand, but did not get up.

"You're early afield," he said, and went on rubbing the sand on the helmet.

"It's such a pretty day," said Elfrida. "May we go out?"

"And welcome," said the man simply; "but go not beyond the twelve acre, for fear of rough folk and Egyptians. And go not far. But breakfast will have a strong voice to call you back."

They went out, and instead of stepping straight on to the turf of the downs, their stout shoes struck echoing notes from the wooden planks of a bridge.

"It's a drawbridge," said Edred, in tones of awe; "and there's a moat, look—and it's covered with cat-ice at the edges."

There was, and it was. And at the moat's far edge, their feet fast in the cat-ice, were reeds and sedge—brown and yellow and dried, that rustled and whispered as a wild duck flew out of them.

"How lovely!" said Elfrida. "I do *wish* Arden had a moat now."

"If we found out where the water comes from," said Edred practically, "we might get the moat back when we'd found the treasure."

So when they had crossed the moat, and felt the frozen dew crackle under their feet as they trod the grass, they set out, before photographing the castle, to find out where the moat water came from.

The moat, they found, was fed by a stream that came across the field from Arden Knoll and entered the moat at the north-east corner, leaving it at the corner that was in the south-west. They followed the stream, and it was not till they had got quite into the middle of the field, and well away from the castle, that they saw how very beautiful the castle really was. It was quite perfect—no crumbled arches, no broken pillars, no shattered, battered walls.

"Oh," said Edred, "how beautiful it is! How glad I am that we've got a castle like this!"

"Our castle isn't like this," said Elfrida.

"No; but it shall be, when we've found the treasure. You've got the two film rolls all right?"

"Yes," said Elfrida, who had got them in a great unwieldy pocket that was hanging and banging against her legs under the full skirt. "Oh, look! Where's the river? It stops short!"

It certainly seemed to. They were walking beside it, and it ran swiftly—looking like a steel-grey ribbon on the green cloth of the field—and half-way across the field it did stop short; there wasn't any more of it—as though the ribbon had been snipped off by a giant pair of scissors, and the rest of it rolled up and put by safely somewhere out of the way.

"My hat!" said Edred; "it does stop short; and no mistake." Curiosity pricked him, and he started running. They both ran. They ran to the spot where the giant scissors seemed to have snipped off the stream, and when they got there they found that the stream seemed to have got tired of running aboveground, and without any warning at all, any sloping of its bed, or any deepening of its banks, plunged straight down into the earth through a hole not eight feet across.

They stood fascinated, watching the water as it shot over the edge of the hole, like a steel band on a driving-wheel, smooth and shining, and moving so swiftly that it hardly seemed to move at all. It was Edred who roused himself to say, "I could watch it for ever. But we'll have it back; we'll have it back. Come along; let's go and see where it comes from."

"Let's photograph this place first," said Elfrida, "so as to know, you know." And the Brownie clicked twice.

Then they retraced their steps beside the stream and round two sides of the moat and across the field to Arden Knoll, and there—oh, wonderful to see!—the stream came straight out of the Knoll at the part where it joined on to the rest of the world—came out under a rough, low arch of stone that lay close against the very lip of the water.

"So that's where it came from and that's where it goes to," said Elfrida. "I wonder what became of it, and why it isn't at Arden now?"

"We'll bring it back," said Edred firmly,—"when we find the treasure."

And again the Brownie clicked.

"And we'll make the castle like it is now," said Elfrida. "Come on; let's photograph it."

So they went back, and they photographed the castle. They photographed it from the north and the south and the east and the west, and the north-east and the south-east, and the north-north-west—and all the rest of the points of the compass that I could easily tell you if I liked; but why be wearisome and instructive?

And they went back across the hollow-echoing drawbridge, and past the soldier, who had now polished his helmet to his complete satisfaction and was wearing it.

There was a brief and ardent conference on the drawbridge; the subject of it, breakfast. Edred wanted to stay; he was curious to see what sort of breakfast people had in the country in James the First's time, Elfrida wanted to get back to 1908, and the certainty of eggs and bacon.

"THE STREAM CAME OUT UNDER A ROUGH, LOW ARCH OF STONE."

"If we stay here we shall only be dragged into some new adventure," she urged, "I know we shall. I never in my life knew such a place as history for adventures to happen in. And I'm tired, besides. Oh, Edred, do come along!"

"I believe it's ducks," said Edred, and he sniffed questioningly; "it smells like onion stuffing."

"Stuff and nonsense," said Elfrida; "that's for dinner, most likely. I expect breakfast for *us* would be bread and water. You'd find we'd done something wrong, as likely as not. Oh, come along, do, before we get punished for it. Besides, don't you want to know whether what Cousin Richard said about the cricket was right?"

"Well, yes," said Edred, "and we can always come back here, can't we?"

"Of course we can," Elfrida said eagerly. "Oh, come on."

So they climbed up to the twisty-twiny, corkscrew staircase, and found the door of the room where they had slept under the wonderful white coverlets that now were coats. Then they stood still and looked at each other, with a sudden shock.

"How are we to get back?" was the unspoken question that trembled on each lip.

The magic white coats cuddled close round their necks. There was, somehow, comfort and confidence in the soft, friendly touch of that magic fur. When you are wearing that sort of coat, it is quite impossible to feel that everything will not come perfectly right the moment you really, earnestly, and thoroughly wish that it *should* come right.

"Our clothes," said Elfrida.

"Oh, yes, of course," said Edred, "I was forgetting."

"You may as well go on forgetting," said his sister, "because the clothes aren't here. They're the other side of that twisty-twiny, inside-out, upside-down shakiness that turned the attic into the tower. I suppose the tower would turn back into the attic if we could only start that shaky upside-downness going—wrong way before, you know."

"I suppose it would," said Edred, stopping-short, with his fingers between the buttons of his doublet. "Hallo! What's this?"

He pulled out a folded paper.

"It's the thing about cricket that Cousin Richard gave you. Don't bother about that now. I want to get back. I suppose we ought to make some poetry."

But Edred pulled out the paper and unfolded it.

"It might vanish, you know," he said, "or get stuck here, and when we got home we should find it gone when we came to look for it. Let's just see what he says Kent *did* make."

He straightened out the paper, looked at it, looked again, and held it out with a sudden arm's-length gesture.

"Look at that," he said. "If that's true, Richard *has* dreamed our times, and no mistake. And, what's more, he's brought things back here out of our times."

Elfrida took the paper and looked at it, and her mouth dropped open. "If it's true?" said she. "But it *must* be true!" The paper almost fell from her hand, for it was a bill from Gamage's for three ships' guns, a compass, and a half-dozen flags—and the bill was made out to Mr. R. D. Arden, 117, Laurie Grove, New Cross, London, S.E. On the other side was the pencilled record of the runs made by Kent the previous Thursday.

"I *say*," said Elfrida, and was going on to say I don't know what clever and interesting things, when she felt the fur coat creep and wriggle all through its soft length, and along its soft width, and no wriggle that ever was wriggled expressed so completely "Danger! danger! danger! You'd better get off while you can—while you can." A quite violent ruffling of the fur round the neck of her coat said, as plain as it could speak, "Don't stop to jaw. Go now—*now*—*now*!"

When you say a lady is a "true daughter of Eve" you mean that she is inquisitive. Elfrida was enough Eve's daughter to scurry to the window and look out.

A thrill ran right down her backbone and ended in an empty feeling at the ends of her fingers and feet.

"Soldiers!" she cried, "And they're after us—I know they are."

The fur coat knew it too, if knowledge can be expressed by wriggling.

"Oh, and they're pulling up the drawbridge! What for?" said Edred, who had come to the window too. "And, I say, doesn't the portcullis look guillotinish when it comes down like that?"

Through the window one looked straight down on to the drawbridge, and as the tower stuck out beyond the gate, its side window gave an excellent view of the slowly descending portcullis.

"I say," said Elfrida, "my fluffy coat says 'Go!' Doesn't yours?"

"It would if I'd listen to it," said Edred carelessly.

The soldiers were quite near now—so near that Elfrida could see how fierce they looked. And she knew that they were the same soldiers who had hammered so loud and so hard at the door of Arden House, in Soho. They must have ridden all night. So she screwed her mind up to make poetry, just as you screw your muscles up to jump a gate or run a hundred yards. And almost before she knew that she was screwing it up at all the screw had acted and she had screwed out a piece of Mouldiwarp poetry and was saying it aloud—

"Dear Mouldiwarp, since Cousin Dick

Buys his beautiful flags from Gamage's,

Take us away, and take us quick,

Before the soldiers do us any damages."

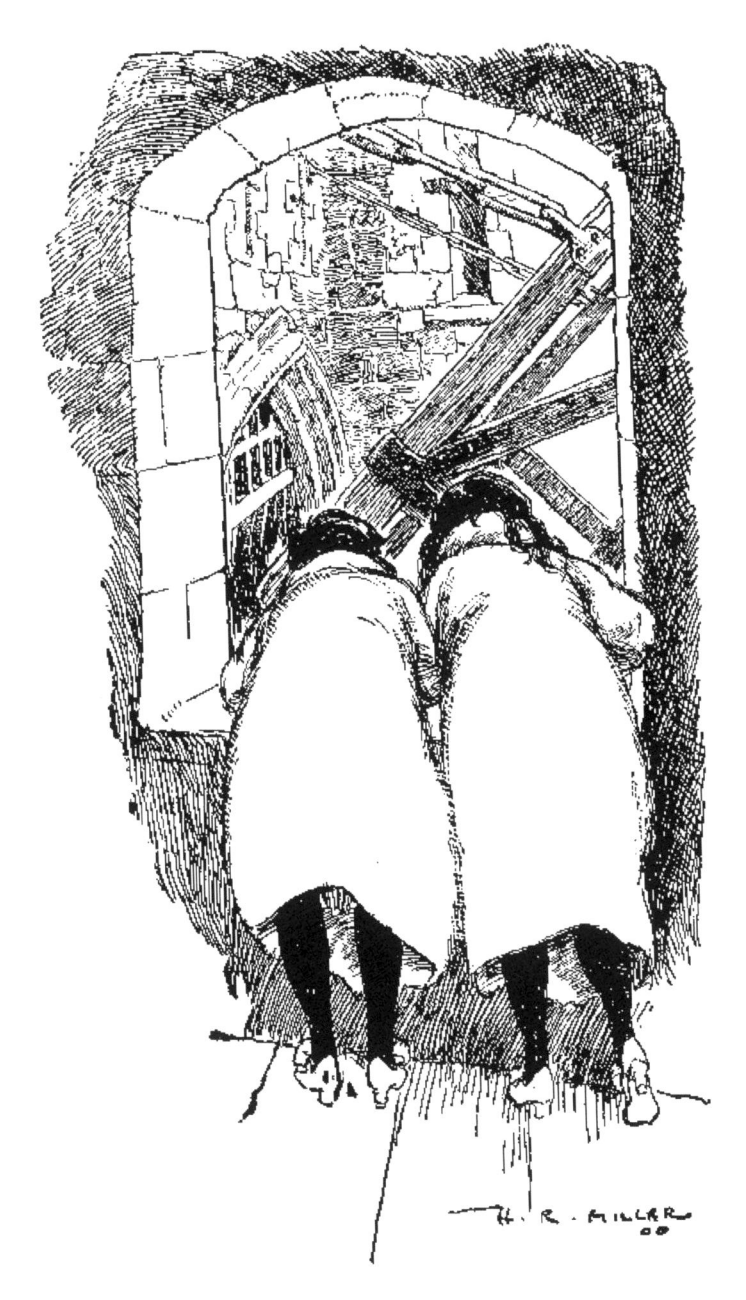

"'SOLDIERS!' SHE CRIED, 'AND THEY'RE AFTER US.'"

And the moment she had said it, the white magic coats grew up and grew down and wrapped the children up as tight and as soft as ever a silkworm wrapped itself when it was tired of being a silkworm and entered into its cocoon, as the first step towards being a person with wings.

Can you imagine what it would be like to have lovely liquid sleep emptied on you by the warm tubful? That is what it felt like inside the white, wonderful cocoons. The children knew that the tower was turning wrong way up and inside out, but it didn't matter a bit. Sleep was raining down on them in magic showers—no; it was closing on them, closer and closer, nearer and nearer, soft, delicious layers of warm delight. A soft, humming sound was in their ears, like the sound of bees when you push through a bed of Canterbury bells, and the next thing that happened was that they came out of the past into the present with a sort of snap of light and a twist of sound. It was like coming out of a railway tunnel into daylight.

The magic coverlet-coat-cocoons had even saved them the trouble of changing into their own clothes, for they found that the stiff, heavy clothes had gone, and they were dressed in the little ordinary things that they had always been used to.

"And now," said Elfrida, "let's have another look at that Gamage paper, if it hasn't disappeared. I expect it has though."

But it hadn't.

"I should like to meet Dick again," said Edred, as they went downstairs. "He was much the jolliest boy I ever met."

"Perhaps we shall," Elfrida said hopefully. "You see he *does* come into our times. I expect that New Cross time he stayed quite a long while, like we did when we went to Gunpowder Plot times. Or we might go back there, a little later, when the Gunpowder Plot has all died away and been forgotten."

"It isn't forgotten *yet*," said Edred, "and it's three hundred years ago. Now let's develop our films; I'm not at all sure about those films. You see, we took the films with us, and of course we've brought them back, but the *picture* that's on the films—we didn't take that with us. I shouldn't be a bit surprised if the films are all blank."

"It's very, very clever of you to think of it," said Elfrida respectfully; "but I do hope it's a perfectly silly idea of yours. Let's ask Mrs. Honeysett if we may use the old room she said used to be the still-room to develop them in. It'll be a ripping dark-room when the shutters are up."

"Course you may," said Mrs. Honeysett. "Yes; an' I'll carry you in a couple of pails of water. The floor's stone; so it won't matter if you do slop a bit. You pump, my lord, and I'll hold the pails."

"Why was that part of the house let to go all dirty and cobwebby?" asked Elfrida, when the hoarse voice of the pump had ceased to be heard.

"It's always been so," said Mrs. Honeysett. "I couldn't take upon me to clear up without Miss Edith's orders. Not but what my fingers itch to be at it with a broom and a scrubbing brush."

"But *why*?" Elfrida persisted.

"Oh, it's one of them old, ancient tales," said Mrs. Honeysett. "Old Beale could tell you, if any one could."

"We'll go down to old Beale's," said Edred decidedly, "as soon as we've developed our pictures of the castle—if there *are* any pictures," he added.

"You never can tell with them photo-machines, can you?" said Mrs. Honeysett sympathetically. "My husband's cousin's wife was took, with all her family, by her own back door, and when they come to wash out the picture it turned out they'd took the next door people's water-butt by mistake, owing to their billy-goat jogging the young man's elbow that had got the camera. And it wasn't a bit like any of them."

CHAPTER XI
DEVELOPMENTS

"Come on," said Edred, "you measure out the hypo and put the four pie-dishes ready. I'll get the water."

He got it, with Mrs. Honeysett's help—two brimming pails full.

"You mustn't come in for anything, will you, Mrs. Honeysett?" he earnestly urged. "You see, if the door's open ever so little, all the photographs will be done for."

"Law, love a duck!" said Mrs. Honeysett, holding her fat waist with her fat hands. "*I* shan't come in; I ain't got nothing to come in *for*."

"We'll bolt the door, all the same," said Edred, when she was gone, "in case she was to think of something."

He shot the great wooden bolt.

"Now it'll be quite dark," he said.

And, of course, it wasn't. You know the aggravating way rooms have of pretending to be quite dark until you want them to *be* dark—and then—by no means! This room didn't even pretend to be dark, to begin with. Its shutters had two heart-shaped holes, high up, through which the light showed quite dazzlingly. Edred had to climb up on to the window-seat and stuff up the holes very tight with crushed newspaper, to get which he had to unbolt the door.

"There," he said, as he pulled and patted the newspaper till it really and darkly filled the heart-shaped holes, "now it will be quite dark."

"MRS. HONEYSETT WAS SITTING IN A LITTLE LOW CHAIR AT THE BACK DOOR PLUCKING A WHITE CHICKEN."

And again it wasn't! Long, dusty rays of light came through the cracks where the hinges of the shutters were. Newspapers were no good for them. The door had to be unbolted and Mrs. Honeysett found. She was sitting in a little low chair at the back door plucking a white chicken. The sight of the little white feathers floating fluffing about brought wonderful memories to Edred. But he only said—

"I say, you haven't any old curtains, have you? Thick ones—or thin, if they were red."

Mrs. Honeysett laid the chicken down among his white feathers and went to a chest of drawers that stood in the kitchen.

"Here you are," she said, handing out two old red velvet curtains, with which he disappeared. But he was back again quite quickly.

"You haven't got a hammer, I suppose?" said he.

The dresser-drawer yielded a hammer, and Edred took it away, to return almost at once with—

"I suppose there aren't any tacks———?"

"I suppose," said Mrs. Honeysett, laughing, "there ain't much sense locking that still-room door on the inside when it ain't me that keeps all a-popping in, but you that keeps all a-popping out."

However, she gave him the tacks—rusty ones, in a damp screw of paper.

When he had hammered his fingers a good deal and the tacks a little the tacks consented to hold up the curtain, or the curtain condescended to be held up by the tacks.

"And now," said Edred, shutting the door, "it really *is*———"

Dark, he meant. But of course it wasn't. There was a gap under the door so wide, as Elfrida said, that you could have almost crawled through it. *That* meant another appeal to Mrs. Honeysett for another curtain, and this time Mrs. Honeysett told him to go along with him for a little worrit, and threw a handful of downy soft white feathers at him. But she laughed, too, and gave him the curtain.

At last it really *was* dark, and then they had to unbolt the door again, because Elfrida had forgotten where she had put the matches.

You will readily understand that, after all this preparation, the children were at the last point of impatience, and everything seemed to go slowly. The lamp with the red shade burned up presently, and then the four pie-dishes were filled with water that looked pink in that strange light.

"One good thing," said Edred, "the hypo has had time to melt."

And now there was careful snipping, and long ribbons of black paper curled unheeded round the legs of the operators.

"I wish we were born photographers like the man who took Aunt Edith and you on the beach with the donkey," said Edred nervously, as he began to pass the film in and out of the water in pie-dish Number One.

"Oh, be sure there are no air-bubbles!" said Elfrida; "you might let me do some of it."

"You shall do the next one," said Edred, almost holding his breath.

Dear reader, do you recall the agitating moment when you pass the film through the hypo—and hold it up to the light—and nothing happens? Do you remember the painful wonder whether you may have forgotten to set the shutter? Or whether you have got hold of an unexposed film by mistake? Your breath comes with difficulty, your fingers feel awkward, and the film is unnaturally slippery. You dip it into the hypo-bath again, and draw it through and through with the calmness of despair.

"I don't believe it's coming out at all," you say.

And then comes the glorious moment when you hold it up again to the red light and murmur rapturously, "Ah! it is beginning to show!"

If you will kindly remember all the emotions of those exciting moments—on an occasion, let us say, when you had not had your camera very long—then multiply by seven million, add x—an unknown quantity of an emotion quite different from anything you have ever felt—and you will have some idea of what Edred and Elfrida felt when the first faint, grey, formless patches began to appear on the film.

But you might multiply till you had used up the multiplication table, and add *x*'s as long as you could afford them, and yet never imagine the rapture with which the two children saw the perfect development of the six little perfect pictures. For they *were* perfect. They were perfect pictures of Arden Castle at a time when it, too, was perfect. No broken arches, no crumbling wall, but every part neat and clear-cut as they had seen it when they went into the past that was three hundred years ago.

They were equally fortunate with the second film. It, too, had its six faultless pictures of Arden Castle three hundred years ago. And the last film developed just as finely. Only, just before the moment which was the right moment for taking the film out of the hypo-bath and beginning to wash it, a tiny white feather fell out of Edred's hair into the dish. It was so tiny that in that dim light he did not notice it. And it did not stick to the film or do any of those things which you might have feared if you had seen the little, white thing flutter down. It may have been the feather's doing; I don't know. I just tell you the thing as it happened.

Of course, you know that films have to be pinned up to dry.

Well, the first film was pinned on the right-hand panel of the door and the second film was pinned on the left-hand panel of the door. And when it came to the third, the one that had had the little white feather dropped near it, there was nothing wooden left to pin it to—for the walls were of stone—nothing wooden except the shutters. And it was pinned across these.

"It doesn't matter," said Edred, "because we needn't open the shutters till it's dry."

And with that he stuck in four pins at its four corners, and turned to blow out the lamp and unbolt the door. He meant to do this, but the door, as a matter of fact, wasn't bolted at all, because Edred had forgotten to do it when he came back with the dusters, so he couldn't have unbolted it anyway.

But he could blow out the red-sided lamp; and he did.

And then the wonderful thing happened. Of course the room ought to have been quite dark. I'm sure enough trouble had been taken to make it so. But it wasn't. The window, the window where the shutters were—the shutters that the film was pinned on—the film on which the little white feather had fallen—the little white feather that had settled on Edred's hair when Mrs. Honeysett was plucking that chicken at the back door—that window now showed as a broad oblong of light. And in that broad oblong was a sort of shining, a faint sparkling movement, like the movement of the light on the sheet of a cinematograph before the pictures begin to show.

"Oh!" said Elfrida, catching at Edred's hand. What she did catch was his hair. She felt her way down his arm, and so caught what she had meant to catch, and held it fast.

"It's *more* magic," said Edred ungratefully. "I do wish——"

"Oh, hush!" said Elfrida; "look—oh, look!"

The light—broad, oblong—suddenly changed from mere light to figures, to movement. It was a living picture—rather like a cinematograph, but much more like something else. The something else that it was more like was *life*.

It seemed as though the window had been opened—as though they could see through it into the world of light and sunshine and blue sky—the world where things happen.

There was the castle, and there were people going across the drawbridge—men with sacks on their backs. And a man with a silver chain round his neck and a tall stick in his hand, was standing under the great gateway telling them where to take the sacks. And a cart drove up, with casks, and they were rolled across the drawbridge and under the tall arch of the gate-tower. The men were dressed. Then something blinked, and the scene changed. It was indoors now—a long room with many pictures on one side of it and many windows on the other; a lady, in a large white collar and beautiful long curls, very like Aunt Edith, was laying fine dresses in a chest. A gentleman, also with long hair, and with a good deal of lace about his collar and cuffs, was putting jugs and plates of gold and silver into another chest; and servants kept bringing more golden grand things, and more and more.

Edred and Elfrida did not say a word. They couldn't. What they were looking at was far too thrilling. But in each heart the same words were uttered—

"That's the treasure!" And each mind held the same thought.

"If it only goes on till the treasure's hidden, we shall see where they put it, and then we can go and find it."

I think myself that the white Mouldiwarp was anxious to help a little. I believe it had arranged the whole of this exhibition so that the children might get an idea of the whereabouts of the treasure, and so cease to call on it at all hours of the day and night with the sort of poetry which even a mole must see not to be so *very* good. However this may be, it was a wonderful show. One seemed to see things better somehow like that, through the window that looked into the past, than one did who was really *in* the past taking an active part in what was going on.

There appeared, at any rate, to be no doubt that this really *was* the treasure, and still less that it was a treasure both plentiful and picturesque. Quickly and more quickly the beautiful rich things were being packed into the chests. More and more pale looked the lady; more and more anxious the gentleman.

The lady was taking from her waiting-woman little boxes and bundles with which the woman's apron was filled, and the chest before which she was kneeling was nearly full when the door at the end of the gallery opened suddenly, and Elfrida and Edred, in the dark in the still-room, were confronted with the spectacle of themselves coming down the long picture-gallery towards that group of chests and treasure, and hurried human people. They saw themselves in blue silk and lace and black velvet, and they saw on their own faces fear and love, and the wonder what was to happen next. They saw themselves embraced by the grown-ups, who were quite plainly father and mother—they saw themselves speak, and the grown-ups reply.

"I'd give all my pocket-money for a year to hear what they're saying," Edred told himself.

"That daddy's just like *my* daddy," Elfrida was telling herself; "and just like the daddy in the Tower that was so like my own daddy."

Then the children in the picture kneeled down, and the daddy in the picture laid his hands on their heads, and the children out of the picture bent their own heads there in the dark still-room, for they knew what was happening in the picture. Elfrida even half held out her arms; but it was no good.

Again the scene changed. A chest was being carried by four men, who strained and staggered under its weight. They were carrying it along a vaulted passage by ropes that passed under the chest and over their shoulders. Every now and then they set it down and stretched, and wiped their faces. And the picture kept on changing so that the children seemed to be going with the men down a flight of stairs into a spacious hall full of men, all talking, and very busy with armour and big boots, and then across the courtyard, full of more men, very busy too, polishing axes and things that looked like spears, cleaning muskets and fitting new flints to pistols and sharpening swords on a big grindstone. Edred would have loved to stay and watch them do these things, but they and their work were gone quite quickly, and the chest and the men who carried it were going under an archway. Here one of the men wanted to rest again, but the others said it was not worth while—they were almost there. It was quite plain that they said this, though no sound could be heard.

"Now we shall *really* know," said Edred to himself. Elfrida squeezed his hand. That was just what she was thinking, too.

The men stopped at a door, knocked, knocked again, and yet once more. And, curiously enough, the children in the still-room could hear the sound of the knocking quite plainly, though they had heard nothing else.

The men looked at each other across the chest that they had set down. Then one man set his shoulder to the door. There was a scrunching sound and the picture disappeared—went out; and there were the shutters with the film pinned across them, and behind them the door, open, and Mrs. Honeysett telling them that dinner—which was roast rabbit and a boiled hand of pork—would be cold if they didn't make haste and come along.

"Oh, Mrs. Honeysett," said Elfrida, with deep feeling, "you are too bad—you really are!"

"I hope I've not spoiled the photos," said Mrs. Honeysett; "but I did knock three times, and you was that quiet I was afraid something had happened to you—poisoned yourselves without thinking, or something of that."

"It's too bad," said Edred bitterly; "it's much too bad. I don't want any dinner; I don't want anything. Everything's spoiled."

"Perhaps," said Mrs. Honeysett patiently, "I might ha' gone on knocking longer, only I thought the door was bolted—you did so keep on a-bolting of it at the beginning, didn't you? So I just got hold of the handle to try, and it come open in my hand. Come along, lovey; don't bear malice now. I didn't go for to do it. An' I'll get you some more of whatever it is that's spoiled, and you can take some more photos tomorrow."

"You might have known we were all right," said Edred, still furious; but both thought it only fair to say, "It wasn't the *photographs* that were spoiled"—and they said it at the same moment.

"Then what was it?" said Mrs. Honeysett. "And do come along, for goodness' sake, and eat your dinner while it's hot."

"It was—it was a different sort of picture," said Elfrida, with a gulp, "and it *was* a pity."

"Never mind, love," said Mrs. Honeysett, who was as kind as a grandmother, and I can't say more than that; "there's a lovely surprise coming by and by for good little gells and boys, and the rabbit'll be stone cold if you don't make haste—leastways, it would have been if I hadn't thought to pop it in the oven when I came to call you, knowing full well what your hands would be like after all that messing about with poison in dishes; and if I was your aunt I'd forbid it downright. And now come along and wash your hands, and don't let's have any more nonsense about it. Do you hear?"

I daresay you notice that Mrs. Honeysett was quite cross at the end of this speech and quite coaxing and kind at the beginning. She had just talked herself into being cross. It's quite easy. I daresay you have often done it.

It was a silent dinner—the first silent meal since the children had come to Arden Castle. You can judge of Edred's feelings when I tell you that he felt as though the rabbit would choke him, and refused a second helping of gooseberry pie with heartfelt sincerity. Elfrida did not eat so much as usual either. It really was a bitter disappointment. To have been so near seeing where the treasure was, and then—just because they hadn't happened to bolt the door that last time—all was in vain. Mrs.

Honeysett thought they were sulking about a silly trifle, and nearly said so when Edred refused the pie.

It was at the end of dinner that Elfrida, as she got down from her chair, saw Mrs. Honeysett's face, and saw how different it looked from the kind face that she usually wore. She went over to her very slowly, and very quickly threw her arms round her and kissed her.

"I'm sorry we've been so piggy," she said. "It's not your fault that you're not clever enough to know about pictures and things, is it?"

If Mrs. Honeysett hadn't been a perfect dear, this apology would have been worse than none. But she *was* a perfect dear, so she laughed and hugged Elfrida, and somehow Edred got caught into the hug and the laugh, and the three were friends again. The sky was blue and the sun began to shine.

And then the two children went down to old Beale's.

There were roses in his garden now, and white English flags and lupins and tall foxgloves bordering the little brick path. Old Beale was sitting "on a brown Windsor chair," as Edred said, in the sun by his front door. Over his head was a jackdaw in a wicker cage, and Elfrida did not approve of this till she saw the cage door was open, and that the jackdaw was sitting in the cage because he liked it, and not because he must. She had been in prison in the Tower, you remember, and people who have been in prison never like to see live things in cages. There was a tabby and white cat of squarish shape sitting on the wooden threshold. (Why are cats who live in country cottages almost always tabby and white and squarish?) The feathery tail of a brown spaniel flogged the flags lazily in the patch of shade made by the water-butt. It was a picture of rural peace, and old Beale was asleep in the middle of it. I am glad to tell you that Lord Arden and his sister were polite enough to wait till he awoke of his own accord, instead of shouting "hi!" or rattling the smooth brown iron latch of the gate, as some children would have done.

They just sat down on the dry, grassy bank, opposite his gate, and looked at the blue and white butterflies and the flowers and the green potato-tops through the green-grey garden palings.

And while they sat there Elfrida had an idea—so sudden and so good that it made her jump. But she said nothing, and Edred said—

"Pinch the place hard, and if it's still there you'll kill it perhaps"—for he thought she had jumped because she had been bitten by an ant.

When they had finished looking at the butterflies and the red roses and the green-growing things, they looked long and steadily at old Beale, and, of course, he awoke, as people always do if you look at them long enough and hard enough. And he got up, rather shaking, and put his hand to his forehead, and said—

"My lord——"

"How are you?" said Elfrida. "We haven't found the treasure yet."

"But ye will, ye will," said old Beale. "Come into the house now; or will ye come round along to the arbour and have a drink of milk?"

"We'd as soon stay here," said Edred—they had come through the gate now, and Edred was patting the brown spaniel, while Elfrida stroked the squarish cat. "Mrs. Honeysett said you knew all the stories."

"Ah," said old Beale, "a fine girl, Mrs. Honeysett. Her father had Sellinge Farm, where the fairies churn the butter for the bride so long as there's no cross words. They don't ever get too much to do, them fairies." He chuckled, sighed, and said—

"I know a power of tales. And I know, always I do, which it is that people want. What you're after's the story of the East House. Isn't it now? Is the old man a-failing of his wits, or isn't he?"

"'AH,' SAID OLD BEALE ADMIRINGLY, 'YOU'LL BE A-BUSTING WITH BOOK-LARNIN' AFORE YOU COME TO YOUR TWENTY-ONE, I LAY.'"

"We want to know," said Edred, companionably sharing the flagstone with the feather-tailed spaniel, "the story about why that part of the house in the castle is shut up and all cobwebby and dusty and rusty and musty, and whether there's any reason why it shouldn't be all cleaned up and made nice again, if we find the treasure so that we've got enough money to pay for new curtains and carpets and things?"

"It's a sad tale, that," said old Beale, "a tale for old folks—or middle-aged folks, let's say—not for children. You'd never understand it if I was to tell it you, likely as not."

"We *like* grown-up stories," said Elfrida, with dignity; and Edred added—

"We can understand *anything* that grown-ups understand if it's told us properly. I understand all about the laws of gravitation, and why the sun doesn't go round the earth but does the opposite; I understood *that* directly Aunt Edith explained it, and about fixed stars, and the spectroscope, and microbes, and the Equator not being real, and—and heaps of things."

"Ah," said old Beale admiringly, "you'll be a-busting with book-larnin' afore you come to your twenty-one, I lay. I only hope the half of it's true and they're not deceiving of you, a trusting innocent. I never did hold myself with that about the sun not moving. Why, you can see it a-doin' of it with your own naked eyes any day of the week."

"*You* wouldn't deceive any one," said Elfrida gently. "*Do* tell us the story."

So old Beale began, and he began like this—

"It was a long time ago—before my time even, it was, but not so long afore, 'cause I can recomember my father talking about it. He was coachman at the castle when it all happened, so, of course, he knew everything there was to know, my mother having been the housekeeper and gone through it all with the family. There was a Miss Elfrida then, same as there is now, only she was older'n what you are, missy. And the gentlemen lads from far and near they come a-courting her, for she was a fine girl—a real beauty—with hair as black as a coal and eyes like the sea when it's beating up for a storm, before the white horses comes along. So I've heard my father say—not that I ever see her myself. And she kept her pretty head in the air and wouldn't turn it this way or that for e'er a one of them all. And the old lord he loved her too dear to press her against her wish and will, and her so young. So she stayed single and watched the sea."

"What did she do that for?" Edred asked.

"To see if her sweetheart's ship wasn't a-coming home. For she'd got a sweetheart right enough, she had, unbeknown to all. It was her cousin Dick—a ne'er-do-weel, if ever there was one—and it turned out afterwards she'd broken the sixpence with him and swore to be ever true, and he'd gone overseas to find a fortune. And so she watched the sea every day regular, and every day regular he didn't come. But every day another young chap used to come a-riding—a fine young gentleman and well-to-do, but he was the same kidney as Master Dick, only he'd got a fine fortune, so his wild oats never got a chance to grow strong like Dick's."

"Poor Dick!" said Elfrida.

"Not so fast, missy," said the old man. "Well, her father and mother, they said, 'Have him that's here and loves you, dear,' as the saying is—a Frewin he was, and his christened name Arnold. And she says 'No.' But they keeps on saying 'Yes,' and he keeps on saying 'Do!' So they wears her down, telling her Dick was drowned dead for sure, and I don't know what all. And at last she says, 'Very well, then, I'll marry you—if you can stand to marry a girl that's got all her heart in the sea along of a dead young chap as she was promised to.' And the wedding was set for

Christmas. Miss Elfrida, she slep' in the room in the East House that looks out towards Arden Knoll, and the servants in the attics, and the old people in the other part of the house.

"And that night, when all was asleep, I think she heard a tap, tap at her window, and at first she'd think it was the ivy—but no. So presently she'd take heart to go to the window, and there was a face outside that had climbed up by the ivy, and it was her own true love that they'd told her was drowned."

"How splendid!" said Edred.

"How dreadful for Mr. Frewin," said Elfrida.

"That's what she thought, miss, and she couldn't face it. So she puts on her riding-coat and she gets out of window and down the ivy with him, and off to London. And in the morning, when the bells began to ring for her wedding, and the bridegroom came, there wasn't no bride for him. She left a letter to say she was very sorry, but it had to be. So then they shut up the East House."

"So that's the story," said Elfrida.

"Half of it, miss," said old Beale, and he took out a black clay pipe and a screw of tobacco, and very slowly and carefully filled the pipe and lighted it, before he went on, "They shut up the East House, where she'd been used to sleep; but it was kep' swep' and dusted, and the old folks was broken-hearted, for never a word come from Miss Elfrida. An' if I know anything of the feelings of a parent, they kept on saying to each other, 'She might ha' trusted us. She might 'a' known we'd never 'a' denied her nothing.' And then one night there was a knock at the door, and there was Miss Elfrida that was—Mrs. Dick now—with her baby in her arms. Mr. Dick was dead, sudden in a accident, and she'd come home to her father and mother. They couldn't make enough of the poor young thing and her baby. She had her old rooms and there she lived, and she was getting a bit happier and worshipping of her baby and the old people worshipping it and her too. And then one night some one comes up the ivy, same as Master Dick did, and takes away—not her—but the baby."

"How dreadful!" breathed Elfrida. "Did they get it back?"

"Never. And never a word was ever found out about who took it, or why, or where they took it to. Only a week or two after Mr. Frewin was killed in the hunting-field, and as they picked him up he said, 'Elfrida; tell Elfrida———' and he was trying to say what they was to tell her, when he died. Some folks hold as 'twas him stole the baby, to be even with her for jilting of him, or else to pretend to find it and get her to marry him out of gratitude. But no one'll ever know. And the baby's mother, she wore away bit by bit, to a shadow, and then she died, and after that the East House was shut up for good and all, to fall into rot and ruin like it is now. Don't you cry, missie. I know'd you wouldn't like the story, but you would have it; but don't you cry. It's all long ago, and she and her baby and her young husband's all been happy together in heaven this long time now, I lay."

"I *do* like the story," said Elfrida, gulping, "but it *is* sad, isn't it?"

"Thank you for telling it," Edred said; "but I don't think it's any good, really, being unhappy about things that are so long ago, and all over and done with."

"I wish we could go back into the past and find the baby for her," Elfrida whispered—and Edred whispered back—

"It's the treasure we've got to find. Excuse our whispering, Mr. Beale. Thank you for the story—oh, and I wanted to ask you who owns the land now—all the land about here, I mean, that used to belong to us Ardens?"

"That Jackson chap," said old Beale, "him that made a fortune in the soap boiling. The Tallow King, they call him. But he's got too rich for the house he's got. He's bought a bigger place in Yorkshire, that used to belong to the Duke of Sanderstead, and the Arden lands are to be sold next year, so I'm told."

"Oh," said Edred, clasping his hands, "if we could only find the treasure, and buy back the land! We haven't forgotten what we said the first time: if we found the treasure we'd make all the cottages comfortable, and new thatch everywhere."

"That's a good lad," said old Beale, "you make haste and find the treasure. And if you don't find it, never fret; there's ways of helping other folks without finding of treasure, so there is. You come and see old Beale again, my lord, and I shouldn't wonder but what I'd have a white rabbit for you next time you come along this way."

"He *is* an old dear," said Elfrida, as they went home, "and I do think the films will be dry by the time we get back; but perhaps we'd better not print them till to-morrow morning."

"There's plenty of light to-day," said Edred, and Elfrida said—

"I say?"

"Well?"

"Did you notice the kind of clothes we wore in those pictures—where they were stowing away the treasure?"

"*Oh!*" groaned Edred, recalled to a sense of his wrongs. "If only Mrs. Honeysett hadn't opened the door just when she did, we should know exactly where the treasure was. It was the West Tower they took it to, wasn't it?"

"I'm not sure," said Elfrida, "but———"

"And if it had gone on we *should* have been sure—we should have seen them come away again."

"Yes," said Elfrida, and again she remarked, "I say?"

Edred again said, "Well——?"

"Well—suppose we looked in the chests we should be sure to find clothes like *those*, and then we should be back there—living in those times, and we could *see* the treasure put away, and then we really *should* know."

"A1, first class, ripping!" was Edred's enthusiastic rejoinder. "Come on—I'll race you to the gate."

He did race her, and won by about thirty white Mouldiwarp's lengths.

There had been no quarrel now for quite a long time—if you count as time the days spent in the Gunpowder Plot adventure—so the attic was easily found, and once more the children stood among the chests, with the dusty roof, and the dusty sunbeams, and the clittering pigeon feet, and the soft pigeon noises overhead.

"Come on," cried Elfrida joyously. "I shall know the dress directly I see it. Mine was blue silk with sloping shoulders, and yours was black velvet and a Vandyke collar."

Together they flung back the lid of a chest they had not yet opened. It held clothes far richer than any they had seen yet. The doublets and cloaks and bodices were stiff with gold embroidery and jewels. But there was no blue silk dress with sloping shoulders and no black velvet suit and Vandyke collar.

"Oh, never mind," said Edred, bundling the splendid clothes back by double armfuls. "Help me to smooth these down so that the lid will shut properly, and we'll try the next chest."

But the lid would not shut at all till Elfrida had taken all the things out and folded them properly, and then it shut quite easily.

Then they went on to the next chest.

"I have a magic inside feeling that they're in *this* one," said Elfrida gaily. And so they may have been. The children never knew—for the next chest was *locked*, and the utmost efforts of four small arms failed to move the lid a hair's breadth.

"Oh, bother!" said Edred; "we'll try the next."

But the next was locked, too—and the next, and the one after that, and the one beyond, and——Well, the fact is, they were *all* locked.

The children looked at each other in something quite like despair.

"I feel," said the boy, "like a baffled burglar."

"I feel," said the girl, "as if I was just going to understand something. Oh, wait a minute; it's coming. I think," she added very slowly,—"I think it means if we go anywhere we've got to go wherever it was they wore those glorious stiff gold clothes. That's what the chest's open for; that's what the others are locked for. See?"

"Then let's put them on and go," said Edred.

"I don't think I want any more Tower of Londons," said Elfrida doubtfully.

"I don't mind what it is," said Edred. "I've found out one thing. We always come safe out of it, whatever it is. And besides," he added, remembering many talks with his good friend, Sir Walter Raleigh, "an English gentleman must be afraid of nothing save God and his conscience."

"IT HELD CLOTHES FAR RICHER THAN ANY THEY HAD SEEN YET."

"All right," said Elfrida, laying hands on the chest-lid that hid the golden splendour. "You might help," she said.

But Edred couldn't. He laid hands on the chest, of course, and he pulled and Elfrida pulled, but the chest-lid was as fast now as any of the others.

"Done in the eye!" said Edred. It was a very vulgar expression, and I can't think where he picked it up.

"'He that will not when he may,

He shall not when he would—a,'"

said Elfrida—and I do know where she learned that. It was from an old song Mrs. Honeysett used to sing when she blackleaded the stoves.

"I suppose we must chuck it for to-day," said Edred, when he had quite hurt his fingers by trying all the chests once more, and had found that every single one was shut tight as wax. "Come on—we'll print the photographs."

But the films were not dry enough. They never are when you just expect them to be; so they locked the still-room door on the outside, and hung the key on a nail high up in the kitchen chimney. Mrs. Honeysett was not in the kitchen at that moment, but she came hurrying in the next.

"Here you are, my lambs," she said cheerily, "and just in time for the surprise."

"Oh, I'd forgotten the surprise. That makes two of it, doesn't it?" said Elfrida. "Do tell us what it is. We need a nice surprise to make up for everything, if you only knew."

"Ah," said Mrs. Honeysett, "you mean because of me opening that there door. Well, there *is* two surprises. One's roast chicken. For *supper*," she added impressively.

"Then I know the other," said Edred. "Aunt Edith's coming."

And she was—indeed, at that very moment, as they looked through the window, they saw her blue dress coming over the hill, and joyously tore out to meet her.

It was after the roast chicken, when it was nearly dark and almost bedtime, that Aunt Edith said, suddenly—

"Children, there's something I wanted to tell you. I've hesitated about it a good deal, but I think we oughtn't to have any secrets from each other."

Edred and Elfrida exchanged guilty glances.

"Not *real* secrets, of course," said Edred, hastily; "but you don't mind our having magic secrets, do you?"

"Of course not," said Aunt Edith, smiling; "and what I'm going to tell you is rather like magic—if it's true. I don't know yet whether it's true or not."

Here Aunt Edith put an arm round each of the children as they sat on the broad window-seat, and swallowed something in her throat and sniffed.

"Oh, it's *not* bad news, is it?" Elfrida cried. "Oh, darling auntie, don't be miserable, and don't say that they've found out that Arden isn't ours, or that Edred isn't really Lord Arden, or something."

"Would you mind so very much," said Aunt Edith gently, "if you weren't Lord Arden, Edred? Because——"

CHAPTER XII
FILMS AND CLOUDS

The films were quite dry by bedtime, when, after a delightful evening with no magic in it at all but the magic of undisturbed jolliness, Edred slipped away, unpinned them and hid them in Elfrida's corner drawer, which he rightly judged to be a cleaner resting-place for them than his own was likely to be. So there the precious films lay between Elfrida's best lace collar and the handkerchief-case with three fat buttercups embroidered on it that Aunt Edith had given her at Christmas. And Edred went back to the parlour for one last game of Proverbs before bed. As he took up his cards he thought how strange it was that he, who had been imprisoned in the Tower and had talked with Sir Walter Raleigh, should be sitting there quietly playing Proverbs with his aunt and his sister, just like any other little boy.

"Aha!" said Edred to himself, "I am living a double life, that's what I'm doing."

He had seen the expression in a book and the idea charmed him.

"How pleased Edred looks with himself!" said Aunt Edith; "I'm sure he's got a whole proverb, or nearly, in his hand already."

"You'll be looking pleased presently," he said; "you always win."

And win she did, for Edred's thoughts were wandering off after the idea how pleased Aunt Edith would look when he and Elfrida should come to her, take her by the hand, and lead her to the hiding-place of the treasure, and then say, "Behold the treasure of our house! Now we can rebuild the castle and mend the broken thatch on the cottages, and I can go to Eton and Oxford, and you can have a diamond tiara, and Elfrida can have a pony to ride, and so can I."

Elfrida's thoughts were not unlike his—so Aunt Edith won the game of Proverbs.

"You have been very good children, Mrs. Honeysett tells me," said Aunt Edith, putting the cards together.

"Not so extra," said Edred; "I mean it's easy to be good when everything's so jolly."

"We have quarrelled once or twice, you know," said Elfrida virtuously.

"Yes, we have," said Edred firmly.

They needn't, they felt, have confessed this—and that made them feel that they were good now, if never before.

"Well, don't quarrel any more. I shall be coming over for good quite soon, then we'll have glorious times. Perhaps we'll find the treasure. You've heard about the treasure?"

"I should jolly well think we had," Edred couldn't help saying. And Elfrida added—

"And looked for it, too—but we haven't found it. Did *you* ever look for it?"

"No," said Aunt Edith, "but I always wanted to. My grandfather used to look for it when he was a little boy."

"Was your grandfather Lord Arden?" Edred asked.

"No; he was the grandson of the Lord Arden who fought for King James the Third, as they called him—the Pretender, you know—when he was quite a boy. And they let him off because of his being so young. And then he mortgaged all the Arden lands to keep the Young Pretender—Prince Charlie, you know, in the ballads. He got money to send to him, and of course Prince Charlie was going to pay it back when he was king. Only he never *was* king," she sighed.

"And is that why the Tallow King got all the Arden land?"

"Yes, dear—that's why English people prefer Tallow kings to Stuart kings. And old Lord Arden mortgaged everything. That means he borrowed money, and if he didn't pay back the money by a certain time he agreed to let them take the land instead. And he couldn't pay; so they took the land—all except a bit in the village and Arden Knoll—that was fixed so that he couldn't part from it."

"When we get the treasure we'll buy back the land again," said Edred. "The Tallow King's going to sell it. He's got so tallowy that Arden land isn't good enough for him. Old Beale told us. And, I say, Auntie, we'll rebuild the castle, too, won't we, and mend the holes in the thatch—where the rain comes in—in people's cottages, I mean."

"Have you been much into people's cottages?" Aunt Edith asked anxiously—with the strange fear of infection which seems a part of a grown-up's nature.

"Every one in the village, I think," said Elfrida cheerfully. "Old Beale told us we ought to—in case we found the treasure—so as to know what to do. The people are such dears. I believe they like us because we're Ardens. Or is it because Edred's a lord?"

"We *must* find the treasure," said Edred, looking as he always did when he was very much in earnest, so like his lost father that Aunt Edith could hardly bear it—"so as to be able to look after our people properly."

"And to kick out the Tallow King," said Elfrida.

"But you won't be discontented if you *don't* find it," said Aunt Edith. "It's only a sort of game really. No one *I* ever knew ever found a treasure. And think what we've found already! Arden Castle instead of Sea View Terrace—and the lodgers. Good-night, chicks."

She was gone before they were up in the morning, and the morning's first business was the printing of the photographs.

They printed them in the kitchen, because Mrs. Honeysett was turning out the parlour, and besides the kitchen window was wide and sunny, and the old table, scoured again and again till the grain of the wood stood up in ridges, was a nice, big, clear place to stand toning dishes on. They printed on matt paper, because it seemed somehow less common, and more like a picture than the shiny kind. The printing took the whole morning, and they had only one frame. And when they had done there were eighteen brown prints of the castle from all sorts of points of the compass—north and south and——but I explained all this to you before. When the prints were dried—which, as you know, is best done by sticking them up on the windows—it became necessary to find a place to put them in. One could not gloat over them forever, though for quite a long time it seemed better to look at them again and again, and to say, "That's how it ought to be—that's the way we'll have it," than to do anything else.

Elfrida and Edred took the prints into the parlour, which was now neat as a new pin, and smelt almost *too* much of beeswax and turpentine, spread them on the polished oval dining-table and gloated over them.

"You can see every little bit exactly right," said Elfrida. "They're a little tiny bit muzzy. I expect our distance wasn't right or something, but that only makes them look more like real pictures, and us having printed them on paper that's too big makes it more pictury too. And any one who knew about how buildings are built would know how to set it up. It would be like putting the bricks back into the box from the pattern inside the lid."

Here Mrs. Honeysett called from the kitchen, "You done with all this litter?" and both children shouted "Yes!" and went on looking at the pictures. It was well that the shout was from both. If only one had done it there might have been what Mrs. Honeysett called "words" about the matter later; for next moment both said, "The films!" and rushed to the kitchen—just in time to see the kitchen fire enlivened by that peculiar crackling flare which fire and films alone can produce. Mrs. Honeysett had thrown the films on the fire with the other "litter," and it was no one's fault but the children's, as Mrs. Honeysett pointed out.

"I ask you if you done with it all, an' you says 'Yes'—only yourselves to thank," she repeated again and again amid their lamentations, and they had to own that she was right.

"We must take extra special care of the prints, that's all," said Edred, and the "History of the Ardens" was chosen as a hiding-place both safe and appropriate.

"It doesn't matter so much about the films," said Elfrida, "because we could never have shown them to any one. If we find the treasure we'll arrange for Auntie to find these prints—leave the History about or something—and she'll think they're photographs of painted pictures. So *that'll* be all right."

As they arranged the prints between the leaves of the History Elfrida's eye was caught by the words "moat" and "water-supply," and she read on and turned the page.

"Don't stop to read," said Edred, but she waved him away.

"I say, listen," she said, turning back; and she read—

"'In ancient times Arden Castle was surrounded by a moat. The original architects of the venerable pile, with that ingenuity whose fruits the thinking world so much admires in the lasting monuments of their labours, diverted from its subterraneous course a stream which rose through the chalk in the hills of the vicinity, and is said to debouch into the sea about fifty yards below high-water mark. The engineering works necessary for this triumph of mind over matter endured till 1647, when the castle was besieged by the troops of that monster in human form Oliver Cromwell. To facilitate his attack on the castle the officer in command gave orders that the stream should be diverted once more into its original channel. This order was accordingly executed by his myrmidons, and the moat was left dry, this assisting materially the treacherous designs of the detestable regicides. It is rumoured that the stream, despite the lapse of centuries, still maintains its subterranean course; but the present author, on visiting, during the autumn of 1821, the residence of the present Earl of Arden, and by his permission, most courteously granted, exploring the site thoroughly, was unable to find any trace of its existence. The rural denizens of the district denied any knowledge of such a stream, but they are sunk in ignorance and superstition, and have no admiration for the works of philosophy or the awe-inspiring beauties of Nature.'"

"What a dull chap he is!" said Edred. "But, I say, when was it printed—1822? . . . I believe I know why the rural What's-his-names wouldn't let on about the stream. Don't you see, it's the stream that runs through the smugglers' cave? and they were smuggling then for all they were worth."

"That's clever of you," said Elfrida.

"Well, I bet we find traces of its existence, when we've found the treasure. Come on; let's try the chests again. We'll put on the first things we find, and chance it, this time. There's nothing to stop us. We haven't quarrelled or anything."

They had not quarrelled, but there was something to stop them, all the same. And that something was the fact that they could not find The Door. It simply was not there.

"And we haven't quarrelled or anything," said Elfrida, despairing when they had searched the East House again and again, and found no door that would consent to lead them to the wonderful attic where the chests stood in their two wonderful rows. She sat down on the top step of the attic stairs, quite regardless of the dust that lay there thick.

"It's all up—I can see that," said Edred. "We've muffed it somehow. I wonder whether we oughtn't to have taken those photographs."

"Do you think perhaps . . . *could* we have dreamed it all?"

"*No*," said Edred, "there *are* the prints—at least, I suppose they're there. We'll go down and see."

Miserably doubting, they went down and saw that the photographs were where they had put them, in between the pages of the "History of Arden."

"I don't see *what* we can do. Do you?" said Edred forlornly. It was a miserable ending to the happenings that had succeeded each other in such a lively procession ever since they had been at Arden. It seemed as though a door had been shut in their faces, and "Not any more," written in very plain letters across the chapter of their adventures.

"I wish we could find the witch again," said Elfrida; "but she said she couldn't come into these times more than once."

"I wonder why," said Edred, kicking his boots miserably against the leg of the table on which he sat. "That Dicky chap must have been here pretty often, to have an address at New Cross. I say, suppose we wrote to him. It would be something to do."

So they wrote. At least Elfrida did, and they both signed it. This was the letter:—

"DEAR COUSIN RICHARD,—You remember meeting us at the Gunpowder Plot. If you are at these modern times again we should like to know you and to know how you get into the future. Perhaps we could get into the past the same way, because the way we used to get we can't any more.

"Perhaps you could come here next time instead of New Cross.

"Your affectionate friends at a distance,

(MISS) ELFRIDA ARDEN,

(LORD) EDRED ARDEN.

"PS.—I don't know how lords sign letters because I have not been it long, but you'll know who it is.

"PSS.—Remember old Parrot-nose."

They walked down to the post with this, and as they went they remembered how they had gone to the "George" with old Lady Arden's letter in Boney's time; and Edred remarked, listlessly, that it would be rather fun to find the smugglers' cave. So when they had bought a stamp and licked it and put it on the letter they went up on the cliff and looked among the furze-bushes for the entrance to the smugglers' cave. But they did not find it. Nothing makes you hotter than looking for things that you can't find—and there is no hotter place to look for things than a furze forest on the downs on a sunny summer afternoon. The children were glad to sit down on a clean, smooth, grassy space and look out at the faint blue line of the sea.

They had not really enjoyed looking for the smugglers' cave. Vain regrets were busy in each breast. Edred gave voice to them when he said—

"Oh, if only we had put those gold clothes on when we had the chance!"

And Elfrida echoed the useless heartfelt wail with, "Oh, if we only had!"

And then they sat in silence and looked at the sea for quite a long time.

Now, if you sit perfectly silent for a long time and look at the sea, or the sky, or the running water of a river, something happens to you—a sort of magic. Not the violent magic that makes the kind of adventures that I have been telling you about, but a kind of gentle but very strong *inside* magic, that makes things clear, and shows you what things are important, and what are not. You try it next time you are in a very bad temper, or when you think some one has been very unjust to you, or when you are very disappointed and hurt about anything.

The magic worked in Edred and Elfrida till Edred said—

"After all, we've got the castle;" and Elfrida said—

"And we have had some ripping times."

And then they looked at the sea in more silence, during which Hope came and whispered to Elfrida, who instantly said—

"The Mouldiwarp! Perhaps it's not all over. It told us to find the door. And we did find the door. Perhaps it would tell us something new if we called it now—and if it came."

"And if it came," said Edred.

"Don't talk—make poetry," said Elfrida. But that was one of the things that Edred never could do. Trying to make poetry was, to him, like trying to remember a name you have never heard, or to multiply a number that you've forgotten by another number that you don't recollect.

But Elfrida, that youthful poet, frowned and bit her lips and twisted her hands, and reached out in her mind to words that she just couldn't quite think of, till the words grew tame and flew within reach, and she caught them and caged them behind the bars of rhyme. This was her poem—

"Dear Mouldiwarp, do come if you can,

And tell us if there is any plan

That you can tell us of for us two

To get into the past like we used to do.

Dear Mouldiwarp, we don't want to worry

You—but we *are* in a frightful hurry."

"So you be always," said the white Mouldiwarp, suddenly appearing between them on the yellowy dry grass. "Well, well! Youth's the season for silliness. What's to do now? I be turble tired of all this. I wish I'd only got to give ye the treasure and go my ways. You don't give a poor Mouldiwarp a minute's rest. You do terrify me same's flies, you do."

"Is there any other way," said Elfrida, "to get back into the past? We can't find the door now."

"Course you can't," said the mole. "That's a chance gone, and gone for ever.

"'He that will not when he may,

He shall not when he would-a.'

Well, tell me where you want to go, and I'll make you a backways-working white clock."

"Anywhere you like," said Edred incautiously.

"Tch, tch!" said the mole, rubbing its nose with vexation. "There's another chance gone, and gone for ever. You be terrible spending with your chances, you be. Now, answer sharp as weasel's nose. Be there any one in the past you'd like to see?

"'If you don't know,

Then you don't go.'

And that's poetry as good as yours any day of the week."

"Cousin Richard," said Elfrida and Edred together. This was the only name they could think of.

"Bide ye still, my dears," said the Mouldiwarp, "and I'll make you a white road right to where he is."

So they sat still, all but their tongues.

"Is he in the past?" said Elfrida; "because if he *is*, it wasn't much good our writing to him."

"You hold your little tongues," said the Mouldiwarp, "and keep your little mouths shut, and your little eyes open, and wish well to the white magic. There never was a magic yet," the mole went on, "that was the worse for being well-wished."

"May I say something," said Elfrida, "without its stopping the magic?"

"Put your white handkerchief over your face and talk through it, and then you may."

By a most fortunate and unusual chance, Elfrida's handkerchief *was* white: it was, in fact, still folded in the sixteen blameless squares into which the laundress had ironed it. She threw it over her face as she lay back on the turf and spoke through it.

"I'd like to see the nurse witch again," she said.

"Instead of Cousin Richard?"

"No: as well as."

"That's right," said the magic mole. "You shouldn't *change* your wishes; but there's no rule against enlarging them—on the contrary. Now look!"

Elfrida whisked away the handkerchief and looked.

Have you ever noticed the way the bath water runs away when you pull up the bath tap? Have you ever seen bottles filled through a funnel?

The white Mouldiwarp reached up its hands—its front feet I ought perhaps to say—towards the deep-blue sky, where white clouds herded together like giant sheep.

And it spoke. At least, it did not speak, but it sang. Yet I don't know that you could call it singing either. It was more like the first notes that a violin yields to the bow wielded by the hand of a master musician. And the white clouds stooped to answer it. Round and round in the blue sky they circled, drawing together and swirling down, as the bath water draws and swirls when you pull up the knob labelled "Waste"—round and round till they showed like a vast white funnel whose neck hung, a great ring, above the group on the dry grass of the downs. It stooped and stooped. The ring fitted down over them, they were in a white tower, narrow at its base where that base touched the grass, but widening to the blue sky overhead.

"Take hands," cried the Mouldiwarp. "Always hold hands when there is magic about."

The children clasped hands.

"Both hands," said the Mouldiwarp; and each child reached out a hand, that was caught and held. Round and round, incredibly swifter and swifter, went the cloud funnel, and the voice of the mole at their feet sounded faint and far away.

"Up!" it cried, "up! Shall the very clouds dance for your delight, and you alone refrain and tread not a measure?"

The children leaped up—and through the cloud came something that was certainly music, though it was so vague and far away that the sharpest music-master you ever had could not have made out the tune. But the rhythm of it was there, an insistent beat, beat, beat—and a beat that made your feet long to keep time to it. And through the rhythm presently the tune pierced, as the sound of the pipes pierces the sound of the drums when you see the Church Brigade boys go by when you are on your holiday by the sea near their white-tented, happy camps. And that time the children's feet could not resist. They danced steps that they had not known they knew. And they knew, for the first time, the delight of real dancing: none of your waltzes, or even minuets, but the dancing that means youth and gaiety, and being out for a holiday, and determined to enjoy everything to the last breath.

And as they danced the white cloud funnel came down and closed about them, so that they danced, as it were, in a wrapping of white cotton-wool too soft for them even to feel it. And there was a sweet scent in the air. They did not know in that cloudy, soft whiteness, what flower bore that scent, but they knew that it smelt of the spring, and of fields and hedges far away from the ugliness of towns. The cloud thinned as the scent thickened, and green lights showed through it.

The green lights grew, the cloud funnel lifted. And Edred and Elfrida, still dancing, found themselves but two in a ring of some thirty children, dancing on a carpet of green turf between walls of green branches. And every child wore a wreath of white May-blossoms on its head. And that was the magic scene that had come to them through the white cloud of the white Mouldiwarp's magic.

"What is it? Why are we dancing?" Edred incautiously asked of the little girl whose hand—and not Elfrida's—he found that his left hand was holding. The child laughed—just laughed, she did not answer. It was Elfrida who had his right hand, and her own right hand was clasped in that of a boy dressed in green.

"Oh!" she said, with a note of glad recognition. "It's you! I'm so glad! What is it? Why are we dancing?"

"It's May-day," said Cousin Richard, "and the King is coming to look on at the revels."

"What king?" she asked.

"Who but King Harry?" he said. "King Harry and his new Queen, that but of late was the Lady Anna Boleyn."

"I say, Dick," said Edred across his sister, "I am jolly glad to see you again. We——"

"Not now," said Dick earnestly; "not a word now. It is not safe. And besides—here comes the King!"

CHAPTER XIII
MAY-BLOSSOM AND PEARLS

The King came slowly on a great black horse, riding between the green trees. He himself wore white and green like the May-bushes, and so did the gracious lady who rode beside him on a white horse, whose long tail almost swept the ground and whose long mane fluttered in the breeze like a tattered banner.

The lady had a fine face—proud and smiling—and as her brave eyes met the King's even the children could see that, for the time at least, she and the King were all the world to each other. They saw that in the brief moment when, in the whirl of the ringed dance, their eyes were turned the way by which the King came with his Queen.

"I wish I didn't know so much history," gasped Elfrida through the quick music. "It's dreadful to know that her head——" She broke off in obedience to an imperative twitch of Richard's hand on hers.

"Don't!" he said. "I have *not* to think. And I've heard that history's all lies. Perhaps they'll always be happy like they are now. The only way to enjoy the past is not to think of the future—the past's future, I mean—and I've got something else to say to you presently," he added rather sternly.

The ring broke up into an elaborate figure. The children found themselves fingering the coloured ribbons that hung from the Maypole that was the centre of their dance, twining, intertwining, handing on the streamers to other small, competent fingers. In and out, in and out—a most complicated dance. It was pleasant to find that one's feet knew it, though one's brain could not have foreseen, any more than it could have remembered, how the figures went. There were two rings round the Maypole—the inner ring, where Edred and Elfrida were, of noble children in very fine clothes, and the outer ring, of village children in clothes less fine but quite as pretty. Music from a band of musicians on a raised platform decked with May-boughs and swinging cowslip balls inspired the dancers. The King and Queen had reined up their horses and watched the play, well pleased.

And suddenly the dance ended and the children, formed into line, were saluting the royal onlookers.

"A fair dance and footed right featly," said the King in a great, jolly voice. "Now get you wind, my merry men all, and give us a song for the honour of the May Queen and of my dear lady here."

There was whispering and discussion. Then Richard Arden stepped out in front of the group of green-clad noble children.

"With a willing heart, my liege," he said, "but first a song of the King's good Majesty."

And with that all the children began to sing—

"The hunt is up, the hunt is up,

And it is well-nigh day,

And Harry our King is gone a-hunting

To bring his deer to bay."

It is a rousing tune, and it was only afterwards that Edred and Elfrida were surprised to find that they knew it quite well.

But even while they were singing Elfrida was turning over in her mind the old question, Could anything they did have any effect on the past? It seemed impossible that it should not be so. If one could get a word alone with that happy, stately lady on the white horse, if one could warn her, could help somehow! The thought of the bare scaffold and the black block came to Elfrida so strongly that she almost thought she saw them darkling among the swayed, sun-dappled leaves of the greenwood.

Somebody was pulling at her green skirt. An old woman in a cap that fitted tightly and hid all her hair—an old woman who was saying, "Go to her! go!" and pushing her forward. Some one else put a big bunch of wild flowers into her hand, and this person also pushed her forward. And forward she had to go, quite alone, the nosegay in her hand, across the open space of greensward under the eyes of several hundreds of people, all in their best clothes and all watching her.

She went on till she came to the spot where the King and Queen were, and then she paused and dropped two curtsies, one to each of them. Then, quite without meaning to do it, she found herself saying—

"May-day! May-day!

This is the happy play day!

All the woods with flowers are gay,

Lords and ladies, come and play!

Lords and ladies, rich and poor,

Come to the wild woods' open door!

Hinds and yeomen, Queen and King,

Come do honour to the Spring!

And join us in our merrymaking."

And when she had said that she made two more nice little curtsies and handed up the flowers to the Queen.

"If we had known your Majesties' purpose," said a tall, narrow-faced man in a long gown, "your Majesties had had another than this rustic welcome."

"Our purpose," said the King, "was to surprise you. The Earl of Arden, you say, is hence?"

"His son and daughter are here to do homage to your Highness," said the gowned man, and then Elfrida saw that Edred was beside her.

"Hither, lad," said the King, and reaching down a hand caught Edred's. "Your foot on mine," said his Majesty. "So!" and he swung Edred up on to the saddle in front of him. Elfrida drew nearer to the white horse as the Queen beckoned her, and the Queen stooped low over her saddle to ask her name. Now was the moment that Elfrida had wished for, now was the chance, if ever, to warn the Queen.

"Elfrida Arden's my name," she said. "Your Majesty, may I say something?"

"Say on," said the Queen, raising fine eyebrows, but smiling too.

"I should like to come quite close and whisper," said Elfrida stoutly.

"Thou'rt a bold lass," said the Queen, but she stooped still lower.

"I want to warn you," said Elfrida, quickly whispering, "and *don't* not pay attention because I'm only a little girl. I *know*. You may think I don't know, but I do. I want to warn you——"

"Already once, this morning I have been warned," said the Queen. "What croaking voices for May-day!"

"Who warned you, your Majesty?"

"An old hag who came to my chamber in spite of my maids, said she had a May charm to keep my looks and my lord's love."

"What was the charm?" Elfrida asked eagerly, forgetting to say "Majesty" again.

"It was quite simple," said the Queen. "I was to keep my looks and my love so long as I *never dropped a kerchief*. But if I dropped a kerchief I should lose more than my looks and my love; she said I should lose my head,"—the Queen laughed low,—"within certain days from the dropping of that kerchief—this head you see here;" she laughed again.

"Don't, oh, don't!" said Elfrida. "Nineteen days, that's the warning—I do hope it'll do some good. I do like you, dear Queen. You are so strong and splendid. I would like to be like you when I grow up."

The Queen's fine face looked troubled.

"Please Heaven, thou'lt be better than I," she said, stooping lower still from her horse; Elfrida standing on tip-toe, she kissed her.

"Oh, do be careful," said Elfrida. "Your darling head!" and the Queen kissed her again.

Then a noise rather like bagpipes rose shrill and sudden, and all drew back, making room for the rustic maids and swains to tread the country dance. Other instruments joined in, and suddenly the King cried, "A merry tune that calls to the feet. Come, my sweeting, shall we tread a measure with the rest?" So down they came from their horses, King and Queen, and led the country dance, laughing and gay as any country lad and lass.

Elfrida could have cried. It seemed such a pity that everybody should not always be good and happy, as everybody looked to-day.

The King had sprung from his horse with Edred in his arms, and now he and his sister drew back towards Cousin Richard.

"How pretty it all is!" said Edred. "I should like to stay here for ever."

"If I were you," said Richard, very disagreeably indeed, "I would not stay here an hour."

"Why? Is it dangerous? Will they cut our heads off?"

"Not that I know of," said Cousin Richard, still thoroughly disagreeable. "I wasn't thinking about your heads. There are more important things than your heads in the world, I should think."

"Not so very much more," said Elfrida meekly,—"to us, I mean. And what are you so cross about?"

"I should have thought," Richard was beginning, when the old woman who told Elfrida to go forward with the nosegay of ceremony sidled up to them.

"Into the woods, my children," she whispered quickly,—"into the woods. In a moment the Queen will burst into tears, and the King will have scant kindness for those whose warnings have set his Queen to weeping."

They backed into the bushes, and the green leaves closed behind the four.

"Quick!" said the witch; "this way." They followed her through the wood under oaks and yew-trees, pressing through hazels and chestnuts to a path.

"Now run!" she said, and herself led the way nimbly enough for one of her great age. Their run brought them to a thinning of the wood—then out of it—on to the downs, whence they could see Arden Castle and its moat, and the sea.

"'NOW RUN!' SHE SAID, AND HERSELF LED THE WAY."

"Now," the old woman said, "mark well the spot where the moat stream rises. It is there that the smugglers' cave was, when Betty Lovell foretold the landing of the French."

"Why," said Edred and Elfrida, "you're the witch again! You're Betty Lovell!"

"Who else?" said the old woman. "Now, call on the Mouldiwarp and hasten back to your own time. For the King will raise the country against the child who has made his sweeting to shed tears. And she will tell him, she keeps nothing from him, and . . . yet——"

"She won't tell him about the kerchief?"

"She will, and when she drops it on that other May-day at Greenwich he will remember. Come, call your Mouldiwarp and haste away."

"But we've only just come," said Edred, "and what's Elfrida been up to?"

"Oh, bother!" said Elfrida. "I want to know what Richard meant about our heads not being important."

"Your heads will be most important if you wait here much longer!" said the witch sharply. "Come, shall I call the Mouldiwarp, or will you?"

"You do," said Elfrida. "I say, Dicky, what did you mean? Do tell us—there's a dear."

Betty Lovell was tearing up the short turf in patches, and pulling the lumps of chalk from under it.

"Help me," she cried, "or I shan't be in time!" So they all helped.

"Couldn't Dick go with us—if we *have* to go?" said Elfrida suddenly.

"No," said Richard, "I'm not going to—so there!"

"Why?" Elfrida gasped, tugging at a great piece of chalk.

"Because I shan't."

"Then tell us what you meant before the Mouldiwarp comes."

"You can't," said a little voice, "because it's come now."

Every one sat back on its heels, and watched where out of the earth the white Mouldiwarp was squeezing itself between two blocks of chalk, into the sunlight.

"Why, I hadn't said any poetry," said Elfrida.

"I hadn't made the triangle and the arch," said old Betty Lovell. "Well, if ever I did!"

"I've been here," said the mole, looking round with something astonishingly like a smile of triumph, "all the time. Why shouldn't I go where I do please, nows and again? Why should I allus wait on your bidding—eh?" it asked a little pettishly.

"No reason at all," said Elfrida kindly; "and now, dear, dear Mouldiwarp, please take us away."

A confused sound of shouting mixed with the barking of dogs hurried her words a little.

"The hunt is up," said the old witch-nurse.

"I don't hold with hunting," said the Mouldiwarp hastily, "nor yet with dogs. I never could abide dogs, drat the nasty, noisy, toothy things! Here, come inside."

"Inside where?" said Edred.

"Inside my house," said the mole.

And then, whether they all got smaller or whether the crack in the chalk got bigger they never quite knew, but they found themselves walking that crack one by one. Only Elfrida got hold of Richard's hand and held it fast, though he wriggled and twisted to get it free.

"I'm not going back to your own times with you," he said. "I'll go my own way."

"Where to?" said Elfrida.

"To wherever I choose," said Richard savagely, and regained possession of his own hand. It was too late—the chalk had closed over them all.

As the chalk had closed so thoroughly that not a gleam of daylight could be seen, you might have expected the air they had to breathe to be close and stuffy. Not a bit of it! Coming into the Mouldiwarp's house out of the May sunshine was like coming out of a human house into the freshness of a May night. But it was darker than any night that ever was. Elfrida got hold of Edred's hand and then of Richard's. She always tried to remember what she was told, and the Mouldiwarp had said, "Always hold hands when there's magic about."

Richard let his hand be taken, but he said, quite sternly, "You understand I mean what I say: I won't go back to their times with them."

"You were much nicer in James the First's time," said Elfrida.

Then a sound like thunder shook the earth overhead, an almost deafening noise that made them thrill and hold each other very tight.

"It's only the King's horses and the King's men hunting after you," said the Mouldiwarp cheerfully. "Now I'll go and make a white clock for you to go home on. You set where you be, and don't touch nothing till I be come back again."

Left alone in the fresh, deep darkness, Elfrida persisted in her questions.

"Why don't you want to come with us to our times?"

"I hate your times. They're ugly, they're cruel," said Richard.

"They don't cut your head off for nothing anyhow in our times," said Edred, "and shut you up in the Tower."

"They do worse things," Richard said. "*I* know. They make people work fourteen hours a day for nine shillings a week, so that they never have enough to eat or wear, and no time to sleep or to be happy in. They won't give people food or clothes, or let them work to get them; and then they put the people in prison if they take enough to keep them alive. They let people get horrid diseases, till their jaws drop off, so as to have a particular kind of china. Women have to go out to work instead of looking after their babies, and the little girl that's left in charge drops the baby and it's crippled for life. Oh! I know. I won't go back with you. You might keep me there for ever." He shuddered.

"I wouldn't. And I can't help about people working, and not enough money and that," said Edred.

"If *I* were Lord Arden," said Richard, through the darkness, "I'd make a vow, and I'd keep it too, never to have a day's holiday or do a single thing I liked till all those things were stopped. But in *your* time nobody cares."

"It's not true," said Elfrida; "we do care—when we know about it. Only we can't do anything."

"I *am* Lord Arden," said Edred, "and when I grow up I'll do what you say. I shall be in the House of Lords, I think, and of course the House of Lords would have to pay attention to me when I said things. I'll remember everything you say, and tell them about it."

"You're not grown up yet," said Richard, "and your father's Lord Arden, not you."

"Father's dead, you know," said Elfrida, in a hushed voice.

"How do you know?" asked Richard.

"There was a letter——"

"Do you think *I'd* trust a letter?" Richard asked indignantly. "If I hadn't seen my daddy lying dead, do you think I'd believe it? Not till I'd gone back and seen how he died, and where, and had vengeance on the man who'd killed him."

"But he wasn't killed."

"How do you know? You've been hunting for the beastly treasure, and never even tried to go back to the time when he was alive—such a little time ago—and find out what really did happen to him."

"I didn't know we *could*," said Elfrida, choking. "And even if we could, it wouldn't be right, would it? Aunt Edith said he was in heaven. We couldn't go there, you know. It isn't like history—it's all different."

"Well, then," said Richard, "I shall have to tell you. You know, I rather took a fancy to you two kids that Gunpowder Plot time; and after you'd gone back to your own times asked Betty Lovell who you were, and she said you were Lord Arden. So the next time I wanted to get away from—from where I was—I gave orders to be taken to Lord Arden. And it——"

"Come along, do, dear," said the sudden voice of the Mouldiwarp. "The clock's all ready."

A soft light was pressing against their eyes—growing, growing. They saw now that they were in a great chalk cave—the smugglers' cave, Edred had hardly a doubt. And in the middle of its floor of smooth sand was a great clock-face—figures and hands and all—made of softly gleaming pearls set in ivory. Light seemed to flow from this, and to be reflected back on it by the white chalk walls. It was the most beautiful piece of jeweller's work that the children—or, I imagine, any one else—had ever seen.

"Sit on the minute hand," said the Mouldiwarp, "and home you go."

"But I can't go," said Edred grimly, "till I've heard what Richard was saying."

"You'll be caught, then, by the King and his soldiers," said the witch.

"I must risk that," said Edred quite quietly. "I will not go near the white clock till Richard has told me what he means."

"I'll give him one minute," said the Mouldiwarp crossly, "not no more than that. I'm sick to death of it, so I am."

"Oh, *don't* be cross," said Elfrida.

"I bain't," said the Mouldiwarp, "not under my fur. It's this Chop-and-change, and I-will-and-I-won't as makes me so worritable."

"Tell me, what did you mean—about my father?" Edred said again.

"I tried to find you—I asked for Lord Arden. What I found wasn't you—it was your father. And the time was *your* time, July, 1908."

"WHAT!" cried Edred and Elfrida together.

"Your father—he's alive—don't you understand? And you've been bothering about finding treasure instead of about finding him."

"Daddy—alive!" Elfrida clung to her brother. "Oh, it's not right, mixing *him* up with magic and things. Oh, you're cruel—I hate you! I know well enough I shall never see my daddy again."

"You will if you aren't little cowards as well as little duffers," said Richard scornfully. "You go and find him, that's what you've got to do. So long!"

And with that, before the Mouldiwarp or the nurse could interfere, he had leapt on to the long pearl and ivory minute hand of the clock and said, "Home!" just as duchesses (and other people) do to their coachmen (or footmen).

And before anything could be done the hands of the clock began to go round, slowly at first, then faster and faster, till at last they went so fast that they became quite invisible. The ivory and pearl figures of the clock could still be seen on the sand of the cave.

Edred and Elfrida, still clinging together, turned appealing eyes to the Mouldiwarp. They expected it to be very angry indeed, instead of which it seemed to be smiling. (Did you ever see a white mole smile? No? But then, perhaps you have never seen a white mole, and you cannot see a smile without seeing the smiler, except of course in the case of Cheshire cats.)

"He's a bold boy, a brave boy," said the witch.

"Ah!" said the Mouldiwarp, "he be summat like an Arden, he be."

Edred detached himself from Elfrida and stiffened with a resolve to show the Mouldiwarp that he too was not so unlike an Arden as it had too hastily supposed.

"Can't we get home?" Elfrida asked timidly. "Can't you make us another white clock, or something?"

"Waste not, want not," said the mole. "Always wear out your old clocks afore you buys new 'uns. Soon's he gets off the hand the clock'll stop; then you can get on it and go safe home."

"But suppose the King finds us?" said Elfrida.

"He shan't," said Betty Lovell. "You open the chalky door, Mouldy, my love, and I'll keep the King quiet till the young people's gone home."

"THEY ALL JUMPED ON THE WHITE CLOCK."

"They'll duck you for a witch," said the Mouldiwarp, and it did not seem to mind the familiar way in which Betty spoke to it.

"Well, it's a warm day," said Betty; "by the time they get me to the pond you'll be safe away. And the water'll be nice and cool."

"Oh, *no*," said Edred and Elfrida together. "You'll be drowned." And Edred added, "I couldn't allow that."

"Bless your silly little hearts," said the Mouldiwarp, "*she* won't drown. She'll just get home by the back door, that's all. There's a door at the bottom of every pond, if you can only find it."

So Betty Lovell went out through the chalk to meet the anger of the King, with two kisses on her cheeks.

And suddenly there was the pearl and ivory clock again, all complete, minute hand and hour hand and second hand.

Edred and Elfrida sat down on the minute hand, and before the Mouldiwarp could open its long, narrow mouth to say a word Edred called out in a firm voice, "Take us to where Daddy is;" for he had learned from Richard that white clocks can be ordered about.

And the minute hand of pearl and ivory began to move, faster and faster and faster, till, if there had been any one to look at it, it would have been invisible.

But there wasn't any one to look at it, for the Mouldiwarp had leaped on to the hour hand at the last moment, and was hanging on there by all its claws.

CHAPTER XIV
THE FINDING OF THE TREASURE

"To Richard Arden!" shouted the Mouldiwarp of Arden as it leaped on the hour hand of the pearl and ivory clock. And then the hands went round far too fast for speech to be possible. When the clock stopped, which it did quite suddenly, Edred caught his breath and shouted, "To my daddy!" at the top of his voice. And the hands began to move again so quickly that neither of the children had time to see where they had stopped. They just saw that they were in a room, and that the Mouldiwarp, who seemed suddenly to have grown to the size of an enormous Polar bear, leaned over the edge of the clock and caught at something with a paw a foot long. And then some one called out something that they couldn't hear, and almost at once the clock stopped, and they saw something climb off the clock. And the clock was in the cave again. And there was Cousin Richard in quite different clothes from those he had worn at King Henry the Eighth's maying. They were the kind of clothes Edred had worn in Boney's time, and the cave was just as it had been then, with kegs and bales, and the stream running through it.

"You *must* come with us," said the Mouldiwarp, slowly resuming its ordinary size. "Don't you see? If these children let their father see them, they'll have to explain the whole magic, and when once magic's explained all the magic's gone, like the scent out of scent when you leave the cork out of the bottle. But *you* can see him and help—if he wants help—without having to explain anything."

"All right," said Richard, and muttered something about "the Head of the House." "Only," he added, "I dropped *my* magic here." He stooped to the sand and picked up a little stick with silver bells hung round it, like the one that Folly carries at a carnival. "It's got the Arden arms and crest on it," he said, pointing, and by the light of the pearl and ivory clock the children could see the shield and the chequers and the Mouldiwarp above. "Now I'm ready. Cousins, I take back everything I said. You see, *my* father's dead . . . and if I'd only had half your chance. . . . That was what I thought. See? So give us your hand."

The hands were given.

"But oh," said Elfrida, "this is different from all the rest; that was a game, and this is—this is———"

"This is real, my sock-lamb," said the Mouldiwarp, with unusual kindness. "Now your Cousin Richard will help you, and when you get your father back, as I make no doubts but what you will, then your Cousin Dick he'll go back to his own time and generation, and be seen no more, and your father won't never guess that you was there so close to him as you will be."

"I don't believe we shall," said Elfrida, nodding stubbornly, and for the first time in this story she did *not* believe.

"Oh, well," said the Mouldiwarp bitterly, "of course if you don't believe you'll find him, you'll not find him. That's plain as a currant loaf."

"But *I* believe we shall find him," said Edred, "and Elfrida's only a girl. It might be only a dream, of course," he added thoughtfully. "Don't you think I don't know that. But if it's a dream, I'm going to stay in it. I'm not going back to Arden without my father."

"Do you understand," said the Mouldiwarp, "that if I take you into any other time or place in your own century, it's the full stop? There isn't any more."

"It means there's no chance of our getting into the past again, to look for treasure or anything?"

"Oh, *chance*!" said the Mouldiwarp. "I mean no magic clock'll not never be made for you no more, that's what I mean. And if you find your father you'll not be Lord Arden any more, either!"

I hope it will not shock you very much when I tell you that at that thought a distinct pang shot through Edred's breast. He really felt it, in his flesh-and-blood breast, like a sharp knife. It was dreadful of him to think of such a thing, when there was a chance of his getting his daddy in exchange for just a title. It *was* dreadful; but I am a truthful writer, and I must own the truth. In one moment he felt the most dreadful things—that it was all nonsense, and perhaps daddy wasn't there, and it was no good looking for him any way, and he wanted to go on being Lord Arden, and hadn't they better go home.

The thoughts came quite without his meaning them to, and Edred pushed them from him with both hands, so to speak, hating himself because they had come to him. And he will hate himself for those thoughts, though he did not mean or wish to have them, as long as he lives, every time he remembers them. That is the worst of thoughts, they live for ever.

"I don't want to be Lord Arden," was what he instantly said—"I want my father." And what he said was true, in spite of those thoughts that he didn't mean to have and can never forget.

"Shall I come along of you?" said the Mouldiwarp, and every one said "Yes," very earnestly. A friendly Mouldiwarp is a very useful thing to have at hand when you are going you don't know where.

"Now, you won't make any mistake," the mole went on. "This is the wind-up and the end-all. So it is. No more chestses in atticses. No more fine clotheses out of 'em neither. An' no more white clocks."

"All right," said Edred impatiently, "we understand. Now let's go."

"You wait a bit," said the Mouldiwarp aggravatingly. "You've got to settle what you'll be, and what way your father'd better come out. *I* think through the chink of the chalk."

"Any way you like," said Elfrida. "And Mouldiwarp, dear, shan't we ever see *you* again?"

"Oh, I don't say *that*," it said. "You'll see me at dinner every day."

"At dinner?"

"I'm on all the spoons and forks, anyhow," it said, and sniggered more aggravatingly than ever.

"Mouldie!" cried Edred suddenly, "I've got it. You disguise us so that father won't know us, and then we shan't be out of it all, whatever it is."

"I think that's a first-rate idea," said Richard; "and me too."

"Not you," said the Mouldiwarp. But it waved a white paw at Edred and Elfrida, and at once they found themselves dressed in tight-fitting white fur dresses. Their hands even wore fat, white fur gloves with tiger claws at the ends of the fingers. At the same moment the Mouldiwarp grew big again—to the size of a very small Polar bear, while Cousin Richard suddenly assumed the proportions of a giant.

"Now!" said the Mouldiwarp, and they all leaped on the white clock, which started at once.

When it stopped, and they stepped off it, it was on to a carpet of thick moss. Overhead, through the branches of enormous trees, there shone stars of a wonderful golden brightness. The air was warm-scented as if with flowers, and warm to breathe, yet they did not feel that their fur coats were a bit too warm for the weather. The moss was so soft to their feet that Edred and Elfrida wanted to feel it with their hands as well, so down they went on all fours. Then they longed to lie down and roll on it; they longed so much that they had to do it. It was a delicious sensation, rolling in the soft moss.

Cousin Richard, still very much too big, stood looking down on them and laughing. They were too busy rolling to look at each other.

"This," he said, "is a first-class lark. Now for the cleft in the chalk. Shall I carry you?" he added politely, addressing the Mouldiwarp, who, rather surprisingly, consented.

"Come on," he said to the children, and as he went they followed him.

There was something about the moss, or about the fur coats or the fur gloves, that somehow made it seem easier and more natural to follow on all fours—and really their hands were quite as useful to walk on as their feet. Never had they felt so light, so gay, never had walking been such easy work. They followed Richard through the forest till quite abruptly, like the wall at the end of a shrubbery, a great cliff rose in front of them, ending the forest. There was a cleft in it, they saw the darkness of it rising above them as the moon came out from a cloud and shone full on the cliff's white face—and the face of the cliff and the shape of the cleft were very like that little cleft in the chalk that the Mouldiwarp had made when it had pulled up turf on the Sussex downs at home. And all this time Edred and Elfrida had never looked at each other. There had been so many other things to look at.

"That's the way," said Cousin Richard, pointing up the dark cleft. Though it was so dark Edred and Elfrida could see quite plainly that there were no steps—only ledges that a very polite goat might have said were a foothold.

"You couldn't climb up there," Edred said to the great Richard; yet somehow he never doubted that he and Elfrida could.

"No," said the Mouldiwarp, leaping from Richard's arms to the ground, "I must carry him"—and it grew to Polar bear size quite calmly before their very eyes.

"They don't see it—even yet," said Richard to the mole.

"See what?" Elfrida asked.

"Why, what your disguise is. You're cats, my dear cousins, white cats!"

Then Edred and Elfrida did look at each other, and it was quite true, they *were*.

"I'll tell you what my plan is," Richard went on. "The people of this country have never seen tame cats. They think a person who can tame animals is a magician. I found that out when I was here before. So now I've got three tame animals, all white too, that is, if you'll play," he added to the Mouldiwarp. "You *will* play, won't you?"

"Oh, yes, I'll play!" it said, snarling a little.

"And you cats must only mew and purr, and do whatever I tell you. You'll see how I work it. Don't do anything for any one but me and your father."

"Is father really here?" asked Elfrida, trembling a little.

"He's on the other side of the great cliff," said Richard,—"the cliff no man can climb. But *you* can come."

He got on the Mouldiwarp's back and put his arms round its Polar-bear-like neck, and it began to climb. That *was* a climb. Even the cats, which Edred and Elfrida now could not help seeing that they were, found it as much as they could do to keep their footing on those little, smooth, shelving ledges. If it had not been that they had cat's eyes, and so could see in the dark, they never could have done it. And it was such a long, long climb too; it seemed as though it would last for ever.

"I've heard of foreign climbs," said Elfrida, "but I never thought they would be like this. I suppose it *is* foreign?"

"South American," said Richard. "You can look for it on the map when you get home—but you won't find it. Come on!"

And then when they had climbed to the top of the cliff they had to go down on the other side. For the cliff rose like a wall between the forest and a wide plain, and by the time they reached that plain the sun was looking down at them over the cliff.

The plain was very large and very wonderful, and a towering wall of cliff ran all round it. The plain was all laid out in roads and avenues and fields and parks. Towns and palaces were dotted about it—a tall aqueduct on hundreds of pillars brought water from an arch in the face of the cliff to the middle of the plain, and from these canals ran out to the cliff wall that bounded the plain all round, even and straight, like the spokes of a wheel, and disappeared under low arches of stone, back under the cliff. There were lakes, there were gardens, there were great stone buildings whose roofs shone like gold where the rising sun struck them.

In the fields were long-horned cattle and strange, high-shouldered sheep, which Richard said were llamas.

"I know," he explained, "from seeing them on the postage stamps."

They advanced into the plain and sat down under a spreading tree.

"We must just wait till we're found," said Richard. He had assumed entire command of the expedition, and Edred and Elfrida, being cats, had to submit, but they did not like it.

Presently shepherds coming early to attend to their flocks found a boy in strange clothes, attended by a great white bear and two white cats, sitting under a tree.

The shepherds did not seem afraid of the bear—only curious and interested; but when the Mouldiwarp had stood up on its hind legs and bowed gravely and the cats had stood up and lain down and shaken paws and turned somersaults at the word of command one of the shepherds wrapped his red woollen cloak round him with an air of determination and, making signs that Richard was to follow, set off with all his might for the nearest town.

Quite soon they found themselves in the central square of one of the most beautiful towns in the world. I wish I had time to tell you exactly what it was like, but I have not. I can only say that it was at once clean and grand, splendid and comfortable. There was not a dirty corner nor a sad face from one end of the town to the other. The houses were made of great blocks of stone inlaid wonderfully with gold and silver; clear streams—or baby canals—ran by the side of every street, and each street had a double row of trees running all along its wide length. There were open, grassy spaces and flower-beds set with flowers, some glowing with their natural and lovely colours and some cunningly fashioned of gold and silver and jewels. There were fountains and miniature waterfalls. The faces of the people were dark, but kind and unwrinkled. There was a market with stalls of pleasant fruits and cakes and bright-coloured, soft clothes. There was a great Hall in the middle of the town with a garden on its flat roof, and to this Hall the shepherd led the party.

The big doors of inlaid wood were set wide and a crowd, all dressed in soft stuffs of beautiful colours, filled the long room inside. The room was open to the sky; a wrinkled awning drawn close at one side showed that the people could have a roof when it suited them.

"THE HOUSES WERE MADE OF GREAT BLOCKS OF STONE."

There was a raised stone platform at one end, and on this three chairs. The crowd made way for the shepherd and his following, and as they drew near to the raised platform the two white cats, who were Edred and Elfrida, looked up and saw in the middle and biggest chair a splendid, dark-faced man in a kind of fringed turban with two long feathers in it, and in the two chairs to right and left of him, clothed in beautiful embroidered stuffs, with shining collars of jewels about their necks, Father and Uncle Jim!

"Not a word!" said Cousin Dick, just in time to restrain the voices of the children who were cats. Their actions he could not restrain. Every one in that Hall saw two white cats spring forward and rub themselves against the legs of the man who sat in the right-hand chair. Compelled to silence as they were by the danger of their position, Edred and Elfrida rubbed their white-cat bodies against their father's legs in a rapture which I cannot describe and purred enthusiastically. It was a wonderful relief to be able to purr, since they must not speak.

The King—he who sat on the high seat—stood up, looking down on them with wise, kind eyes, and spoke, seeming to ask a question.

Quite as wonderfully as any trained bear, and far more gracefully, the white Mouldiwarp danced before the King of that mysterious hidden kingdom.

Then Dick whistled, and Edred and Elfrida withdrew themselves from their passionate caresses of the only parts of their father that they could get at, and stood upon their white-hind-cat-feet.

"The minuet," said Edred, in a rapid whisper. Dick whistled a tune that they had never heard, but the tune was right; and now was seen the spectacle of two white cats slowly and solemnly going through the figures of that complicated dance, to the music of Dick's clear whistling, turning, bowing, pacing with all the graces that Aunt Edith had taught them when they were Edred and Elfrida and not white cats.

When the last bow and curtsey ended the dance, the King himself shouted some word that they were sure meant, "Well done!" All the people shouted the same word, and only father and Uncle Jim shouted "Bravo!"

Then the King questioned Dick.

No answer. He laid his finger on his lips.

Then the King spoke to father, and he in turn tried questions, in English and French and then in other languages. And still Dick kept on laying his finger on his lips, and the white bear shook its head quite sadly, and the white cats purred aloud with their eyes on their father.

Richard stooped. "When your father goes out, follow him," he whispered.

And so, when the King rose from his throne and went out, and every one else did the same, the white cats, deserting Dick, followed close on their father's footsteps. When the King saw this, he spoke to the men about him, who were leading Richard in another direction, and presently the cats and the bear that was the Mouldiwarp, and Richard found themselves alone with Uncle Jim and the father of Elfrida on a beautiful terrace shaded by trees, and set all along its edge with wonderful trailing flowers of red and white and purple that grew out of vases of solid silver.

And now, there being none of the brown people near, Richard looked full in the eyes of the father of Edred and Elfrida, and said in a very low voice—

"I am English. I've come to rescue you."

"You're a bold boy," said Edred and Elfrida's father, "but rescue's impossible."

"There's not much time," said Richard again; "they've only let us come here just to see if you know us. I expect they're listening. You are Lord Arden now—the old lord is dead. I can get you out if you do exactly as I say."

"It's worth trying," said Uncle Jim,—"it's worth trying anyhow, whatever it is."

"Are you free to go where you like?"

"Yes," said Lord Arden—not Edred, but Edred's father, for Edred was now no longer Lord Arden. "You see there's no way out but the one, and that's guarded by a hundred men with poisoned arrows."

"There *is* another way," said Richard; "the way we came. The white bear can carry you, one at a time."

"Shall we risk it?" said Lord Arden, a little doubtfully.

"Rather!" said Uncle Jim; "think of Edith and the kids."

"That's what I *am* thinking of," said Lord Arden; "while we're alive there's a chance. If we try this and fail, they'll kill us."

"You won't fail," said Richard. "I'll help you to get home; but I would like to know how you got into this fix. It's only curiosity. But I wish you'd tell me. Perhaps I shan't see you again after to-day."

"We stumbled on the entrance, the only entrance to the golden plain," said Lord Arden, "prospecting for gold among these mountains. They have kept us prisoners ever since, because they are determined not to let the world know of the existence of the plain. There are always rumours of it, but so far no 'civilised' people have found it. Every King when he comes to the throne takes an oath that he will die sooner than allow the plain to be infected by the wicked cruelties of modern civilisation."

"I think so too," said Dick.

"This is an older civilisation than that of the Incas," said Lord Arden, "and it is the most beautiful life I have ever dreamed of. If they had trusted me, I would never have betrayed them. If I escape, I will never betray them. If I let in our horrible system of trusts and syndicates, and commercialism and crime, on this golden life, I should know myself to be as great a criminal as though I had thrown a little child to wild beasts."

The white cats noticed with wonder and respect that their father addressed Richard exactly as though he had been a grown-up.

"We managed to send one line to a newspaper, to say that we were taken by bandits," Lord Arden went on; "it was all that they would allow us to do. But except that we have not been free, we have had everything—food, clothes, kindness, justice, affection. We *must* escape, if we can, because of my sister and the children, but it is like going out of Eden into the Black Country."

"That's so," said Uncle Jim.

"And if we're not to see you again," Lord Arden went on, "tell me why you have come—at great risk it must be—to help us."

"I owe a debt," said Richard, in a low voice, "to all who bear the name of Arden." His voice sank so low that the two cats could only hear the words "head of the house."

"And now," Richard went on, "you see that black chink over there?" he pointed to the crevice in the cliff. "Be there, both of you, at moonrise, and you shall get away safely to Arden Castle."

"You must come with us, of course," said Lord Arden. "I might be of service to you. We have quite a respectable little fortune in a bank at

Lima—not in our own names—but we can get it out, if you can get *us* out. You've brought us luck, I'm certain of it. Won't you go with us, and share it?"

"I can't," said Richard. "I must go back to my own time, my own place, I mean. Now I'll go. Come on, cats."

The cats looked imploringly at their father, but they went and stood by Richard.

"I suppose we *may* go?" he asked.

"Every one is perfectly free here," said Lord Arden. "The only thing you may not do is to leave the golden plain. It is very strange. There are hardly any laws. We are all free to do as we like, and no one seems to like to do anything that hurts any one else. Only if, any one is caught trying to get into the outer world, or to let the outer world in, he is killed—without pain, and not as vengeance but as necessity."

The white cats looked at each other rather ruefully. This was not at all the way in which they remembered their daddy's talking to them.

"But," said Lord Arden, "for the children and my sister we must risk it. I trust you completely, and we will be at the crevice when the moon rises."

So Richard and his three white animals went out down steps cut in the solid rock, and the townspeople crowded round them with fruits and maize-cakes for Richard, and milk in golden platters for the cats.

And later Richard made signs of being sleepy, and they let him go away among the fields, followed by the three white creatures. And at the appointed hour they all met under the vast cliff that was the natural wall and guardian of the golden plain.

And the Mouldiwarp carried Uncle Jim up to the top, and then came back for Lord Arden and Richard. But before there was time to do more a shout went up, and a thousand torches sprang to life in the city they had left, and they knew that their flight had been discovered.

"There's no time," the white Bear-Mouldiwarp, to the utter astonishment of Lord Arden, opened its long mouth and spoke. And the white cats also opened their mouths and cried, "Oh, daddy, how awful! what shall we do?"

"Hold your silly tongues," said the Mouldiwarp crossly. "You was told not to go gossiping. Here! scratch a way out with them white paws of yours."

It set the example, scratching at the enormous cliff with those strong, blunt, curved front feet of it. And the cats scratched too, with their white, padded gloves that had tiger claws to them. And the rock yielded—there was a white crack—wider, wider. And the swaying, swirling torches came nearer and nearer across the plain.

"In with you!" cried the Mouldiwarp; "in with you!"

"Jim!" said Lord Arden. "I'll not go without Jim!"

"He's half-way there already," said the Mouldiwarp, pushing Lord Arden with its great white shoulder. "Come, I say, come!" It pushed them all into the crack of the rock, and the cliff closed firm and fast behind them, an unanswerable "*No*" set up in the face of their pursuers.

"This way out," said the Mouldiwarp, pointing its dusty claw to where ahead light showed.

"Why," said Edred, "it's the smugglers' cave—and there's the clock!"

Next moment there it wasn't, for Richard had leapt on it, and he and it had vanished together, the Mouldiwarp clinging to the hour hand at the last moment.

The white cats, which were Edred and Elfrida, drew back from the whirl of the hands that was the first step towards vanishment. They saw their father and Uncle Jim go up the steps that led to the rude wooden door whose key was like a church key—the door that led to the opening among the furze that they had never been able to find again.

When the vanishing of the clock allowed them to follow, and they regained the sunny outer air where the skylarks were singing as usual, they were just in time to see two figures going towards the castle and very near it.

They turned to look at each other.

"Why," said Edred, "you're not a cat any more!"

"No more are you, if it comes to that," said Elfrida. "Oh, Edred, they're going in at the big gate! Do you think it's really real—or have we just dreamed it—this time? It was much more dreamish than any of the other things."

"I feel," said Edred, sitting down abruptly, "as if I'd been a cat all my life, and been swung round by my tail every day of my life. I think I'll sit here till I'm quite sure whether I'm a white cat or Edred Arden."

"I know which *I* am," said Elfrida; but she, too, was not sorry to sit down.

"That's easy. You aren't either of them," said Edred.

. . . . .

When, half an hour later, they slowly went down to the castle, still doubtful whether anything magic had ever really happened, or whether all the magic things that had seemed to happen had really been only a sort of double, or twin, dream. They were met at the door by Aunt Edith, pale as the pearl and ivory of the white clock, and with eyes that shone like the dewdrops on the wild flowers that Elfrida had given to the Queen.

"Oh, kiddies!" she cried. "Oh, dear, darling kiddies!"

And she went down on her knees so that she should be nearer their own height and could embrace them on more equal terms.

"Something lovely's happened," she said; "something so beautiful that you won't be able to believe it."

They kissed her heartily, partly out of affection, and partly to conceal their want of surprise.

"Darlings, it's the loveliest thing that could possibly happen. What do you think?"

"Daddy's come home," said Elfrida, feeling dreadfully deceitful.

"Yes," said Aunt Edith. "How clever of you, my pet! And Uncle Jim. They've been kept prisoners in South America, and an English boy with a performing bear helped them to escape."

No mention of cats. The children felt hurt.

"And they had the most dreadful time—months and months and months—coming across the interior—no water, and Indians and all sorts of adventures; and daddy had fever, and would insist that the bear was the Mouldiwarp—our crest, you know—come to life, and talking just like you or me, and that there were white cats that had your voices, and called him daddy. But he's all right now, only very weak. That's why

I'm telling you all this. You must be very quiet and gentle. Oh, my dears, it's too good to be true, too good to be true!"

. . . . .

Now, was it the father of Edred and Elfrida who had brain fever and fancied things? Or did they, blameless of fever, and not too guilty of brains, imagine it all? Uncle Jim can tell you exactly how it all happened. There is no magic in *his* story. Father—I mean Lord Arden—does not talk of what he dreamed when he had brain fever. And Edred and Elfrida do not talk of what happened when they hadn't. At least they do, but only to me.

It is all very wonderful and mysterious, as all life is apt to be if you go a little below the crust, and are not content just to read newspapers and go by the Tube Railway, and buy your clothes ready-made, and think nothing can be true unless it is uninteresting.

. . . . .

"I've found the most wonderful photographs of pictures of Arden Castle," said Aunt Edith, later on. "We can restore the castle perfectly from them. I do wish I knew where the original pictures were."

"I'm afraid we can't restore the castle," said Lord Arden laughing; "our little fortune's enough to keep us going quite comfortably—but it won't rebuild Norman masonry."

"I do wish we could have found the buried treasure," said Edred.

"We've got treasure enough," said Aunt Edith, looking at Uncle Jim.

As for what Elfrida thinks—well, I wish you could have seen her face when she went into the parlour that evening after Aunt Edith had knelt down to meet them on equal terms, and tell them of the treasure of love and joy that had come home to Arden.

There was Lord Arden, looking exactly like the Lord Arden she had known in the Gunpowder Plot days, and also exactly like the daddy she had known all her life, sitting at ease in the big chair just underneath the secret panel behind which Sir Edward Talbot had hidden when he was pretending to be the Chevalier St. George. His dear face was just the same and the smile on it was her own smile—the merry, tender, twinkling smile that was for her and for no one else in the world. It was just a moment that she stood at the door. But it was one of these moments that are as short as a watch-tick, and as long as a year. She stood there and asked herself, "Have I dreamed it all? Isn't there really any Mouldiwarp or any treasure?"

And then a great wave of love and longing caught at her, and she knew that, Mouldiwarp or no Mouldiwarp, the treasure was hers, and in one flash she was across the room and in her father's arms, sobbing and laughing and saying again and again—

"Oh, my daddy! Oh, my daddy, my daddy!"

THE END

Made in the USA
Columbia, SC
07 January 2025